"Are you going to deny the passion you felt for my father?"

"You have no right—" Hope whispered.

"Oh really?" Chase knew, feeling as he did about her, that he had every right. "Just what constitutes passion in your view, Hope? A touch? A kiss?" He slanted his lips over hers, all the need he held back surging to the surface. "Is this passion enough for you, Hope?" His mouth brushed hers. "What about this?" Pulling her closer, Chase trailed his lips over her jaw, tasting the flavor of her skin. "Or this?"

Hope's legs buckled as her body went fluid. Needing something to hold on to, she reached out to Chase, seduced by the promise of his arms. "I want you," she whispered.

Suddenly, Chase closed his eyes. He'd never meant to go this far. He whispered, in a low, tortured voice, racked with guilt, "But we can't—"

ABOUT THE AUTHOR

Cathy Gillen Thacker is a veteran full-time novelist. Besides her stories for Harlequin American Romance, she has written several novels of romantic suspense for Harlequin Intrigue. After attending Miami University, Cathy taught piano to children, then turned to fiction writing. She now resides with her husband and children in Texas.

Books by Cathy Gillen Thacker

Don't miss any of our special offers. Write to us at the following address for information on our newest releases.

Harlequin Reader Service
P.O. Box 1397, Buffalo, NY 14240
Canadian address: P.O. Box 603,
Fort Erie, Ont. L2A 5X3

CATHY GILLEN THACKER

TANGLED WEB

Harlequin Books

TORONTO • NEW YORK • LONDON
AMSTERDAM • PARIS • SYDNEY • HAMBURG
STOCKHOLM • ATHENS • TOKYO • MILAN

Published January 1992

ISBN 0-373-16423-8

TANGLED WEB

Chapter One

"Chase, can you hear me?" Rosemary Barrister shouted.

"Barely," Chase shouted back, holding the field telephone up to his face. A caterpillar dropped from a nearby tree and crawled up his arm. He swatted at it irritably, then wiped at the sweat dripping down the back of his neck. He hated having his work interrupted, and knowing his mother, despite the trouble she'd had to go through to track him down, this was something trivial. "What's up?" he asked, trying his best to keep the terseness out of his tone.

"That trollop is ruining your father's store, that's what!" His mother shouted back hysterically, the static on the long-distance line covering none of her intense dislike for his father's second wife. "I want you to come back to the States immediately!"

Chase emitted a heavy sigh and swore silently. Rosemary's timing was the pits, as always. He was right in the middle of important medical research and getting out of the Costa Rican rain forest was no easy trick. And if this call went as usual, he'd make no headway with her at all. "Mom, I can't do that right now—"

"Fine!" Rosemary countered, her faint voice rising stridently. "But don't come crying to me when Barrister's goes bankrupt next month and we both lose our sole source of support."

"Mom, it can't be that bad—" Chase said in the most soothing tone he could manage. Mesmerized by the sheer beauty of it, he watched a sunbird fly from branch to branch in the canopy of trees above him where raindrops glinted like shiny pearls at the ends of pointed leaves. Damn, but he loved it here, where there were no phones, no family hassles, nothing but the work he loved....

"The hell it can't! Barrister's lost money last month, Chase, and the month before that! Haven't you been reading your statements?"

Chase tore his eyes from the hanging orchids above him and concentrated on what his mother was saying. "Well, no." He had no interest in the family department store; she knew that.

"The rent on my villa is due, Chase. I'll be evicted if I don't come up with some cash soon."

Now that was a problem. "Where are you?" Chase asked, frowning. The way Rosemary flitted around, there was no telling.

"Monte Carlo. Chase, are you coming home or not?"

Chase groped for the canteen fastened to his waist, put it to his lips and drank deeply of the cool water. He didn't want to go home. He never was in Houston for more than a day or so if he could help it, and usually he could. But this time it looked as if he had no choice. If he didn't get things straightened out at the store, then he'd have no income and his mother would have no income. Which meant Rosemary would be on his back constantly, and he'd have to stop his research.

"Yes, I'll go home." He heaved a reluctant sigh, promising silently that he would only stay as long as it took to get the trouble settled.

THERE'S NO REASON this should be so hard, Chase told himself several days later as he parked his Jeep in front of the River Oaks mansion where he'd grown up. But it was hard, now that his father was gone. He hadn't been back to

Houston since the funeral over a year ago, and even then he'd avoided coming to the house, staying in town only long enough to attend the memorial service and say a last private goodbye to a man he'd never really known.

It shouldn't have ended that way, with the two of them being more or less estranged, but there'd been no choice. They couldn't lie to each other, and even if they had, they still would've both known the truth, that Chase felt disloyal being anywhere near the woman who had broken up his parents' twenty-six-year marriage. Maybe it wouldn't have been so bad had Hope not been so damn young—nineteen when she first married his father, and twenty when her son, Joey, was born. Or if she hadn't been such a striking, sensual beauty, with her wide blue eyes, generous mouth and full lips, silky dark hair and fair skin.

She was so damn gorgeous and ripe-looking she could have married anyone she wanted. So much so that from the very beginning Chase had been unable to help but be aware of her, and he still felt guilty as hell about that. Now that she was single again she would be open to involvement and sending out signals, unconscious or otherwise, to that effect. He wondered how he would respond. It wouldn't be easy seeing her look at another man or even him as a potential suitor. There was no way he would ever have wanted to desire his father's young wife, but he had. Not that she had tried to make him notice her. If anything, Hope downplayed her physicality, retaining that mysterious air of innocence she had in her most unguarded moments.

Chase shook his head in confusion. He still wondered how his father could have robbed the cradle that way. If it had been him—hell, he would've felt like a lecherous old man going after someone half his age, especially someone as sensual and hauntingly beautiful as Hope. Whether she realized it or not, she needed a real partner in her life, someone who could take her to the limits of her physicality and back, not a father-figure who'd treat her like a china doll on a shelf, one who was pretty to look at but too fragile to touch. But apparently the difference in their ages hadn't bothered Edmond or Hope because they'd seemed happy enough together, even a decade after their marriage. Never passionate exactly in the healthy, unconsciously sexy way he would have expected Hope to be, but happy in a gentle, familial way.

Well, none of that mattered now, Chase thought wearily, pushing from his Jeep. He was here because the family-owned department store was in trouble. And like it or not, he would have to stay until matters were resolved. He owed his father at least that much.

"Mom, you'll never guess what happened today! The neatest thing!" Joey said, the moment Hope picked him up from school. "I got asked to go hiking and camping with a bunch of guys from school. In New Mexico, even! Isn't that neat?"

No, Hope thought, troubled, for more reasons than she could count. Deciding not to jump to conclusions, she put her white Mercedes SL coupe into drive and eased carefully back into the congested late-afternoon traffic. "When is this trip?" she asked, working hard to keep her tone conversational and light.

"Spring break."

Frowning, Hope braked as they approached a crosswalk. "Honey, that's mid-March. It's still cold in the mountains."

"I know, but we're gonna go to a low elevation, where there's no snow. I can go," Joey pleaded passionately. "Can't I? Mom?"

As much as she wanted to say yes, she knew she couldn't. Working hard to keep the worry from her voice, Hope pointed out what he already knew. "Joey, your asthma would be aggravated." Worse, he would probably get sick, and he'd been sick so much already this past winter. He'd lost weight he couldn't afford to lose and sometimes missed school more than he was there.

"I'll take my medicine or get a shot or whatever the doctor says I need to do," Joey promised earnestly. "And I won't complain, either."

Hope wished that was all it would take to make her son be able to lead a normal life, but she knew it wasn't so. "Honey, that won't work," she reminded him with gentle reluctance. "I'm sorry. But the answer has to be no. Maybe we could work out something else you could do instead."

Realizing by the firm yet pleasant tone of her voice there was no arguing with her, Joey hung his head. He was silent and visibly depressed the rest of the trip home. Guilt assailed her. "Do you have a lot of homework?" Hope asked as she turned the car onto their street.

"The usual," Joey muttered.

Which meant a lot, Hope thought. She couldn't believe how much homework they were giving these days.

"Dude. Whose Jeep it that?" Joey said. He pointed to the dull blue Jeep parked in the circular driveway in front of their home. Dented and splattered with red-brown mud, the vehicle looked incongruous next to the elegant white brick early Georgian mansion with the dark green shutters.

As always, Hope felt a sense of pride and accomplishment when she looked at her home. Three stories high, it was surrounded by beautifully landscaped flowers, evergreen shrubs, and towering live oak trees with Spanish moss. At either end of the three-story structure, was an octagonal-shaped wing with floor-to-ceiling casement windows on all sides. Four columns supported the two-story-high front porch. And there were shady terraces, rimmed with waist-high white balustrade, leading off the second floor of both octagonal wings.

She might have grown up poor, but there was no trace here of her impoverished, difficult beginnings or the heartbreak she had suffered years ago.

Realizing her son was still waiting for an answer, Hope said, "I don't know whose Jeep that is." Service people were required to park in the back, as did her help. Nor was there any identifying insignia on the Jeep. Still puzzling over who it might be, she added in a bemused voice, "I'm not expecting company." Indeed, after a long day at the store, that was the last thing she needed or wanted. She spent most evenings with Joey, helping him with his homework, watching television or playing board games. And that was the way she liked her evenings; quiet, with a solid sense of family.

Nevertheless, she touched a hand to her dark upswept hair, making sure the thick waves were still securely pinned into the loose French twist she favored for work. A cautious glance in her rearview mirror revealed her makeup to still be intact, except for a smudge of mascara beneath one lash, which she promptly took care of with one quick brush of her little finger. Her blue eyes showed no sign of the normal end-of-day fatigue she felt inside. Satisfied that she was outwardly prepared to greet a visitor with the Texas charm and graciousness expected of all the Barristers, she gathered her things from inside the car.

As she did so, she saw him, sitting on one of the cushioned wicker sofas that sat on either end of the front porch. Chase Barrister. Her husband's son. He was her stepson, though she had never been able to think of him as such. Just four years older than she, he was sexy and rugged and possessed the blatant sexuality and intense interest in all things physical his father had always lacked. Making love with Chase, she sensed, would be like being caught up in the center of a hurricane. There'd be calm, but it would be deceptive. One step too far in any direction and a woman would be in for the ride of her life—only to get drawn back into the tranquil center, then seduced to the dangerous edge again. With Chase, she sensed, there would never be an end. He'd enjoy a love affair to the hilt, with the same limitless verve he did everything else, and he'd make sure his woman enjoyed it, too.

It was her woman's intuition about him, that had always kept her as far away from him as possible. Had she met

Chase before she'd married her husband, she doubted she would have married Edmond. It would have been too hard. Chase was too attractive in an intensely primal way. Never mind trying to think of Chase as her stepson, for she knew no matter what she could never think of him as that. And Chase, for all his icy distrust of her, knew it, too.

Fortunately, in the ten years she had been married to Edmond, Chase had astutely kept his distance, using the demands of his work as excuse, and had remained as much a self-contained enigma to her now as the day they had first met. She blessed him for that. If he had been around constantly and tried to get close to her, she didn't know what would have happened. And that fear of involvement with him had weighed on her heart and soul for years. She owed Edmond a lot. She had loved and respected him. As long as she'd been his wife, she'd done nothing to dishonor him, except one thing. She had desired his son, Chase, in a way she had never been able to desire his father. And for that she felt deeply guilty.

Chase stood and viewed her with the usual remote disregard as she and Joey got out of the Mercedes. She knew Chase thought she had married his father for his money, and although she knew it wasn't true—she had married Edmond for his heart—it still hurt.

But she wouldn't dwell on that, or let Chase put her on edge. At lease she'd try not to, she promised herself silently, as she took in everything about him. In soft denim jeans and a rumpled khaki shirt, he looked as ruggedly casual and defiantly at ease as ever. Remembering how unimpressed he was with ceremony, Hope felt a little swell of apprehension in her chest as he strode laconically toward her.

She didn't know how this meeting was going to go. Even though she was still some ways away from her wide front porch, she did know he hadn't shaved in at least twenty-four hours and there were telltale signs of travel fatigue both on his angular face and in the slow, weary movements of his lean, well-toned body. That probably meant he was just back in-country. He hadn't cut his dark ash-blond hair in heaven knows when, and though the fine but abundant strands were combed neatly in a side part and pushed behind his ears, the unshorn style gave him a sexy, untamed look. He was so close to her own age, so different from Edmond, *and* so exciting.

In his professional and private life, Chase seemed to dare anything and for all his innate kindness and generosity, he seemed intent on pleasing only himself. And yet, she sensed, there was a part of him that seemed restless and unfulfilled and she wondered absently what it would take to make him feel replete. Not that he was inclined to give her any clue, of course. She had never had even the most cursory conversation with him one-on-one, never seen him look rattled. Never angry. Always cool and collected and somehow untouchable, emotionally as well as physically. And his enforced distance from her hurt as well as entranced. She knew he resented her for marrying his father, and also that he had no reason to resent her. But she could never tell him that, not without betraying Edmond. She had promised her husband that she would carry his secret with her to the grave. It was a promise she meant to keep.

"Mom, who is that?" Joey repeated, nudging her slightly.

Hope glanced back at her young son. He was still wearing his private-school uniform of gray slacks, navy blazer, white shirt. Puny in stature and bespectacled, he looked the antithesis of the healthy, robust, very laid-back and casual Chase. Chase had attended private school, too, albeit reluctantly. And maybe those years of forced formality were why he always refused to dress up now, unless it was absolutely unavoidable.

Putting her leather briefcase in one hand, her bag in the other, Hope said, "It's your half brother, Chase, honey. You remember him, don't you?"

"Oh," Joey said in a voice that indicated he clearly did not remember Chase. "Yeah, sure."

Of course, Hope thought, sighing inwardly, there was no reason why Joey should have remembered Chase. The funeral had been overflowing with people, she and Chase had made an art out of tactfully avoiding each other for years, and when he was in town, he'd managed to see his father only briefly before swiftly moving on.

So why was he here now? she wondered. What could he possibly want? And he did want something from her; she could tell by the look on his ruggedly handsome, sun-weathered face.

"Hope." He nodded at her formally, making no effort to extend his hand.

Feeling ill at ease but determined not to show it, Hope nodded back stiffly. "Chase." The moment drew out awkwardly, stretching her nerves unbearably thin as she realized close up, he was still as breathtakingly attractive as ever, still as able to wreak havoc on her senses. "I wasn't aware you were in town." Or that he still wore the deliciously rich, woodsy after-shave he had always favored.

He shoved a hand into his back pocket, the motion drawing his jeans tighter against the flatness of his abdomen, and fastened his hazel eyes on her face. "Just got in this afternoon," he said laconically. His voice was a gravelly drawl and his eyes probed hers for a reaction.

He'd headed right over to see her, Hope realized with amazement, trying hard not to notice how soft and worn and snug those jeans were or how nicely they clung to the muscled contours of his trim waist, lean hips and long legs. Aware he was looking her over with the same in-depth appraisal, boldly examining every inch of her, it was all Hope could do to hold her ground.

Having apparently picked up her unaccustomed nervousness, Joey cast her a curious glance. "Is he gonna be staying with us, Mom?"

Chase can't want to, Hope thought nervously, unable to tell from his defiantly impassive expression whether he found her changed or not. Because of Edmond, she had to offer her reluctant hospitality, "This is your home, too, Chase, and you're welcome here anytime." *No matter how uncomfortably lonely you make me feel.* Judging from the state of his clothes and his Jeep, he was as perennially short of cash as ever. He spent the yearly income from his lifetime trust almost as soon as it came. Usually, of course, he had quarterly profits from Barrister's to tide him over as well, but Hope knew there had been no profits this quarter—or last. Which meant he was probably down to his last nickel.

"Thanks for the offer," Chase said with a politeness as forced as her own, "but I wouldn't want to impose."

"You wouldn't be imposing," Hope countered cordially, again for her husband's sake. She never wanted it said she hadn't at least tried to make Chase welcome. While her husband had been alive, Chase had sometimes quartered in the guest house, however briefly. He'd maintained minimal contact with his father, none whatsoever with her and Joey. As far as she was concerned, he could continue to do the same. The guest house had a private entrance and driveway. As for her attraction to him, well, it was just something she would have to fight. She had conquered it before. She could conquer it again.

"Well," Chase said awkwardly, confirming by his actions that he was indeed as short of cash as she suspected, "if you're sure it's no trouble and the guest house is available—"

"It is," Joey cut in gregariously before Hope could verify the same.

"Well, fine, then. I'll only be here a day or so, anyway," Chase continued.

Hope tried very hard not to show her relief at that bit of news. One day of having him around she could handle, but not any more than that.

Aware her thoughts were straying into forbidden territory, she forced her mind back to the reason for his quick departure. "Still doing research in Brazil?" she asked, hoping fervently he hadn't been able to read her thoughts.

"Costa Rica now. I'm not sure where I'll be next."

Joey touched Hope's sleeve, subtly commanding her attention. "Mom, is it okay if I go in now? I'm hungry."

"Sure, honey. Just have Carmelita give you a snack. But don't eat too much. Dinner's going to be soon." She looked at Chase, forcing herself to offer, even as she hoped he would refuse, "Will you be dining with us or do you have other plans?"

"No plans," Chase said candidly, watching as Joey disappeared into the house. He turned back to Hope, his gaze intent and all encompassing, his purpose for being there as much a mystery as ever. He frowned and released a long, uneven breath, then seemed to have forced himself to speak. "Actually, Hope, a family dinner would be just the thing."

For what? Hope wondered in complete unmitigated shock.

I'M HANDLING THIS all wrong, Chase thought, as he stood under the shower in the guest house, the hot clean water streaming over his skin. "Pretending that I feel like family when I don't. Pretending I'm here for no reason in particular." Yet try as he might, he had been unable to cut to the heart of the matter and ask her just what the hell was going on with the store. Especially with Joey standing there.

For one thing, he knew the economy in Texas was bad. The oil bust in the late eighties had affected everything and everyone. Businesses had gone under by the handful. People who had been millionaires all their lives had lost everything. Entire shopping centers had closed, and real-estate foreclosures occurred by the hundreds. But Barrister's had not only survived, it had continued to do well, at least while his father was alive. Now, a year later, it was a different story. Now Hope was at the helm. Worse, she was as beautiful as ever and that wouldn't make things easy.

He couldn't stand by and let the business his father had built go down the drain, but he couldn't just walk in and take the business away from Hope either. Not when he knew his father had wanted her to have it. Chase had no real interest in it, save keeping it afloat, but it was Hope's life.

He had to find a way to turn things around, to ensure the livelihood for all of them continued. And he had to do it in a way that would've been okay with his father, which meant not getting rid of Hope. Realizing that, he swore roundly and grabbed for a towel. If this wasn't an impossible task, he didn't know what was.

"SO YOU GET TO SPEND weeks and weeks in the jungles, looking for cures for stuff like cancer and arthritis? And you don't have to take a bath except when you want to and you get to sleep in a tent and cook on a camp fire every single night?" Joey asked Chase incredulously.

Chase chuckled. "That about sums it up, yeah, but it's not nearly as glamorous as it sounds."

The dry note in her stepson's voice completely escaped her son, who was thrilled by Chase's adventures. "Wow," Joey continued, shaking his head admiringly. "I wish my mom would let me do stuff like that, but right now she won't even let me go camping in New Mexico."

Chase slanted Hope a measuring look. "You don't approve of the great outdoors?"

It wasn't that, although Chase was right to assume she wouldn't want her son to ever have the kind of nomadic, no-ties life Chase reveled in. As far as she knew, Chase had never lacked in female companions, but he had never been serious about any woman except Lucy, and their brief engagement had ended almost as quickly and mysteriously as it had begun, years before. "Joey has asthma. He's allergic to many of the tree and plant pollens. That's why he can't go camping." A doctor himself, Chase should understand the risks.

Joey scowled. "If Dad were still here, he'd let me go."

Unfortunately, Hope knew that was true. Edmond had been optimistic to a fault, in that regard. And because of that they'd had to continually deal with the consequences. "Joey—"

His pleasure in the meal with his half brother diminished, Joey said abruptly, "May I be excused, please?"

Realizing this was no time to get into a prolonged argument, Hope nodded her permission. "Be sure you finish your homework before you watch any television."

"I will." Joey put his napkin down next to his plate, then shoulders hunched in silent misery, marched off.

Embarrassed, Hope turned back to Chase. Suddenly the air between them was charged with electricity and none of it had to do with the emotional departure of her son. "Would you care for more coffee or dessert?" She was aware her voice and manners were stiff and mannequinlike, but was unable to do anything about it. She feared if she relaxed, even a tad, Chase would see through her flimsy defenses and realize how uneasy and self-conscious she felt, being there alone with him, especially now that she was single again.

He had eaten everything Carmelita put before him, as if he'd been starved for months. And she supposed where he had been, there had been a lack of elegant cuisine.

"I'll pass on the seconds. Thanks. I do need to speak to you—privately."

She had been expecting this. "Very well," she said. She led the way to the heavy paneled library. Once inside, she shut the double oak doors firmly behind them and Chase got straight to the point.

"I'm concerned about Barrister's."

Hope felt her spine stiffen. As disinterested as Chase had always been in the store, she hadn't expected this. Unable to keep the defensive note out of her voice, she retorted, "So am I."

Chase smoothed his blond hair, then let his palm rest idly on the back of his neck.

Just shampooed, the sun-streaked strands gleamed like
gold in the soft inside light, appearing very touchable and
distracting in their sexy disarray. And he smelled just as
fresh and male.

"Look, Hope," he began rather gruffly, as he passed her
in a wake of rich, woodsy after-shave, "I doubt I can say
this without offending you—"

From the reluctant look on his face, she doubted it too.
"Just get on with it," she advised tensely, expecting the
worst.

He dropped his hand and leaned against the marble fire-
place. "All right." More comfortable now, he met her gaze
and continued flatly, "Popular opinion is you're misman-
aging Barrister's."

Hope hung on to her escalating temper with all her might.
"Then popular opinion is wrong," she corrected, just as
bluntly.

His fair brow lifted slightly at her tone. "I wish I could
believe that," he said tersely. Then in a softer, more resigned tone, he added, "Try to understand. This isn't personal, but I can't let my father's work end in Chapter
Eleven."

As the threat of what he was saying became real, Hope's
shock abated. "I'm well aware of what happened to Frost
Brothers," she said icily. She got up and moved around the
room restlessly. Then she whirled to face Chase, the awkward silence doing nothing to diffuse her anger. "You can
rest assured I won't let Barrister's end in bankruptcy." The
business meant too much to her. Apart from Joey, it was her
whole life.

He crossed his arms at his waist and looked at her frankly.
He wasn't about to give in to every whim. Unlike Edmond,
he didn't care if she was displeased or not. "Neither will I,"
he said flatly.

Aware her hands were shaking, she shoved them into the
pockets of her skirt. Although she knew him to be a formidable opponent, she had never expected this from Chase,

and it threw her. "What do you mean?" With effort, she kept her voice harsh, exacting.

His hazel eyes darkened in a similar show of emotion. "I inherited thirty percent of the stock, Hope. My mother owns ten percent of it."

Her pulse thudded faster. "Are you asking me to buy your shares?" She faced him in disbelief, disappointment stabbing at her like a knife.

"No." He shook his head grimly. "I'm asking you to step down as president, effective immediately, and let the board of directors appoint someone else to run it."

Hope stared at him, feeling both shocked and annoyed at his matter-of-fact tone. Once the conversation had turned to the store, she had braced herself for complaints from Chase about the lack of profits in the past two quarters, but she had never expected this. Knowing Chase and Rosemary Barrister, perhaps she should have expected it. Neither had ever liked her. Neither had been happy when Edmond left forty-eight percent of the stock to her and recommended she replace him as president. But until now, neither had fought her, either. Knowing how rich people liked to hold onto what they had, as well as what they didn't, she supposed she should have seen this coming.

"Your father wanted me to run the store, Chase," she pointed out reasonably. "He spent ten years grooming me to do just that."

Again, Chase managed to look torn. "I know how hard you've worked," he soothed. "I'm sorry it hasn't worked out."

Silence fell between them once more and she studied him relentlessly. As hard as it was for her to admit, Hope saw this wasn't revenge on his part. He wasn't trying to hurt her, just to salvage what was left of the business. What he didn't know was that she was already one step ahead of him, and had been for several months.

"I don't agree that it hasn't worked out," she countered practically. "But I do share your concern. That's why I've called a meeting with the buyers tomorrow morning at nine sharp, to outline some immediate changes that will turn business around. You're welcome to sit in if you like."

His mouth twisted unhappily. "One meeting with the buyers isn't going to change anything, Hope."

He was underestimating her. In a crisp businesslike tone, she repeated firmly, "The meeting's at nine sharp, Chase. I assume I'll see you there?"

Realizing evidently he owed her at least that much, he held her gaze a long moment, looking into her eyes until she flushed and had to fight herself not to back away. Then he nodded his agreement circumspectly.

She hadn't changed his mind, but what the hell, he thought, he'd give her one more day. For his dad's sake and for Joey's. But then he would have to lower the ax. Like it or not, he had no choice. "I'll be there," he promised inexorably, letting none of his emotions show. "You can count on it."

Chapter Two

Knowing she had a battle in front of her, Hope walked into the conference room with her head held high. She took her place at the head of the table and motioned for everyone else in the room to sit. Among the buyers was Chase Barrister. In a dark blue suit and tie, he looked very somber and businesslike. He'd also had a haircut, and the dark ash-blond layers were arranged in a neat, preppy style. Used to seeing him more casually dressed, his blond hair rumpled, his posture defiantly casual and laid-back, Hope was disconcerted by his formal attire and exacting attitude. For the first time, he looked a lot like Edmond—powerful, observant, demanding. And though Chase had always possessed Edmond's wit, intelligence and consummate people-sense, he had never shown the slightest inclination to indulge her the way Edmond had. Realizing that, Hope felt her nerves jangle. And she wasn't the only one on edge.

She could see that the seasoned staff was wondering at Chase's presence, too. Although he had worked at the store, summers, while in college, he had not expressed any interest since. He never attended board meetings, never mind Hope's weekly conferences with the staff. Deciding the only way to get through this was to plunge right in, she said, "You're all aware of the lack of recent profits. To survive, Barrister's is going to have to change. We can no longer cater strictly to the socialites. We're going to have to try to capture some of the yuppie market, too.''

"You're not serious, are you?'' Steve Supack asked, his look both astonished and grim. Informal spokesperson for group, Steve was in his mid-forties. He had been with the the company for over twenty years, working his way up steadily from clerk to head buyer for menswear. Although he did not have a college degree, his sense of style and ability to please even the rudest, most discriminating customer had proved invaluable. Edmond had trusted him implicitly.

"I never kid about anything this important,'' Hope said, meeting Steve's level gaze. She knew they were all thinking that if the prices and quality of the merchandise went down, so would the size of their sales commissions. She had also known for some time that this had to be done and that it was going to be an uphill battle. Change was never easy, even when it was necessary. She would face criticism from every source—clients, rival businesspeople, and her own employees. But it was the only way she knew to save what had been her late husband's life work, and preserve her young son's inheritance. So persevere she must, no matter how formidable the odds or how disbelieving her employees.

"The changes will be effective immediately. We are going to cater to a broader range of clients, carry fewer high-ticket items, do away with all in-store displays of whimsical gifts, and become a more mainstream department store.''

She glanced at the sea of apprehensive faces, purposefully avoiding Chase's steady, intent gaze. This was hard enough without worrying about what he thought of her ability to run the business, too. She would deal with him later, only when she absolutely had to. Right now, she was concerned about her employees.

She understood and shared the fear of the thirty buyers in front of her. If her plan didn't work, they would doubtless join the stream of other elitist family-owned department stores that had filed for bankruptcy in recent years. But she also understood what they didn't, and what she hoped Chase would soon, that this was the only chance they had to survive. "We'll begin with the Houston Galleria store. If the changes test successfully here, we will change all the other Barrister's around the country in the fall."

"What do the Board of Directors have to say about this?" a feminine voice from the back challenged openly.

Hope looked up and her heart sank as she focused on the thin blond socialite. It was Rosemary Barrister, Edmond's first wife! When had she walked in?

Chase turned at the sound of his mother's voice. Hope noted, with something akin to satisfaction and surprise, that he didn't look any happier to see his jet-setting mother than she felt. Holding her voice steady, despite the hatred and resentment she felt emanating from the other woman, Hope answered firmly, "The Board has already approved my plan."

Rosemary shook her head. "You're going to ruin the reputation of this store."

Everyone whispered, apparently agreeing with Rosemary.

Hope struggled to control the meeting. "There won't be a Barrister's if we don't make the changes necessary to survive in today's more competitive marketplace."

Apparently she succeeded in getting across just how desperate their situation was, for the staff fell silent. Feeling drained, and fearing another rude outburst from the volatile Rosemary, Hope dismissed the group of buyers, adding, "I'll expect to see your revised stock orders on my desk one week from today."

The mood somber, everyone filed out. Some, like Steve Supack, who had known the family for years, paused to say hello to Rosemary. Chase got up and walked to the window overlooking Westheimer.

Wishing to avoid a run-in with Rosemary, Hope began stuffing papers into her briefcase. To no avail. The minute the conference room had cleared out, a belligerent Rosemary shut the heavy oak doors and faced Hope and Chase.

"I'll see you in hell before I let you destroy Barrister's!" she warned.

"Mother," Chase said curtly, looking as aggrieved as Hope felt. "I told you I'd handle this."

"Look at her!" Rosemary said. "Barrister's is being ruined. And she still looks like she has the world by the tail!"

Chase looked at Hope. His mother was right about that. Hope did look fantastic, even under fire. But then she always had. That had been part of the problem. Even at a very young, naive nineteen she had possessed a strikingly sensual beauty that had doubtless haunted every man who'd ever come in contact with her. She had wide, vulnerable blue eyes, a generous mouth, bee-stung lips, and pearly white teeth. Those features along with the silky thickness of her dark hair and fair skin never failed to command a second, and third look from men and women alike. And though Chase had tried to remain unaffected, he had noticed. He had always noticed, even to his considerable guilt, when his father was alive.

It didn't help matters to notice that in the years since Joey's birth, her slim figure had filled out. Now, her curves were more lush and womanly beneath her white wool dress and red blazer.

If they'd met under any other circumstances, he wouldn't have bothered to hide how he felt, but would have pursued her with everything he had, not stopping until she was his. But that hadn't happened. He'd met her as his father's wife and he still had to try to think of her that way, out of respect. To do otherwise would be wrong.

Oblivious to his traitorous thoughts, Hope turned to his mother and said in a soothing tone, "I'm sorry you're upset, Rosemary. Believe me, this pains me as much as it does you."

"I doubt that," Rosemary said, making no effort to hide the malevolence in her voice.

Chase saw a flash of hurt, then anger, in Hope's eyes. Knowing his mother's formidable temper, and fearing this would turn into an out and out brawl if left unchecked, Chase touched his mother's arm in a calming gesture. He may not have wanted her here, but now that she was, he would have to deal with her, too. "Mother, I'd like to speak to Hope alone."

Rosemary hesitated, then nodded stiffly. "Shall I wait for you outside?"

"Please."

He waited until his mother had departed, then aware they hadn't much time, turned to Hope and got straight to the point. "I agree with Steve Supack and my mother. Changing the image of the store may do more harm than good, at this point."

Striding back to her briefcase, Hope clicked it open, pulled out a sheaf of papers and handed it to him. "Those are the demographics on our latest sales figures and the market projections for the rest of the year, as well as the next decade. I think, Chase, if you study them you'll see I am well-advised to make the changes I've outlined."

Surprised by her professionalism and her calm in the light of so much tension, Chase hooked a booted foot beneath the lower rung of a wheeled conference chair and pulled it out. He sank into it. He was aware of her standing behind him, so closely he could hear her soft, steady breaths and inhale the sophisticated sexy scent of her perfume. He tried to glance through the papers.

Unfortunately, with Hope so close, it was all but impossible for him to concentrate. Briefly he considered asking her to wait outside while he read, then promptly discarded that idea. If he did so, Rosemary would wonder why, and he didn't need his mother's prurient curiosity. Finally, with a great deal of effort, he managed to scan the reports, he saw she'd done a thorough, accurate job. Market projections were just that, however, projections. His mind on business once again, he frowned. "It's still a risk." And more to the point, he wasn't sure hers was a course his father would ever have condoned.

"A risk I'm willing to take," she pointed out calmly. "Suppose I'm not?"

"It isn't up to you," she pointed out levelly. As much as he searched he could find no bitterness or resentment in her eyes, just a quiet practicality that was almost as unnerving as her beauty.

Realizing he was thinking of her as a desirable woman again, one he had no right to yearn for or to know more intimately, Chase pushed the thoughts away. He had to think about business, nothing more. If he didn't, his feelings of guilt and disloyalty would eat him alive.

Chase turned his gaze back to the papers with a grimace of concentration. He knew that Hope held the upper hand in terms of stock; for the moment anyway. She had the controlling interest. If the Board of Directors was behind her, she had the power to do anything she wanted.

Besides, maybe Hope was right. She had been here, working diligently for the past ten years. Her commitment to Barrister's granted her this chance to try to save it her way. "All right," he conceded finally, feeling in his gut he was doing the only decent thing. "I'll make no move to stop you from executing your plans."

Hope didn't so much as blink. She faced him quietly. "What about Rosemary?"

Hope was clearly worried about his mother, and she had every right to be. "I'll see she gives you a clear path, too. For a short time," he specified firmly.

Hope frowned and her blue eyes grew troubled. "How short a time?"

Chase did some rapid calculations. "Three months ought to be enough to turn it around." *If your plan is going to work,* he added mentally.

She heaved a sigh of unmasked exasperation. "I'll need at least six months, Chase, with no interference from either of you."

He shook his head. "Three is all I'm offering, Hope. Take it or leave it."

Silence fell between them. "I'll take it," she retorted glumly. He started to return the papers, but she shook her head and waved her hand, indicating she didn't want them. "Your mother might want to see those. Perhaps they'll reassure her."

Chase doubted that. Rosemary's resentment of Hope was deep and unrelenting; he suspected it always would be. But he said nothing as Hope snapped the locks on either side of her briefcase handle.

"Now that this is settled, I presume you'll be leaving for Costa Rica?"

He only wished it were that easy. "Not exactly. I'm short of funds. The lack of profits caught us unaware. I loaned money to my mother to pay the rent on her villa in Monte Carlo. So, until I can scrounge up more money for my research, I'll be staying in Houston, keeping tabs on what's going on here personally."

Staying on, she thought. If he did that, they'd be seeing each other almost twenty-four hours a day, both at work and at home. They'd take meals together. Where she may have wanted to be closer to Chase for Edmond's sake and for the reunification of the Barrister family, she had never wanted this. Especially not when she knew how attracted she was to him, that she had only to look at him or be near to him to feel a resurgence of desire. And yet, because he was Edmond's son and had once lived there, too, she could hardly tell him to go.

Feeling like she'd sustained a strong blow to the chest, Hope struggled to catch her breath and keep her voice noncommittal and even. "How long?"

Looking totally unaffected by her reluctance to have him underfoot, Chase shrugged. "Until I get enough to underwrite another expedition."

That could take weeks, even months, Hope knew. Weeks of unbearable tension, of dealing with him, and of seeing him at all hours of the day and night, maybe even in his pajamas! *If* he wore pajamas. Something told her he *didn't*.

What was she going to do? Simultaneously desperate to get him out from underfoot, and feeling she owed him whatever financial help she could spare, because of Edmond, she offered to help speed him on his way. "Look, I don't have a lot of ready cash available to me either right now, but if your returning to Costa Rica is a matter of a simple plane fare and a few months provisions, a guide, I could—"

"Why would you want to do that for me?" he cut in abruptly, regarding her suspiciously. He knew, she felt, that she very much wanted to get rid of him A.S.A.P.

"Because you're Edmond's son." *Because I find you distracting and attractive and it's killing me inside because even though I'm single now it makes me feel disloyal to Edmond. Because I know you think the worst of me, that I married Edmond for his money when in reality money never had anything to do with my feelings for your father.* But knowing she'd never convince anyone of that, never mind Chase, she decided to concentrate on the aspects of their relationship they could discuss.

"So?" he challenged mildly. "I'm Edmond's son? I'm not yours."

How well she knew that. Struggling for equilibrium, Hope said, "You're family, Chase." *Neither of us might have chosen it, but there it is. I have to do what Edmond would have wanted.* And beyond that, for reasons she couldn't really define, she wanted to help Chase achieve his goals and be happy. After all, their family difficulties aside, he was a kind, selfless person, in ways that she truly admired. It felt right somehow that she help him. "You're family," she repeated.

He shook his head in mute disagreement, denying it with all he was worth. "That bond ended when my father died."

What bond? Hope wanted to say. He had never so much as given her the time of day. And that had hurt, knowing that he wouldn't give her a chance.

He wished she didn't look so hurt, dejected and crushed. Brushing her off wasn't something he *wanted* to do; it was a familial decency that was required of him.

To his chagrin, Hope's expression remained desolate, as if she were taking his rejection personally. He sighed regretfully. He felt a lot of things for Hope; he didn't want to add guilt for hurting her feelings to the list. And he didn't think his Dad would've wanted it, either. "But you're right," Chase said, picking up the thread of the conversation uncomfortably. "I am anxious to be out of here." *Away from the temptation of you.* "But as much as I want to get back to work I can't take your money, Hope." Not knowing that despite all their best efforts, the store might fold anyway. She would still have Joey to raise, and thus would need every cent she had.

Hope was silent, remembering, he expected, that he had never taken money from his father for his expeditions, either. Chase noticed with relief that her hurt expression was beginning to fade.

"I understand," she empathized softly.

Good. "Which leaves me only one choice," Chase continued.

"For you to stay on at the house with me," Hope guessed in a voice quavering with unspoken emotion.

Silence fell between them. For a moment, neither spoke. Neither needed to. They both knew how difficult it would be for the two of them to share space for even a short period of time, never mind the weeks or months he was proposing.

"I won't get in your way," Chase promised gruffly. "Or Joey's—"

"I know."

"And tell Carmelita not to worry about me, either. I don't want her trooping over to make my bed."

Hope felt her cheeks warm. "All right," she murmured in agreement. She didn't want to know what was going on or not going on in Chase's bedroom, either.

He shoved his suit coat back and put his hands on his hips. He assessed her bluntly. "It'll still be awkward for you, won't it?"

"A little," she agreed, working to keep the heat out of her cheeks. Lamely, she added, "Joey and I aren't used to having anyone else around except Carmelita. But I'm sure we can cope," she said hastily after a moment, embarrassed again.

He nodded his understanding, looking both grateful for the hospitality and wary of the probable complications to come and suddenly Hope knew. He's attracted to me, too, she thought, seeing it in the abrupt tenseness of his frame and the way he suddenly wouldn't look into her eyes. But because of Edmond he wouldn't do anything about it, either, she noted with equally strong feelings of relief and disappointment.

"Hope?" Leigh Olney, the new buyer for Children's Wear, interrupted them. Although she had only been hired recently, Leigh had quickly made herself indispensable. She was already the most flexible of the staff. "Sorry to interrupt but there's—" Leigh looked at Chase and faltered. "A *surprise* in your office that—uh—needs your attention right away."

It was clear to Hope from the excited look on Leigh's face that the twenty-four-year old thought she was doing her a giant favor. And also that the surprise couldn't wait another moment. Glad for the reason to excuse herself from Chase, and from the unexpected realization that he was as uncomfortably aware of her as a woman as she was of him as a man, she said, "I'm sorry, Chase, I've got to go."

Still puzzling over Leigh's excited expression, she walked to her office, wondering all the while what the surprise could be. It wasn't her birthday or her anniversary with the store, or even the date she had taken over as president of Barrister's. Yet the usually unflappable Leigh had acted as if she had an entire surprise party awaiting her. Shrugging it off, she stepped inside her office and closed the door behind her.

And it was then that she saw him, standing next to the polished oak sideboard Edmond had installed in the far corner. Although expertly cut, the jazzy teal blazer, white slacks and shirt, did little to disguise the fact he was now a good twenty pounds overweight. Above the knot of his silk tie, his deeply tanned face had the pinched look of recent plastic surgery. Years had passed and he had aged badly, but as long as she lived she would never forget Russell Morris's aristocratic face or his soulless deep blue eyes.

Her stomach churning with long suppressed memories, she drew on every ounce of gentility she had worked to possess and asked crisply, "How may I be of help to you?" She knew, from reading the *Wall Street Journal,* that his family-owned firm was in big trouble, too. It had been since the day he'd inherited it five years prior. Currently, if she guessed right, Russell Morris was probably close to losing everything, too.

Russell turned, a handful of the Godiva chocolates she kept just for Joey in his palm. "Is this any way to greet an old friend?" he asked. He voluptuously downed one of the expensive treats.

First off, we were never friends, she thought. A friend would never have done to me what you did. Her back stiffened in a way that let him know she wasn't about to be taken advantage of by him again. No longer an innocent young girl, she was stronger now, smarter. She gave him a warning look and said briskly, "I'm very busy—"

"I imagine you are, Hope," he interrupted smoothly. The cruel lines of his mouth flattened even more. "All these stores you inherited from that rich husband of yours aren't doing very well." He finished the last of the chocolates he'd pilfered, then dusted off his hands. The look he gave her was smug and insinuating. Remembering the past, it was all she could do to keep from flying at him and flailing him with both fists. She hated him that much.

"Is there a point to this?" she asked stiffly. She wanted nothing more than to get him out before there was a scene and before Chase discovered him there.

"If you'll let me get to it." Briefly Russell's voice held the old autocratic edge she detested, then it dropped even lower, so it was slick and soft and totally insincere. "I can help you, Hope," he said guilelessly, moving two steps nearer.

The smell of his cologne, even at a distance, made her ill, and it was all she could do to swallow the bile rising in her throat.

"I know you need it," Russell continued. "That's why I've come."

Even if the past hadn't stood between them, there was no way she would have ever let anyone as selfish and remorseless as he anywhere near her beloved Barrister's.

"I don't think so," she corrected archly.

Her skin crawling because of his nearness, she turned and moved purposefully to the door. She had to get him out of her office before the loathing she felt inside got the better of her. What had happened in the past was horrible but it was over, she schooled herself firmly. She had to make sure it stayed that way, for all their sakes. She yanked open the door and waved him on his way.

He stayed where he was, as arrogant and presumptuous as ever. "That's it? You're going to dismiss me without even hearing me out?" he asked in disbelief, as if she were the one in the wrong. Straightening lazily, he moved toward her, one manicured hand held out beseechingly.

As the distance between them narrowed, her stomach lurched again. Working hard to hide the insistent trembling of her hands, she gave him a look that spoke volumes about the way she felt. And would always feel. "I see no reason to waste our time."

"I run Morris Fabrics now—"

"I'm well aware of all you have inherited." The sick feeling in the pit of her stomach increased. He'd inherited the power, the wealth, and the complete and utter lack of scruples.

"And?"

Her chin high, she said, "I have no desire to do business with your family firm, now or at any time in the future." She wanted to make that very clear.

Russell's expression turned ugly. "You're making a mistake," he warned, his eyes flashing in anger. "I could have cut you quite a deal."

The only thing she wanted from him was to be left alone. Pasting an official smile on her face, she stalked out, and on her way, asked the nearest security guard to please escort Mr. Morris to his car and see that he got off all right. As always, Russell knew when to cut his losses and move on to greener pastures. He said nothing more, save a falsely cordial public farewell.

"So how was it?" an excited Leigh Olney asked when she saw Hope again an hour later. At Hope's blank look, Leigh elaborated, "Your reunion with your old high-school buddy? Russell Morris said the two of you hadn't seen one another in years."

Hope wished fervently it had stayed that way.

Leigh continued with cheerful candor, "He figured you'd be really surprised, and I guess you were."

Stunned and heartsick was more like it, Hope thought. Gathering her wits, Hope said, "To tell you the truth, Leigh, we weren't that close back then. He's just down on his luck right now. And I can't help him. That being the case, I'd prefer not to see him again."

Leigh looked crushed. "I'm sorry, Hope. The guy led me to believe—I mean he's the heir to Morris Fabrics and all and you're running this place—I just naturally thought—"

"I know you did, and it's okay." Hope knew how charming Russell could be when he put his mind to it. She sighed, "Mr. Morris has a way of implying closeness where none exists."

Leigh nodded, understanding that much very well. It was clear from the look on her face that nothing more needed to be said. "Listen, about the meeting this morning. I want you to know I'm behind you all the way."

"Thanks. I'm going to need every bit of help I can get," Hope said. Especially since neither Chase nor Rosemary was in her corner, she thought.

Unfortunately Hope's day didn't get any better. One by one, buyers came in to express their concerns about the new direction she had charted for Barrister's and the security of their jobs. She felt exhausted and depressed while she was driving home, but began to relax when she entered the house and caught a whiff of Carmelita's delicious lemon chicken.

After a long, hot soak in the tub and a glass of wine, she'd be able to forget all about her horrendous day and Russell Morris. By the time Joey arrived home from Little League practice, all would be back to normal. Or as close as it could be, with Chase living in the guest house out back, she amended wryly.

Unfortunately, Hope hadn't gotten any further than kicking off her heels and putting down her briefcase when the front door banged open and Joey came running in, his head ducked down in shame. Tears streamed down his face. "My God, what happened?" she cried, looking at the swelling bruise that seemed to cover most of his upper cheek and all of his left eye. Where were his glasses?

He tried to shrug it off and escape further maternal scrutiny. "It's nothing."

"Nothing!" Hope cried. She stepped in front of him, latched on to his arm and gently but firmly prevented his escape to his bedroom.

Carmelita gasped as she joined them. In her mid-thirties, the slim housekeeper had lived with them since Joey was born. As emotional as she was kind, the devoted employee loved Joey almost as fiercely as Hope did. "Oh, no, Joey," Carmelita said, wringing her hands.

"This looks wicked," Hope said seriously. She started for the telephone. "I'm calling the doctor."

"Mom, no—" Joey dashed after her and grabbed her sleeve. "Don't—"

Looking more panic-stricken than ever, Carmelita said, "I'll get Mr. Chase. He's a doctor. He will know what to do." Not waiting for Hope's permission, Carmelita took off at a run.

Realizing what a big deal was going to be made out of this, Joey swore, using language a flabbergasted Hope had never heard coming from his mouth. That mouth, now that she looked at it, seemed a little swollen, too. And there was a tear in the sleeve of his T-shirt. Slowly she put down the phone. She still intended to call the doctor if necessary, but later, when she had a bit more information. Hands on her hips, she faced her young son. "What happened to you?"

His lower lip shot out in mutiny. "I got in a fight, okay?" he said rebelliously.

This was a first and completely unlike Joey. She faced him incredulously, bending her knees slightly until she and Joey were at eye level. "Why?" It didn't take a genius to realize Joey didn't want to say, which made her all the more anxious.

"What's going on?" Chase asked breathlessly. He joined them, Carmelita fast on his heels. He'd obviously been dressing when Carmelita summoned him. Rather than finish, he'd merely grabbed his shirt and boots. Even now, the top two buttons on his jeans had been left undone. Hope, concerned only for her son, was not about to point out that omission to Chase as he pulled on a soft rumpled navy work shirt and began to button it over the broad expanse of his suntanned chest.

Hope turned her gaze up to Chase's face, wishing he weren't here to witness this. "Joey got in a fight," she reported in a highly emotional voice.

Joey rolled his eyes. Too late Hope realized, as evidently did Chase, that smothering concern was not what her son needed or wanted at this moment. Looking as unperturbed as she was upset, Chase grinned at Joey, then shook his head in silent remonstration. Bracing a shoulder against the wall, he asked laconically, with the overt nonchalance only another man could feel at a time like this, "Well, did you lose or win?"

Surprised and pleased by Chase's more understanding reaction to his troubles, Joey had to think about that. "It was a tie, I guess, since one of the twins ended up with a split lip."

Hope whirled on Chase, exasperated. She fixed him with a quelling look he just as deliberately ignored. She realized she had signed up for the misadventure of her life by permitting him to stay. She would have to really work to see he didn't get the upper hand with her or negatively influence her son into adapting his renegade ways. "Chase!" Hope scolded. That he would encourage this kind of macho behavior with her son incensed her. She had wanted him to do the exact opposite. Otherwise, she never would have let Carmelita run to get him.

Chase paused only to give her a look that indicated she was supposed to let him handle this, his way. Whether that was because he was a physician or Joey's brother, she didn't know. Chase gave Hope another I-know-what-I'm-doing look, put a hand on Joey's shoulder and propelled him in the direction of the guest bath that was tucked under the stairs. "Let's get you in here and washed up a bit. Carmelita," he instructed kindly, knowing how anxious Hope's live-in housekeeper was to be helpful, "we could do with an ice pack if you've got one."

"Yes, sir, Mr. Chase." Carmelita scurried off to do his bidding.

Chase ignored Hope and their close proximity to each other in the tiny room. He settled his young patient on the closed seat of the commode, then raided the medicine cabinet for supplies, taking out bandages, antiseptic wipes and antibiotic cream.

Hope wanted to be in the room but she didn't want to be in the way, so she moved back as far as she could go. She found herself braced against the far wall, with her hip wedged against the sink. Chase's shoulder was within a hair's breadth of hers. Maybe I should have stayed in the doorway, she thought, but it was too late. Chase's body was already blocking the only way out. She had no choice but to stay where she was and suffer through their enforced closeness silently.

Watching Chase gently examine Joey's scrapes and bruises was adequate distraction, however. She observed with uncharacteristic helplessness; prior to this she had always been the one who bandaged Joey after a mishap. She was struck by not only Chase's gentleness and physician's expertise, but also by his innate talent for dealing with kids, period. Chase was a very good doctor, she admitted grudgingly, but his ability to handle young patients didn't exactly jibe with his irresponsible, nomadic life-style. Did he miss having kids himself? she wondered absently as Chase took a closer look at a long, rather nasty-looking scrape under Joey's chin. He seemed to find it nothing to worry about and only cleaned it without comment. Would Chase have kids now if his engagement to Lucy had worked out? Chase was so closemouthed about his private life; no one knew why his engagement to Lucy had ended. Certainly she'd been beautiful and intelligent, if a bit aloof and almost superficial at times.

But that was none of her business, Hope reminded herself sternly, turning her attention back to the unfolding drama. From what she could judge as Chase swabbed antiseptic on the scratch beneath Joey's chin, then daubed it with cream and fastened a bandage over it, Joey was in fair shape, all things considered.

That being the case, the conversation shifted back to how Joey had gotten into his predicament. At Chase's gentle, pragmatic urging, the story came tumbling out.

"Well, see, it was like this. The Bateman twins said I was a sissy and shouldn't be allowed to play at all 'cause sometimes I lose my breath and have to stop and use my inhaler. I got mad and called them a name back. A—uh—real bad one, Chase." When Joey admitted this to his half brother, Hope sighed and rolled her eyes.

"And then one of them punched me and I punched one of them. The next thing I knew somebody'd knocked my glasses off and I was on the ground, fighting both of them."

Both Batemans against little Joey! Hope felt color drain from her face. Those twins outweighed him by twenty pounds apiece, and were sturdy and muscular to boot. They could have really hurt him. Or brought on a full-blown asthma attack. But they hadn't, she reminded herself firmly. Hanging on to her composure by a thread, nevertheless, she asked as calmly as possible, "Where are your glasses now?"

"Dunno." Joey shrugged. Apparently that was the least of his worries.

"Well, you defended yourself courageously and held your own and that's something," Chase remarked. He gently cleansed the bruised skin around Joey's left eye. "You're going to have a shiner here, all right." Chase straightened and held up three fingers.

Hope had to flatten herself against the sink to avoid rubbing up against Chase from shoulder to thigh. "How many?" Chase asked, his eyes riveted on her son.

"Three."

Chase nodded in satisfaction then gave Joey his laconic smile. "Well, I guess you'll live."

He might, Hope thought wryly. But she was going to die from lack of oxygen if she didn't get out of there soon. Standing this close to Chase for such a prolonged period of time made it a little difficult to breathe. Fortunately Carmelita was back, ice pack in hand.

Still steadfastly ignoring Hope, Chase put the ice pack in Joey's hand and pressed it to his eye. "You need to keep that on for twenty minutes, then off for twenty, then on again the rest of the night. Got that?'' he instructed his young patient kindly. ''It'll keep the swelling down.''

''Okay.'' Joey started to get up.

''Just a minute, young man,'' Hope said. There was a lot more she wanted to know. ''Where was your coach when all this brawling was going on?''

''Over by the fence. Why?''

''And he let you boys fight?''

Joey shrugged his thin shoulders. ''Well yeah, until the end, then he broke it up.''

''I don't believe this!'' Hope said, turning on her heel. She slipped past Chase, narrowly avoiding a collision, and slipped out into the hall. As far as she was concerned, the fight should have been stopped at the name-calling stage. One punch thrown was too many.

Joey dashed after her, catching up when she reached the telephone table in the hall. ''Mom, you're not going to call the coach, are you?'' he asked anxiously.

''I most certainly am. This is not acceptable behavior. And if he doesn't understand that, then I'm pulling you off the team.''

''You'd make me quit?'' Joey cried. He sounded both incensed and fearful.

''Rather than have you hurt, yes, I would,'' Hope said firmly, reaching for the phone.

''Wait a minute here, Hope.'' Chase put his hand over hers, using just enough pressure to prevent her from picking up the receiver. His hand acted like a bolt of lightning on her already highly charged emotions. She froze, paralyzed both by the cool, adult determination in his hazel eyes and by the extraordinarily sensual heat that radiated from her fingers, through her arm, to her chest. She didn't want to let him, or anyone else for that matter, tell her what to do about her son. Still, Chase's insistent male presence was as hard to fight as his low, persuasive voice. ''Yes, the boys got in a brawl, but there was no real harm done. The other kids were all right, too, weren't they?'' Still touching Hope's hand, Chase looked at Joey for confirmation.

Joey nodded. And where Chase's hand met hers, Hope's skin began to burn and tingle.

"Everyone lost their tempers," Chase continued reassuringly. He looked at Hope, his intent gaze searing hers. "I'm sure it won't happen again."

"You're darn right about that," Hope muttered. Her anger about the indignity her son had suffered returned full force. She still planned to call the coach and tell him exactly what she thought of him but Chase kept his hand squarely on hers. Hope wanted nothing more than to jerk her hand free of his light but implacably confining grip. Not about to tussle with him in front of Joey for ownership of the receiver, however, and knowing Chase wouldn't give it to her willingly, Hope remained where she was, glaring up at Chase all the while.

Joey swallowed. "Mom, you're not going to try to get the twins kicked off the team, are you?" he asked in abject misery, as if the possibility would be unbearably humiliating

Hope considered the call something that had to be done. Those twins had been trouble for a long time. Just because their father owned an oil company, they thought they could do anything and get away with it. Unfortunately, usually they did. Not afraid to take a stand, she said, "Under the circumstances, those Bateman twins shouldn't go unpunished. You could have really been hurt. The next time you, or whoever else they decide to pick on, might not be so lucky."

"Mom, there isn't going to be a next time. Please. Don't do anything!" Joey wailed. Hope said nothing in reply. She wasn't about to commit to any line of action before she'd had time to think it through. Joey glared at her in mute exasperation. To her increasing aggravation, Chase looked equally pained.

"About your glasses—is there any chance they're still at the field?" Chase asked.

"Maybe." Joey shrugged, distracted. "If they're not, am I gonna have to pay for new ones?"

Hope ran her free hand through her hair. She hadn't felt so harried or distressed in a very long time. This wasn't the worst day she had ever had, but it was certainly a close second. Chase seemed to intuit that; he kept his hand squarely over hers, more in empathy now than remonstration. "I don't know, Joey," Hope answered her son tiredly, aware he was still waiting for an answer. "I'll have to think about it." She wanted him to be responsible for his belongings, and not take them or the money it cost to buy them for granted. But was this his fault?

Abruptly Joey looked as emotionally wiped out as she felt. "Can I go up to my room now, Mom? I want to lie down."

Hope shot a concerned glance at her son. It wasn't like him to want to take a nap, even after practice. "You're sure you're okay?" she pressed.

Joey rolled his eyes. "Yes!" He shot a worshipful look at his half brother. "Thanks, Chase. For fixing me up and talking to my mom. You know, calming her down and stuff," Joey said shyly.

Chase held Joey's eyes and touched his shoulder with fraternal affection. "Take care of that eye now, you hear?"

"I will," Joey promised as he moved up the stairs.

Watching him go, Hope was struck by how young he looked. Only when he'd disappeared did Chase let go of her hand. And though she'd resented the way he had physically taken control of her and the situation, Hope found her hand now felt oddly naked and vulnerable without the warm cover of his.

Telling herself she couldn't let Chase affect her this way, especially now that he was staying there, Hope turned her mind back to Joey's troubles. "I'm still calling that coach," she muttered.

"Do so," Chase warned with a daunting raise of his brow, "and that son of yours will never forgive you."

She looked at him in surprise, shocked not only by the quiet vehemence in his voice, but by his unaccustomed willingness to inject himself so fully into her and Joey's lives. The Chase she had known in the past had always watched family dramas from a distance, never risking personal involvement. Was it possible he had changed or matured? Or was this shift due to Edmond's death and to Chase's own decision to assume more responsibility for the Barrister family and business, as a whole? She had no chance to ask; Chase was already heading for the front door.

"I assume Little League still practices at the park down the street?" he asked a trifle impatiently.

Hope stared after him, her feelings in turmoil. "Yes, they do." Her voice sounded as dry and parched as her throat felt.

"I'll run over and see if I can find Joey's glasses. Or what's left of them. And Hope," he reiterated, turning to give her a meaningful look, "I meant what I said. Don't do anything until you've had a chance to calm down." His face looked tanned and healthy in the dwindling sunlight; he fastened his hazel eyes on hers and she knew in that one fleeting instant of visual contact that she had more than met her match. He turned and left.

Hope stared after him, bewildered and confused by his actions and yet oddly and perhaps inappropriately drawn to him all the same. When had he started caring what happened to her or her son? she wondered. And why was just the notion of that as disconcerting as the warm, insistent touch of his hand?

Chapter Three

Short moments later, Hope found Joey curled up on his bed, his baseball mitt and trading cards beside him, the ice pack pressed against his bruised eye. He was watching a college baseball game on ESPN, and although he seemed focused on the pitcher, she knew his mind was still on the scene downstairs. Feeling worse than ever about what had happened and the overly emotional way she had handled it, she sat down beside him and gently touched his shoulder.

"Honey, I'm sorry," she said softly. She knew she had overreacted but he was so small and so physically vulnerable. The idea of the Bateman twins picking on him deliberately made her blood boil. That she had dealt with Chase, Rosemary, and Russell Morris that day had contributed to her losing her composure. And that wasn't fair to Joey. "You really shouldn't have to quit the team because those twins picked a fight with you."

Joey reached for his inhaler. "I really *like* playing Little League, Mom."

"I know." And he liked having Chase around, too. Seeing how well the two of them got on was a surprise to her. Joey worshiped Chase; Chase liked the unchecked adoration. And she hadn't expected that she would like having Chase there, too, at least for a brief while. Even though they had disagreed on how to handle Joey, he had exerted a calming, male influence that had been missing in their lives.

Hope was acutely aware of how much Joey missed Edmond, especially at times like this. Having Chase there had closed that void with remarkable ease. She knew, for that reason alone, she would be as sorry as her son to see him go. But there were other aspects of Chase's presence that she didn't like nearly as much: the probing way he looked at her, his almost overwhelming maleness, and the sexuality and health he exuded. The bottom line was she was never more acutely aware of her womanliness than when she was around him. And those were feelings she didn't want. Not now. Not when she was a widow, and Chase was Edmond's son.

Joey's brow furrowed. "If you yell at the coach, then he might want me to quit. I know the other kids would. And then the twins will get mad, too, and they'll just be meaner than ever—" His shoulders slumped in despair.

"They shouldn't be mean at all." Hope massaged his shoulder gently.

"I know but they are." Joey exhaled loudly, as if exasperated with her lack of understanding about something he considered obvious. "Ain't nothing going to change that, Mom."

"There isn't *anything* that will change that." Hope corrected his grammar absently.

Joey shrugged, and drew on his inhaler again. She watched with relief as he began to breathe a little easier. He lowered the ice pack. His eye didn't look any better, but it didn't look any worse, either. His scratches and scrapes were all tended and neatly bandaged. And with the help of the inhaler, his breathing was still satisfactory. All was okay for the moment, she reassured herself firmly. "Can I get you some dinner?" she urged gently. "No? How about a glass of Gatorade?"

He perked up a bit at her suggestion. "Do we have the orange kind?"

"I'm sure we do. Want me to bring some up?"

Joey nodded, probably grateful he didn't have to go down and get it himself, as was usually the case. Hope didn't allow Carmelita to wait on Joey hand and foot; she didn't want him thinking he was "above all that," just because his family had money. She didn't want him turning into a little jerk; rather to have the same sensible, matter-of-fact up-bringing Chase had had. "Is it okay if I eat later?" Joey asked.

Hope touched his uninjured brow soothingly. "Sure, you can even have a tray in your room if you like." He had been a trooper, she realized. Edmond would have been as proud of him as Chase had been. She closed her eyes briefly, feeling unaccustomed tears well up. On days like this, Joey wasn't the only one who missed Edmond. It was hard to raise a child alone. There were times, like now, when she needed a strong shoulder to lean on, too.

Oblivious to the rush of loneliness she felt, Joey put the ice pack back on his eye, wincing slightly as it touched his tender skin. Looking more exhausted than ever, he yawned and closed his eyes. "Okay. Just don't call the coach," he warned once again.

"I won't," Hope promised. She qualified her statement honestly, "This time. But if it happens again—"

"I know," Joey said. He opened his eyes and finished her sentence for her in a resigned tone that let her know how unacceptable having only a mother could be. "You'll have no choice."

CHASE FOUND JOEY'S glasses in the grass. Although covered with dirty smudges, the lenses and frame were unbroken, but the safety strap that held his sports glasses on had been ripped and would need to be replaced. Obviously, he thought, it had been quite a scuffle, and unless he missed his guess, Joey had done his fair share of swinging and shoving. He probably felt he had something to prove—because of his size, because of his asthma.

Hope didn't understand that, Chase realized. Not that this in itself was surprising. Hope was so soft and feminine, so maternal and kindhearted, she'd be loathe to fight with anyone.

Part of him respected and admired that. He didn't like to fight unnecessarily, either, but this time Joey'd had no choice. He'd had to stand up for himself. Ever the pragmatist, Edmond would've been the first to understand that, and explain it to his gentle-souled wife. But his dad wasn't here to handle this, Chase was. And he knew instinctively what Edmond would've wanted him to do right now—intervene on Joey's behalf and make Hope stop smothering Joey.

Hope wouldn't appreciate that. Hell, she probably wouldn't even listen to anything he had to say. She'd only resent him all the more for butting in at home as well as at the store. If he were smart, he would just grab whatever funding he could for his project and take the nearest plane back to Costa Rica. But that would be self-serving. And Chase had tried very hard to never be the sort of self-centered person his mother was. That left only one option. He'd butt in and give advice where it wasn't wanted. His father would have approved.

He owed his dad that. Why then was it proving so hard to do? he wondered uncomfortably. Was it because Hope was such a smart, independent, vitally interesting woman who he was privately willing to bet had never tapped in to her own latent sexuality? Or was it because he found himself beginning to fantasize about what it would be like to lead her into that unchartered but luscious territory?

HER TEMPLES THROBBING with the beginnings of a fierce tension headache, Hope headed downstairs. It was Carmelita's evening off. The kitchen was blissfully quiet and dark and cool. Hope rummaged in a cabinet for a bottle of aspirin, shook out two and downed them with a glass of water, to little immediate relief.

After some moments, her neck was still stiff with tension, as were her shoulders and spine. Her dinner was in the refrigerator, ready to be microwaved. So was Joey's, but, like him, after the upset of the day, she had little appetite. She fixed herself an icy glass of cola, hoping the mixture of caffeine and aspirin would speed relief to her aching head a little faster than plain water. She headed into the living room, and met Chase, coming in the front door, Joey's glasses in his hand. Seeing his tall, lean body framed in the doorway gave her heart a little pause. Which was, all things considered, she told herself firmly, quite natural. Any woman in her place would have felt a little on edge, physically and emotionally, at the idea of being alone with him. With her, those feelings were intensified. Still, all she had to do was act normally, get through this, and he would go away.

She smiled gratefully, pretending an inner ease she couldn't begin to feel as she accepted Joey's glasses. She felt the brief warm brush of his calloused hand against her softer one. "You found them. Thanks." He had finished buttoning his jeans and tucked in his shirt. His jeans fit snugly at the waist, defining the male contours of his body very well. Too well, she decided, shifting her peripheral vision away from the apex of his thighs.

"Glad to help." His hazel eyes held hers, serious now. And again, she felt her heart skip a beat. "Hope, we need to talk."

No, we don't, she thought. A ripple of unease swept through her. She had been afraid he'd say that. "Chase—"

"It can't wait, Hope."

She knew that tone. Edmond had used it, too, and it wasn't one to be denied. Obviously Chase had made up his mind. Deciding they might as well get it over with, she nodded briefly toward the living room. Though she had shed her shoes and red blazer earlier and taken down her hair so it fell across her shoulders in tousled, naturally waving strands, she was still dressed rather formally in a white merino wool polo sweater and white wool skirt. Her jewelry consisted of a single strand of pearls and pearl earrings. She was glad for the formality of her clothes. She would have felt far too intimate facing Chase in a warm-up suit or jeans. Just having him here in the house felt, at this precise moment, disloyal somehow. Wrong. Maybe because they were too close in age and far apart in outlook for her to be a proper stepmother to Chase. And maybe because he hadn't ever looked at her as if she were his stepmother. He looked at her as an equal, a contemporary, one he didn't particularly like or want to get to know better, but who he was tied to, in a familial sense, just the same. And even though she tried to ignore that, his deliberately remote, vaguely distrustful attitude had hurt her a lot over the years.

Feeling tenser than ever, she sat down on a chair and waited for him to take a seat on the Chesterfield sofa opposite her. "It's about Joey," he said as she took a long, cooling sip of her drink. "You're coddling him unnecessarily in my opinion."

Hope felt herself becoming defensive but was powerless to prevent it. She hated it when other people presumed to know what was best for her son. Putting her drink aside, she hung onto her soaring temper with effort and met his gaze. "Chase, I know you mean well," she said tightly, warning him to back off, "but I don't need your advice on this." Nor do I want it, she thought.

Chase sighed. Knees spread apart, he leaned forward earnestly and clasped both his hands between his thighs. "In this instance, Hope, I think that you do need my advice." He saw the flare of temper in her eyes and felt his own interest stir at the unchecked display of passion. Before she could even begin to cut him off, he interjected autocratically, "He is my half brother."

Now, Hope though, that was rich. Restless and angry at this unexpected intervention, she got up to pace the room. Unable to prevent herself from saying what was on her mind, she pointed out quietly, "With the exception of the last two days, no one would ever have known."

Dammit, she didn't need Chase stepping into her life, into her home and workplace, making her continually uncomfortable and aware of herself. She didn't need him awakening feelings and needs in her she'd forgotten she had. She liked her life simple. She liked being just a mother and a businesswoman. She didn't want to yearn to be someone's woman, too. "You've never acted like his brother."

Chase whitened at her comment, but knowing it was the truth, said nothing to combat her remark.

But now that the subject had come up, she found she couldn't let it go. There had just been too many years of silence on the subject and too much repression of feeling on both their parts. As a consequence, Joey had gotten caught in the crossfire of their withheld resentments. Chase's disinterest in her son hadn't mattered so much before. It had even seemed excusable because Chase was never around to get to know Joey, but now he did know his half brother. If Chase went back to ignoring Joey again, Joey would be terribly hurt. She couldn't let that happen.

Aware he was watching her steadily and unable to bear his relentless scrutiny, she moved to the window. She stared out at the shady tree-lined driveway that led to the street. Not bothering to mask her hurt or resentment, she continued with her blunt assessment of his actions. "In all these years, you never sent him so much as a birthday card or a letter, Chase. Except for when Carmelita brought you over to help tonight, one dinner conversation is the most you've ever given Joey in his entire life. And you only did that last night because you were trying to figure out how to talk to me about the store. If you hadn't needed to do that, you never would have joined us for a meal." He never would have known what a delightful child Joey was, she thought. "You never would have come back to Houston at all."

Hope noted with satisfaction that he didn't try to deny anything she had said. "I admit I haven't been the best sibling," Chase began, visibly embarrassed. Restless now, too, he got up to pace the room.

"You haven't been anything to him," she corrected quietly, with no malice. That was the way they had all figured was best, while Edmond was alive, anyway. "That's why I resent your advice now," she continued calmly.

Chase knew she had a point. Nevertheless, cossetting was not what his father would have wanted for his second child. As difficult as it was, Chase had to do what his father would have expected him to do and make Hope see she was in the wrong here. She was as wrong as he had been in previously denying any and all ties to Joey and Hope. Like it or not, they were family, just like his mother was family. Maybe in the past this hadn't felt like home to him. With his mother gone and Hope living here, he hadn't had much desire to come home. And if he were honest with himself, he still didn't. Given his choice, he would be back in the rain forest right now, instead of leaving everything to his partner to finish up. But he was here. He was involved. And they both had to deal with that fact as best they could.

Moving to stand beside her, he spoke urgently, "I'm trying to right that now—"

Hope shook her head, a defiant light in her dark blue eyes. "It's too late. I know how you feel about me and about him, Chase." Her voice choked and she shook her head in helpless misery. "How you've felt all along—" Her jaw set as her eyes filled with tears. "Why don't you just go ahead and say it, Chase? You think I married your father for his money."

Chase could take a lot of things, but not her playing the victim—not now. "Are you telling me that you didn't?" Chase asked in cool disbelief, his temper rising. "That all this—" he gestured at the Louis XV chairs and the Aubusson rug "—played no part in it?"

Hope wanted to say that was so, but she knew in her heart it wasn't true. Edmond's power and wealth and this River Oaks fortress he had built had been a big part of the attraction when they had first met. She had needed to be taken in and protected at that point in her life. Because of the situation she had been running from, only someone like Edmond had possessed what it had taken to make her feel secure.

Realizing Chase was still waiting for an answer and that she couldn't explain any of her actions without revealing the ugliness and pain in her past, she revealed only the part of the truth she felt she could tell him. "I loved your father, Chase. I loved him with all my heart and soul."

Remembering the way she had broken down at Edmond's funeral, Chase didn't doubt that. Neither could he forget how they'd come together in the first place. "He was old enough to be your father, Hope."

Hope's slender shoulders stiffened defensively. "He was also gentle and good."

Frowning, Chase studied her. "Gentle and good" were only a small part of what Hope needed in a man, whether she realized it or not. There was a hell of a lot more to a fulfilling relationship between a man and a woman than mutual kindness. They needed to be able to turn to one another physically as well and know they'd get a lot more than a lukewarm roll in the hay. "You're telling me there was this great passion between you, that the two of you just couldn't stay out of each other's arms?" He didn't know why, he just didn't buy it. Not with any rich old man and pretty young chick in general and certainly not with Hope and his father. They just hadn't given off those vibes.

Hope turned away, looking angry and upset and uncomfortable. "That," she said flatly, offended by his presumption, "is none of your business, Chase."

Chase supposed she was right about that, too. Nonetheless, her evasion made him all the more certain. Even though Hope clearly had loved his father and had made Edmond very happy, she hadn't loved him in the beginning. Not the way a new bride was *supposed* to love her husband. And that he couldn't condone. Marriage should be more than a business deal or convenient arrangement. Especially for nineteen-year-old girls, even pregnant ones.

Hope ran a hand through her hair, looking even more distressed. She took a drink of her cola. Her back to him, she took a lengthy swallow. "We shouldn't be talking about this, Chase," she continued in a voice that was thick with suppressed emotion. "You obviously resent me and—"

"Can you blame me?" Chase countered incredulously. She was acting like it was all his fault, and it wasn't. "You broke up my parents' marriage, Hope." And not because she hadn't been able to keep her hands off his father, either, but because she had clearly wanted all this and to inherit the store someday.

"You're wrong about that. I never—and I repeat never— came between them!"

His own temper flaring dangerously, he stalked closer. If he got nothing else out of this, he wanted the truth. "Then tell me how it happened," he continued gruffly. "How you started working for Barrister's and six months later my parents' marriage is in a shambles, my father's insisting on a quicky divorce and an even quicker settlement so he can go off and marry you in some tacky Las Vegas chapel. Six months after *that* you present him with a son."

Hope turned white, then red, then white again, but as Chase had expected, she said nothing to defend herself. Chase continued, "Yes, I've resented you all these years. Just as my mother has resented you. But for the sake of everyone, including Joey, I'm trying to do the decent thing now and get past it. Move forward. I know it's what my father would have wanted." And although Chase had let Edmond down in the past, many times, he wasn't going to do so now.

And for his father's sake he had to fight his deep attraction to Hope. God knew he didn't want it, hadn't planned for it, but there it was. He wanted his father's wife in a distinctly man-woman way. And though he felt guilty as hell about it, his feelings weren't going to magically go away. His only choice was to try to work through them, to get to know

Hope and perhaps demystify her and diffuse his desire in the process.

He faced Hope earnestly, trying hard not to notice the tears sparkling in her eyes, or think about what an uphill battle this was bound to be. "The least you could do is help me out here."

Her chin took on a stubborn tilt. "I don't want your charity or your sense of obligation, not with the store or with Joey," she specified flatly.

Chase sighed heavily. His motivations were as pure and chivalrous as he could make them right now, but she was within her rights to resent his presence. Just trying to talk to each other with anything resembling intimacy put them both on edge. If she had anyone else to turn to for help—but she didn't. That meant he had to forge ahead and do his best to be "family" to her now. He hoped like hell that in the long run everything would turn out for the best.

"About Joey," Chase continued doggedly, ignoring her stormy glare. "I know he has asthma. I know he is small for his age. But he's scrappy and smart and he needs to lead the most normal life possible if you don't want him to become a sissy or an invalid. That includes playing Little League and learning to fight his own battles. You can't call the coach and complain every time he has a disagreement with another child."

Her shoulders took on a stiff, unwieldy look. "I don't."

"But you want to," he supposed confidently.

Fighting a guilty flush, she said, "Look, I want Joey to be a man every bit as much as you and Edmond did, but I draw the line at endangering his health." She held up a hand, stop-sign fashion, staving off the refuting comment Chase was about to make. "Because I know how much this means to Joey, however, I've already decided I'll let him continue to play ball, providing he doesn't get beat up again. If he does, all promises are off."

Chase was glad to see she was being reasonable. "If he gets slugged again," Chase vowed, "I'll go talk to the coach myself." An occasional scuffle was to be expected. Habitual brawling was not.

Hope nodded acquiescently, looking grateful for his help now. Like Chase, she seemed to know there were times when Joey missed his father and needed a man. "Fair enough," she conceded reluctantly, accepting his subtle offer of truce.

The silence strung out between them. Chase regarded her flushed, upturned face silently. Strangely and unexpectedly, he was reluctant to leave just yet. Looking at her in the dimming light, he was aware once again of how beautiful she was, how vulnerable. While he admired her boundless love for her son and her strength of purpose in managing the store, he did not like the fact that she always seemed to withhold much, much more than she ever said. He never knew what she was thinking. Only that he was excluded.

Because he had no reason to linger, Chase said a neutral goodbye and headed back to the guest house. Walking across the lawn, he thought about how much he liked women who dealt directly, who weren't afraid to speak their minds. Hope's secretiveness simultaneously disappointed him and made him all the more curious. Was she really the deceiving home wrecker Rosemary claimed? Or the loving angel his father had depicted? Her actions regarding her son seemed to point to the latter, but if that were the case and she indeed had nothing to hide about her relationship with Edmond, then why was she so afraid of divulging more about herself? Was she like his ex-fiancé, Lucy, just incapable of disclosing intimate details about herself? Or was it something else?

Dammit, he thought on a new burst of frustration and pique. Why wouldn't Hope just tell him how, why, when and where she and his dad had gotten involved? Instead, she simply stated over and over that she had loved Edmond. Did she think him hard-hearted and judgmental? Or was there more going on?

Having been around Hope, Chase's heart was telling him to ignore his mother's strident accusations against her, to ignore the facts, and trust in Hope's inherent goodness exactly the way his father had. He didn't know whether that made him a fool, but one way or another he was going to find out the whole truth before he left again. It was the only way he'd ever have any peace.

If Hope wouldn't voluntarily vindicate herself in his eyes, he'd just have to do it for her.

HOURS LATER, Hope stood at her bedroom window looking down at the pool. Chase was swimming laps as intensely as if he were training for the next Olympics. Watching his sturdy body slice through the glistening blue water, she thought she knew precisely how he felt. Their "little talk" about Joey and her marriage had her still strung up tighter than a bow. Had he not been down there swimming off his tension in the pool, she would've been. Going into the adjoining sitting room, she climbed purposefully onto her exercise bike and began to work out. And once again, her thoughts turned back to Chase.

They'd never meant to say even half of what they had. Considering how many years and at what cost they'd been steadfastly avoiding each other, it wasn't surprising that they had finally spoken their minds.

Like almost everyone else in Houston, Chase considered her a gold digger because she'd married a wealthy man twice her age. Unfortunately, no matter how much it grated on her nerves, it was an erroneous assumption she was going to have to let stand. To tell him the truth about her and his father's desperate personal situations at the time of their marriage was unthinkable. She had promised Edmond that no one would ever know the shame and humiliation he had suffered. And that was a promise she was determined to keep for herself and her son, as well as for her late husband. Joey had been devastated by his father's death. He couldn't be expected to weather a scandal as well.

She pedaled harder, her hands gripping the handlebars on the stationary bike. What bothered her most about all this

discord was that, their long-standing differences aside
Chase was such a nice and honorable man. He was remark
ably unspoiled for someone who'd grown up with as much
wealth and power as he. He also knew his own mind, and
hadn't been afraid to go after a career in medical research
even when he'd been continually pressured to do otherwise
and take over the family business. She admired his streng
of character and was certain had they met any other way
that they would've been friends, and possibly much, much
more.

After all, he was good with children and interested in
them; he'd evidenced that with Joey. He cared about peo
ple, as did she, and tried not to hurt anyone voluntarily. Bu
even more compelling than that was the attraction between
them. She couldn't be around him without feeling very
much alive and very much a woman. And like it or not, she
knew those feelings weren't going to go away.

Chapter Four

"Well, it's about time you got here!" Rosemary Barrister said the moment Hope stepped off the elevator the following morning.

Knowing Chase was right behind her—they'd driven to the office separately and met up in the parking garage—Hope tightened her hold on the briefcase in her hand and headed for her office. She did not want to argue with Rosemary in front of the staff. Rosemary looked as if she wanted very much to fight.

Rosemary followed Hope into her office, her stiletto heels clicking on the polished floor. Chase was close on their heels.

"Do you know what this woman has done now?" Rosemary demanded of her son. She pointed an accusatory finger at Hope.

Looking dismayed, Chase shut the door behind them.

Rosemary continued vehemently, "She turned down the chance of a lifetime for silly personal reasons!"

Hope put her briefcase down and moved behind her desk. Although it was barely nine, she could feel the beginnings of a monstrous tension headache. It made her just want to go home and crawl into bed and pull the covers over her head. "What are you talking about?" she asked Rosemary wearily, wishing Edmond's ex had just stayed in Monte Carlo, where she belonged.

"Russell Morris." Rosemary uttered the name in vindictive triumph, then turned to Chase. Hope's heart stopped and the blood drained from her face. "He had a wonderful proposition for Barrister's," Rosemary continued spitefully, "and Hope wouldn't even hear him out."

No emotion readily apparent on his face, Chase looked at Hope for confirmation.

She didn't know what to say. She couldn't very well tell Chase that she hated Russell without revealing why. She couldn't do that without hurting herself even more. Her stomach lurching, she struggled for an excuse. "He didn't have an appointment."

"Oh, for heaven's sake! Russell Morris owns one of the largest textile companies in the entire South! He doesn't need an appointment," Rosemary said.

Hope worked hard to keep her panic hidden. He couldn't hurt her anymore, she schooled herself firmly. Keeping an iron grip on her soaring emotions, she informed Rosemary coolly, "If Mr. Morris wants to meet with me, he does."

Rosemary smiled triumphantly then twisted the knife. "Russell's not having an appointment isn't the issue and you know it," she sneered. "You just didn't want to meet with him because of your thwarted romantic past with the man."

Feeling her legs begin to buckle, Hope put a steadying hand on her desk. Rosemary was wearing an abundance of perfume, and the cloying, heavy smell was making her feel even sicker. "What romantic past?" Hope asked in the most even voice she could manage. If Russell had so much as hinted to Rosemary what had happened, it would be disastrous. Cutting off her deeply troubled thoughts, she demanded, "What did he tell you?"

Rosemary smiled. "That your family used to tenant-farm cotton on Morris land when you were a teenager, and that you had a crush on him he didn't return." She lifted her narrow shoulders in an eloquent shrug. "Obviously you're still holding his good sense against him!"

"Mother!" Chase began, his tone warning her to back off. He looked as if he had heard quite enough, and more importantly still, didn't appreciate Rosemary's attempts to assassinate Hope's character. "What happened then," Chase continued firmly, "has absolutely no bearing on our company problems now."

"I think it does," Rosemary countered smugly, whisking an imaginary piece of lint from the emerald-and-onyx broach she had pinned to the lapel of her Coco Chanel suit. "Hope's refusal to even listen to Russell proves once and for all she is just not capable of running a complex operation like Barrister's."

Chase turned to Hope. He was wearing a stone-colored Armani jacket and pants over a long-sleeved raglan polo, in smoky gray. Loose and unstructured, the softly draped suit flattered the sinewy contours of his tall physique and gave him a breathtakingly understated look. His eyes weren't calm but when he looked at her, they rarely were, and the complex welter of emotions in them was impossible to decipher. She knew he was acutely interested in her and all that was going on. Maybe he was even slightly protective of her with Rosemary on the scene, but that was all she knew. It was all she could allow herself to know, Hope told herself as her stomach muscles tightened.

"Were you unfair to him?" Chase asked.

Considering what Russell Morris had done to her and the way he had ruined her life? "I don't think so, no," Hope answered stiffly.

Chase slid his hands into the pockets of his trousers. His posture was both controlled and lazy as he leaned insouciantly against the other side of her desk. She suppressed the urge to swallow nervously as his hazel eyes fastened on hers and held.

"What did he want?" His voice was casual. Too casual.

Hope really wasn't sure. She wasn't naive enough to think Russell Morris would have appeared in her life again without an ulterior motive. Russell Morris and his family did everything with an ulterior motive. She'd found that out the hard way. But not about to reveal that to Chase and risk further questioning, she moved her shoulders and said evasively, "I don't know. We never got that far."

Chase lifted his brow, making Hope feel all the more embarrassed and strangely inept. It was not as if by letting the store down, she had let Chase down, too. And that was silly because she knew he had never cared much about Barrister's. If he had he would've taken the job as company president, as his father had wanted. Nevertheless, it was humiliating to stand there and let Rosemary put her down in front of Chase. More than anyone, she wanted him to respect her, as a person and a businesswoman. It was clear from the quizzical look on his face he was no longer sure he could do so.

"You see?" Rosemary cut in, taking advantage of her son's shock to press her point. "She wouldn't even listen to him. If Russell hadn't had the moxie to come to me with his proposition, Barrister's might have lost out entirely on what could prove to be a very lucrative arrangement for both our firms."

"Which is?" Chase prodded dryly. Like Hope, he seemed to sense that there had to be a catch somewhere.

"He wants to manufacture an exclusive line of linens and draperies for the Barrister's label. The profit margin would be very high, for both of us." Rosemary's eyes sparkled greedily. "All we'd have to do is put up the capital—"

Hope cut in, "First of all, Barrister's has made its reputation carrying only the finest quality name-brand merchandise. We have no store brand, nor do we plan to have one in the future. Our customers view that with the same disregard they have for anything remotely generic. Second, we're in no position at the moment to undertake anything nearly that risky." And third, she would never ever trust Russell Morris an inch again, no matter how much she or Barrister's supposedly stood to gain. The pain of dealing with him would never be worth it; not in a million years. She couldn't even look at him without thinking about the ugliness of the past, and without resurrecting painful memories.

"I'm afraid she's right on that score, Mother." Chase stepped in, taking up Hope's defense. "It may be a good idea, but right now, the Board of Directors would never go for it. It's just too risky."

Rosemary knew she was outvoted. She wasn't a good loser. Crossing her arms at her waist, she sent an aggrieved look at her son. "Fine. You don't want to go with the idea, I won't pursue it. At least for the moment." She glared at Hope, letting her know the battle between them wasn't over yet. She turned back to her son. "But that doesn't change the facts here, Chase." Her manicured finger stabbed the air between them. "A known businessman, whose family has been a legend in the South for years, went to Hope with a proposition yesterday and she treated him very, very rudely. For silly, juvenile reasons." Rosemary turned to glare at Hope. "Who knows how many other people she has slighted in the past? Why, for all we know this is why Barrister's is going down the drain. And furthermore," Rosemary said, spinning on her heel, "I intend to let our board members know this."

The door slammed behind her. Hope and Chase faced each other in silence. "I have not treated anyone else rudely," Hope said finally, still stinging from Rosemary's insults. She felt frustrated because she was unable to defend herself the way she wanted to, in a way that would vindicate her in his eyes.

Chase latched on to what she didn't say. "But you did treat Russell Morris rudely?" he demanded.

Hope took a deep breath, knowing she had to tell him the whole truth about that much or risk him confirming it another way. "Yes," she admitted finally, turning away from Chase's searing gaze. She clasped her hands together to hide their trembling. "I guess I did." Walking over to the window, she opened the blinds.

In the sunlight, her face looked fragile, her mouth vulnerable, and her eyes sad and scared. Chase felt his heart go out to her. The meeting with Russell Morris had been harder on Hope than she wanted them to know. Knowing something must've happened, and that it wasn't like her to be rude to people, he probed for details.

"Was he rude to you first?" Chase asked, following her. She turned and gave him a hot, bitter look, one he sensed was directed more at Russell and what *he'd* done than at him. Realizing she'd given away more than she intended, Hope pivoted away from him again.

Chase moved, too, not stopping until there was scant space between them and he could see the profile of her face.

Hope drew in a taut breath. Her hands were clenched in front of her again, so tightly the knuckles shone white. "Rude or not," she murmured with a calm she didn't seem to feel, "I can handle Russell Morris."

What secrets was she holding from him? he wondered. And how long would it be before the air between them was cleared, before she trusted him enough to confide in him? Not used to waiting for anything, he wanted to demand answers, but sensing that would only drive her farther away, he said nothing.

She was near enough to see how closely he had shaved that morning. And that the sunlight brought out the sun-streaked gold of his hair as well as the deeply tanned hue of his skin. The constant exposure to the elements of sun, wind and rain had given his skin a faintly weathered, very wholesome look.

He was very curious about her, about Russell. Part of her wanted nothing more than to move into those strong arms of his, take whatever comfort he could give and tell him everything. But she knew she couldn't. What would be cathartic for her, would be devastating for others. And too many people had been hurt by Russell already. She wouldn't be a pawn and inflict more pain.

Realizing after a moment that Chase was still waiting for an explanation from her, Hope jerked from her troubled reverie but still didn't know what to say. Her hatred of Russell went back such a long way. She couldn't get into that without revealing the sordid details of her own past. Even Edmond hadn't known all the details.

"Was he rude?" Chase repeated, looking as though he wanted to find Morris and confront him.

Panicking at the thought of what might be revealed if that happened, Hope shook her head. "No—"

"But he does get to you, doesn't he?" Chase probed casually, looking grim and troubled. "Don't bother to deny it," he continued evenly before she could even begin to form a stalling retort. Stepping closer, he went on matter-of-factly, "You froze up the moment his name was first mentioned."

She knew that, too. She didn't like the fact that Chase had noticed, or that, unlike Edmond, Chase wouldn't let something go simply because she wanted him to. Hating the defensive shift in her posture, she pushed her fingers through her hair. She had to tell him something. Otherwise, he'd never quit. "We were never friends, okay?" she responded passionately. "I know what your mother said, but the truth is I didn't ever know him very well, and what I did find out about him, I didn't like." *In fact, I hated,* she added mentally.

"But the two of you did date once," Chase pressed, more puzzled than ever.

Awash in regret, Hope lifted her head. "Twice." In retrospect, she found it hard to believe she had ever been that foolish and naive.

His eyes pierced hers. "And it didn't work out," he ascertained softly.

That was the understatement of the century. "Right," Hope replied. Both her expression and her voice were as neutral as she could make them.

"And that's why you're holding a grudge against him?"

That, and I don't trust him, Hope thought, aware her heart was thudding heavily in her chest. Admitting only what she felt she could, she evaded Chase's question entirely. "I don't trust him or his motives right now because his firm is in trouble. His family was heavily into land speculation at the time of the oil bust. They lost quite a bit, and from what I've read, have yet to recover. The Morris Fabric Company is about all they have left."

"And that's why you refused to hear him out?" Chase regarded her inscrutably. "Because you think they might be in a panic now or because they've made some bad business decisions in the past?"

No, Hope thought, because Russell hurt me terribly and caused my estrangement from my family. She shrugged indifferently and picked up her calendar. "I've got a very busy day."

He studied her relentlessly, knowing instinctively she was only telling him a small part of the truth. He didn't like that but finally took the hint and headed for the door anyway. As Hope watched him go, it was all she could do not to tell him to wait. She wanted to tell him what had happened, now and in the past. If she did, she would be vindicated. He would know her for the good person she was, rather than the money-grubbing amoral home wrecker circumstances indicated. But she couldn't confide in him about her marriage without breaking her promise to Edmond. Nor could she risk letting her past with Russell Morris be known, for Joey's sake. She remained silent, torn between wanting Chase to know the truth and wanting her future and her son to be protected.

Chase turned at the door, looking as mixed-up as she felt. "I'm sorry about my mother," he said with his hand on the knob. His lips pressed together as he struggled to find the words to express his thoughts. "She speaks before she thinks sometimes."

No, she hates me, Hope thought. She thinks I ruined her marriage. And no matter how often Chase tried to run interference between them, that was never going to change, not unless Rosemary realized that *she* was responsible for the demise of her marriage.

"WE WILL NEVER GAIN control of Barrister's unless you help me, Chase," Rosemary started the moment Chase walked into the sleekly decorated Foulard's and slid into his chair.

Chase swore mentally. "I don't want control." Running the store was a responsibility he was not equipped to handle. Furthermore, after two days of going over the books, he could find nothing Hope had done wrong. Her strategy for saving Barrister's was much more aggressive and in tune with the current economic climate than his would have been.

Rosemary spread her napkin across her lap and signaled the waiter for another Perrier. "Well, I do want it back," she stated emphatically, opening her menu. "Edmond never should have left Barrister's to Hope in the first place."

Chase disagreed. Considering how closely the two had worked together, Edmond had done the only logical thing. "He had faith in Hope."

Rosemary arched a thinly plucked brow. "I think you mean, darling, that he liked having a beautiful young woman on his arm. It enhanced his virility, no doubt."

Chase didn't like the bitterness he heard in his mother's tone. As far as he knew, Edmond's marriage to Hope withstanding, Edmond had never been a skirt chaser. He'd been a monogamous man.

Rosemary continued vehemently, "Joey has no right to Edmond's money anyway."

Though Chase rarely drank at all, and never in the middle of the day, he signaled the waiter and ordered a glass of Bordeaux. "Joey is his son, the same as I," he said after the waiter retreated.

Rosemary assumed a closed but furious expression, as if, Chase thought, that was a fact of life she never intended to accept. "But not the same mother," she corrected, her hand clenching the crystal stem of her water glass. "And I will not be put in the same class with that—that white trash hussy."

"Prejudiced?" Chase asked. Hope was about as far from being a tramp as it was possible for a woman to be, despite the circumstances of her speedy marriage to his father.

Rosemary sniffed. "There is such a thing as breeding, Chase. She doesn't have it."

That, too, he would have liked to differ on. He'd watched the fluid, graceful way Hope walked, and knew the kindness and generosity in her nature. Chase had always felt, even when he resented her the most, that Hope was a very classy young woman. True, she hadn't possessed much of a head for business when she'd met his father, but that had all changed. These days, she had a sharply honed business acumen and a lot more self-esteem. That was due to his dad. Edmond had had a way of making people believe in themselves.

"You're letting her beauty get to you," Rosemary said as their salad plates were brought out.

Chase sighed and picked up his fork. When he had agreed to meet his mother at the exclusive French restaurant for lunch, it was with the express condition that they speak only of business. Hope's looks didn't enter into that. "Mother, please give me a break, would you?" He loved his mother, flaws and all, but lately she was really trying his patience.

"You're not denying you've noticed?"

No, he couldn't deny that. And the years were only enhancing her looks, adding an edge of maturity and perspective and inner calm he found very appealing. It was getting harder to remember she was off limits to him.

"And why did you defend her like that this morning? We had her on the run. If you would've only backed me up, we might have been able to pressure her to resign her position as company president." Rosemary added a bit more lemon juice to her artfully arranged lettuce leaves.

Chase finished his own salad just as the waiter brought out the main course, duckling Normandy, spiced with apples and brandy. "You're dreaming if you think Hope will ever willingly relinquish the reins of Barrister's."

"Then it's up to us to make her so miserable she'll have no choice but to quit. We can stay on there indefinitely, you know, overseeing our interests."

Chase knew that, too. Their holdings in the company came with personal offices on the top floor of the Galleria store. "Can but won't," Chase countered firmly. "I for one am going back to my research as soon as possible."

"Not without some money you won't."

Silence fell between them. Chase realized his mother was right. He might not want to get involved in store business, but he didn't have a choice. His medical research efforts were largely funded by his share of the Barrister's profits.

Nevertheless, the assumption that Hope's looks could distract him was very annoying. True, he had allowed beauty to cloud his judgment before with Lucy, but he'd learned his lesson when their engagement failed. He had no intention of making the same mistake again. His mother of all people should have known that. "Hope is doing the best she can," he finally said.

At his defense of his stepmother, Rosemary reeled as if she had been slapped across the face. Her face white, she hissed, "How can you sit there and defend the woman who was the cause of my divorce from your father? If she hadn't come along we would still be married."

When he had been young, his mother's penchant for drama had inspired a multitude of emotions in Chase; now it only annoyed him. "Would you?" he countered evenly, letting his mother know indirectly he wasn't about to be sucked into any feud, regardless of how much Rosemary felt she had been wronged in the past. "The way I recall it," he continued dryly, "the two of you used to fight all the time. That was, when you were speaking to one another."

"Chase!"

"It's the truth, Mother," he said calmly, remembering his tumultuous childhood. Yes, he'd had plenty of material things, and he had always known his father and mother both loved him fiercely, but it would be stretching the truth to declare they'd ever had anything remotely resembling a tranquil or satisfying family life. That just hadn't happened. The three of them had rarely ever been together. He had been happy going off on fishing and hunting expeditions with his father, or to Europe or Mexico with his mother. But they had never been a cozy family unit, not even on holidays.

"No, that is not the truth," his mother disputed bitterly. "The truth is that your stepmother broke us up. And I can prove it!" Reaching into her purse, Rosemary withdrew a manila envelope. She thrust it at him. "Go ahead. Look inside."

Chase knew instinctively he didn't want to see what was in there; he also knew his mother wouldn't let up until he looked. Suppressing a heavy sigh, he undid the string. Inside were a number of black-and-white photos at least a decade old. His father, entering the Ritz-Carlton hotel in Atlanta, the nineteen-year-old Hope by his side. His father with his arm around Hope, following a bellman, laden with suitcases, into the elevator. Hope and his father dining together intimately, with their heads bent together and their looks intent. He could tell by Hope's waist-length hair that the photos had been taken before they were married. Later, only months after Joey had been born, Hope had cut her hair. Although the basic style had changed from time to time, to his knowledge, she had never worn it longer than shoulder-length since. Sickened by what he realized to be true, he turned away.

"Read the dates on those copies of the hotel bills," his mother said vehemently. "The two of them were away, together, for the weekend, only days before Edmond asked me for a divorce. Now tell me she didn't steal my husband from me and break up my marriage!'' Rosemary finished with tears in her eyes.

Chase recalled Hope saying, the day before, "I never broke up your parents' marriage, Chase! I swear it!'' She had seemed so earnest, so sincere. He had believed her. Now, looking at the evidence his mother offered, he felt like a gullible fool. Had Hope done what Rosemary was accusing her of? Had she purposely set out to steal Edmond away from Rosemary? Had Edmond been sucked into her noble act the same way he had? Was it possible Hope had seduced him and gotten pregnant deliberately, knowing that as gallant a man as Edmond would feel he had to do the right thing and marry her?

Chase didn't want to think so. But he also knew how attracted he was to Hope. Even knowing she had been married to his father had not been enough to circumvent his desire for her. Of course, he hadn't acted on that passion. His father had, despite the fact that he already had a wife at home. Did it matter that Rosemary was shrewish and difficult? Chase thought not. If Edmond had wanted to pursue another woman, he should've ended his marriage first, made a clean break with Rosemary, and then gone after Hope, in that order. But he hadn't. Still, Chase had to admit, like it or not, his own life wasn't always as neatly ordered and well thought out as he'd like it, either. If it were, he'd be back in the rain forest, consumed with his medical research, instead of here in Houston, feeling increasing desire for Hope. If life were logical he'd be able to stop trying to be Hope's white knight and concentrate on saving himself from this tangled web of deceit.

Aware his mother was as lost in private regrets as he, Chase glanced at the photographs again. Hope was so young; his father was old enough to know better. God knew, he didn't want to believe any of this had really happened. It seemed so out of character for Hope and his dad. But Edmond and Hope *had* been in Atlanta together illicitly.

A moment's foolhardiness, an unplanned moment of weakness in Houston, was almost, almost, understandable, given Hope's beauty and Edmond's own unhappy marriage. And if it had been unplanned, unexpected, then the pregnancy was also understandable. A whole weekend away, in Atlanta, at the Ritz-Carlton was something else entirely. The way the two of them had gone into the hotel together, complete with luggage, was no accident. That had to have been well-planned and deliberate; it required plane tickets, reservations, and packing. The idea of them fooling around so blatantly while Edmond was still married to Rosemary sickened him.

His appetite fled. He handed the envelope back to his mother. All the negative feelings he had ever had about Hope were back and hitting him with full force. He still didn't want to deal with this. Not now. Not ever. Because it really wasn't his problem. It was his parents' divorce, not his.

"Why are you bringing this all up now?" he asked his mother wearily, wishing fervently she never had. Years had passed since then. Hope had grown up, matured. Hell, they were all wiser now. Even if he wanted to hold a grudge against her for her foolhardiness then, he couldn't, not knowing the lovely woman and devoted wife and mother she had later become.

Rosemary looked tortured and miserable. As she recovered, though, her eyes took on a determined glint. "I'm bringing this up, Chase, because I want you to be careful around Hope, not get sidetracked into losing sight of our objective, which is to get the store back on track, no matter what it takes."

Chase studied his mother, knowing what she didn't, that since he had been in Houston his objectives had changed, for the better, he felt. He no longer wanted to simply save the store or raise funds for his next research expedition, but to resurrect his family as well. He may not have known it before but he knew it now. As much as he didn't *want* to deal with things, he needed to be close to both Joey and Hope. And he needed to understand Hope, to get her to open up and confide in him. Again, not an easy task. But he knew what Hope had apparently yet to realize. If they were ever to deal with each other in the future, they had to also deal with the past.

"LEAVING, and so soon?" Russell Morris said. He fell into step beside Hope shortly after she entered the dimly lit parking garage. "I was sure you'd put in a full day." He glanced at his watch and made a *tsking* sound. "And here it is only three-thirty."

Hope tightened her hold on her briefcase and increased the speed of her steps. She didn't need this. Determined to show no fear, however, she said briskly, "I thought I made it clear. We have nothing to say to each other, Russell. Nothing." She turned her head and gave him a sharp look, her low words edged with warning, "So leave me alone."

"If I only could." Russell shook his head laconically and looked her up and down. Having reached her Mercedes, Hope reached for the handle. He moved quickly, positioning his body against the side of the car, and blocked her way. "But I can't. I need your help. And by God," he finished with malevolent intent, "you're going to give it to me."

All the anger she'd been withholding pushed to the surface; memories she had worked long and hard to bury rushed to the fore. He had made her life utterly miserable once; he wouldn't do so again. "It'll be a cold day in hell before I ever do anything to help you," she swore.

He laughed, the self-serving sound echoing evilly in the parking garage. "Is that so? I wonder. I had a nice chat with Rosemary yesterday afternoon. I could have an even more *revealing* chat with her tomorrow if I wanted."

Cold chills moved up and down Hope's spine. I'm not going to let him get to me, she instructed herself sternly. I'm not going to let him take advantage. She sighed dramatically and gave him a long-suffering look. "This bullying is pointless, Russell,'' she said, pretending she couldn't care less. ''You can talk to Rosemary all you want but she has very little to say about how Barrister's is run. I have controlling interest. And I am not going to cooperate with you, no matter how much you try to force me to do so. You might as well save yourself a lot of trouble and just give it up right now, before I'm forced to get a restraining order to keep you away from me and the store.''

His eyes darkened and his mouth took on a threatening slant. He crossed his arms against his chest and regarded her smugly. ''You wouldn't go to court. You wouldn't risk the publicity—''

''Watch me.''

''That would mean digging up the past. And you wouldn't want Rosemary to know about that, would you? If she knew, then the whole world would know. Hell, it'd probably turn up in the *Chronicle* or the *Post*.''

Again, Hope felt a chill of uneasiness slide down her spine. If Russell followed through on his threat, he would be hurting himself as much as he was hurting her. But she could see he was desperate; he no longer cared. If he was going to lose everything, he wasn't going to do so alone. No, he'd want to take her and heaven only knew who else, with him.

She swore silently and then emitted a lengthy sigh. For Joey's sake, she would try to reason with him. Running a hand through her hair, she said, ''Barrister's has no capital to put up for such a risky venture.''

He looked unimpressed. ''You could find it.''

Now he was asking the impossible. ''How?''

''Sell a few of your stores.''

She laughed incredulously at his gall. ''That isn't funny.''

''It wasn't meant to be,'' he supplied darkly. ''Or you could talk to the Board of Directors. The bank.''

How was it possible, Hope thought, feeling sick and weak again, that she could have forgotten how relentlessly destructive and self-centered this man was? "I can't," she said firmly. "Even if I wanted to—which I don't—I can't."

"Sure you can. You know how to cooperate." He leaned closer. She could smell the faint odor of whiskey on his breath. "Don't you remember how you cooperated?"

Without warning, Hope felt the bile rise in her throat. It was all she could do to swallow. Her limbs felt like ice; she turned away from Russell. If there had been anyone else in the garage, any chance of gaining help, she would've screamed.

Intending only to buy herself a little time to figure out what to do, she said hoarsely, "All right. I'll think about it."

"I'll give you until Monday to come up with a way to join forces with me. Or then I go to Rosemary," he threatened maliciously. "This time with the whole truth."

Hope knew whatever he said would not be the truth. She doubted he even knew what the truth was. Pushing him aside, she inserted her key in the lock. Despite her best efforts, her hand was trembling slightly.

He touched a hand to her shoulder and she recoiled. "Don't let me down, Hope baby," he said, his hand tightening on her shoulder like a vicious clamp. "I'm counting on you. And you know how *unhappy* I get when I'm thwarted. Monday morning, 9:00 a.m. I'll be waiting for your call."

He walked away. And for the second time in her life, Hope's life took on an unrelenting, nightmarish quality.

Chapter Five

Chase stood in the open doorway to Hope's darkened bedroom several hours later, feeling both uncomfortable and anxious. He didn't want to be there, searching her out. It was too intimate a place. And yet when he'd heard she was ill, he'd wasted no time in getting there. Part of it was obligation. She was Joey's mother, after all. He was here under the same roof, courtesy of her generosity. The other part was more complex and not something he could easily think about when she was lying there so still, like an angel, with her hair spread over the pillow in a halo of dark silk.

At first glance, he thought she was asleep and hence was loath to wake her. Sometimes sleep was the best remedy for the headache Carmelita had told him Hope had. But as he neared, she stirred slightly. She opened her eyes, and sent him a brief but dismissing look. He felt his muscles tighten protectively as he moved to her side and saw how fragile and truly ill she looked at close range.

Carmelita had been right to get him. Hope might want to throw him out of her boudoir—he couldn't blame her if she did—but dammit, she wasn't going to manage it until he had tended to her and made sure she was all right.

"Chase," Hope moaned softly, inhaling the rich familiar scent of his after-shave. His shape seemed blurry to her. "Go away." She didn't want him to see her like this. She didn't want anyone to see her. "I can't talk to you now."

Chase grinned knowingly. Another sign she was ill. Newly sick patients were notoriously cranky and often overemotional. "Then don't talk," he advised softly, already slipping automatically into his physician's mode.

Methodically he let his glance scan over her from head to toe, taking in everything about her. Obviously she felt really sick, for Hope was still in the clothes she had worn to work. The short navy skirt brought out the blue of her eyes and the white silk blouse only served to enhance the creaminess of her fair skin. Her only effort to get comfortable, it seemed, had been to kick off her shoes; they were lying helter-skelter at the bottom of the bed. She'd also removed her longish navy suit jacket and tossed it down next to her on the enormous antique canopy bed. She was lying on top of the ruffled white coverlet rather than beneath it, and a soft white afghan was drawn up to her waist. She looked as pure and untouched as the new-fallen snow against all that white, but up close he could see her full mouth was bare and soft, but drawn taut. It appeared that even the slightest movement caused her an inordinate amount of pain and stress. Realizing this, a surge of compassion flowed through him. He hated seeing her so physically miserable. He kept his voice low and professionally pragmatic as he began to take a routine history of her illness so that he could assess her condition. "Carmelita said you sent her to pick up Joey at school," he remarked casually. She had to have felt very ill to have delegated that, a chore she usually relished.

Hope wet her lips and looked supremely irritated that he hadn't left. Slowly she released a long, exasperated breath, then apparently realizing she wasn't going to get rid of him until she cooperated, answered his question, "Yes," she said, her voice laced with unexpressed pain. "I asked her to do that. Is that a crime?"

No, Chase thought, but looking so beautiful was. Ignoring Hope's grumpy manner, Chase set his medical bag down on the chair next to the bed. Although he didn't often treat patients one-to-one anymore, he was licensed to do so.

Carmelita had summoned him to discover if a call to Hope's private physician was in order. Seeing the amount of distress Hope was in, evidenced as much by her immobility as her attitude, he wondered if maybe they should be considering the emergency room instead.

"Has this ever happened before?" he asked gently. He was aware Hope was trying not to cry now that help had arrived and it was okay to surrender to the inevitable and admit that she was sick.

"Yes. I have a tendency to get migraines, but never this bad." Her whispered admission ended on a groan. "And I really *don't* feel like talking, Chase."

Again he refused to take the hint. "Double vision?"

Hope pressed the heel of her hand between her eyes. "Yes," she said, furious she couldn't get rid of him as easily as she wished. Her voice shook emotionally as she responded, "It's very blurred, almost black."

Looking at her, Chase bet she'd have a hell of a time trying to do anything right now but lie in bed.

"Is it better when you keep your eyes closed?" Chase asked, aware that his own pulse had picked up as rapidly and unconscionably as his thoughts. And that neither should have. Fighting for control of his own spiraling emotions, he reached out to touch a hand to her forehead. Her skin was cool, signifying a reassuring absence of fever. He felt a whisper of relief.

Hope swallowed listlessly and another tear rolled down her cheek. She responded to his question about keeping her eyes closed. "It's a little better when I do close my eyes, yes."

Chase studied her, determined not to overlook anything. "Any other symptoms? A stiff neck? Sore throat? Pain anywhere else?"

They went down a whole list of possibilities. To Chase's unexpressed relief, Hope denied having those symptoms, and a number of others. She hadn't fainted recently. Nor did she have a history of food allergies or anything else that could explain her current disabled state, just a history of migraines and no more. "When was the last one?" he asked, the diagnostician in him already looking for a pattern. He hoped to help her avoid such pain-racked episodes in future, if indeed her headache was stress-related, as Hope seemed to think.

Hope lifted a hand, and let it fall limply across her abdomen. "I don't know. After Edmond's funeral, I think."

Chase wasn't surprised; he knew how emotionally grueling that period had been for them all. "Before that?"

She started to shake her head dismissively, then stopped abruptly, uttering a small despairing moan that made him want to drop down beside her and cradle her in his arms. "It had been years," she murmured hoarsely, fighting not to cry again.

For once, he was glad her eyes were closed. He didn't think he could stand to look into their dark blue depths or get any closer to her bare, trembling mouth.

With supreme effort, Chase forced his attention back to the medical issues at hand. "When did you have them?" he asked gruffly, feeling all the more impatient with himself for his unprecedented lack of concentrated professionalism. It wasn't like him to think about the gender of a patient he was examining in anything but the most clinical way, yet with Hope, as inexcusable as it was, that was *exactly* what was happening.

"I had my first when I was in my late teens," Hope admitted, then grimaced blindly at the renewed burst of pain inside her skull.

Her attacks had started when she was still living on Morris land, and occurred again, during the first months she had lived in Houston, before her marriage to Edmond. Only later, after Joey was born and she was happily settled into her new life, had they stopped for any length of time. But they had stopped before, and they would stop again, Hope reassured herself firmly as a new flood of helpless tears rolled down her cheeks.

And though it was unnerving, having Chase here in her bedroom, letting him see her like this, it was also reassuring. She knew she could lean on him and trust him to help her for just a little while. She had been independent for so long. It was nice to have a man to lean on again, even briefly.

Oblivious to her thoughts, Chase asked with an efficiency that was so brisk it was almost cutting, "What do you usually do for them?"

"I take aspirin. Lie down in a dark room. Wait it out." As she spoke each word, Hope felt a renewed thundering in her skull. It was all she could do not to cry out. She tried not to think about the emotional trauma that had precipitated this attack. It had been being threatened by Russell again that had brought it on. She couldn't tell Chase that, not without telling him the rest, and she wouldn't risk him loathing her for the past anymore than he already did.

Able to tell how miserable she was as she wiped the tears from her cheeks, Chase's heart went out to her. He had always hated to see anyone in pain, and although he could alleviate her suffering easily enough, he wondered curiously what specific stress had brought the attack on this afternoon. Was it the accumulated effect of his renewed presence in her life? His mother's attack on Hope earlier in the day? Or just Hope's own guilt about the past catching up with her? God knew if everything Rosemary asserted about Hope was true, Hope should feel guilty about what she'd done, but somehow Chase didn't feel that alone was it. Had something else happened? Something he should know about? he wondered, his mind moving ahead to a more plausible scenario. Had Rosemary and Hope had it out again, and if they had, was it even something he wanted to know about? He thought not. He'd already been dragged too far into the middle of this tangled mess as it was. If the women were fighting again, and if that was the reason for Hope's migraine, they would just have to sort it out by themselves, without his intervention. That was the only way the situation would ever be resolved.

Forcing himself back to the medical aspects of her dilemma, Chase asked pragmatically, "Do you have anything stronger on hand than aspirin, Hope? Something prescription?" If she did, it was past time to take it.

She grimaced in regret, looking even more fragile and pale. "Nothing."

"Do you want me to give you something?" he asked gently, knowing a shot would provide the quickest relief.

"Will it help?" she asked in a trembling whisper. At that moment she looked as though she needed more than any physician could offer. She needed to be held, loved and taken care of. Not as his father had taken care of her, like a child bride who needed only to be coddled and protected, but as a flesh-and-blood adult woman, with adult needs and feelings and desires. Knowing, however, that he couldn't and shouldn't do that for her, even if she were to give her permission, he once again turned his thoughts back to his duties as a physician.

"I promise it'll help," Chase said softly. He reached out to touch her hand in silent sympathy, letting his touch reassure her that he cared and that relief was on its way. At the moment, he didn't care what she'd done in the past; no one deserved to suffer like this. He didn't care what Rosemary said or thought. He was going to help Hope as much as he was humanly able. If his mother felt he was a traitor to the family for doing so, so be it.

Hope sighed and permission was wrenched from her trembling lips. And in that instant, the die was cast. To her surprise, Chase insisted on staying with her while the medicine took effect. Extremely uncomfortable having him there in the intimacy of her bedroom with her, but in too much pain to get up and move elsewhere, she closed her eyes against his steady presence. Sometime in the next few minutes she fell asleep. When she awakened again, the disabling pain had disappeared, her vision was restored to normal and the blurring and darkness were gone. This should have been a reassuring thing, and it would have been, had Chase not been there with her, looking so handsome and empathetic and concerned about her all at once.

He had been reading, but he put his book down when he saw her stir. He sat forward in the chair he had drawn up beside her bed. "How are you feeling?" His voice was gentle and tender. He was everything a patient would want a doctor to be. But he wasn't her doctor, she reminded herself, or even, really, a friend. He was her stepson. She couldn't take this as anything more than a professional courtesy on his part, especially when she knew how involved Chase got with his patients. He'd gone so far as to get engaged to one during his medical school days.

"I'm much better." Hope shifted slightly. Feeling no resurgence of pain, she sat up slowly, wondering all the while just how long she had been asleep and how closely he had been watching her. She was aware her clothes were rumpled. Her silk blouse was twisted slightly over her breasts and beneath the cover of the soft white afghan, her skirt had slipped high on her thighs. She straightened her clothing self-consciously, deciding for the moment that it might be best just to let her skirt be. He couldn't see much, just an occasional glimpse of stocking-covered leg beneath the open weave of the afghan.

"Still okay?" Chase asked.

She braced her hands behind her, sat up a little bit more, and gave a tentative nod. Again, she felt no pain. Chase leaned forward, to help her prop an additional pillow behind her back. Hope sighed her relief, saying a silent prayer of thanks that the worst of the episode had passed. She waited until Chase had moved free of her, then leaned back against the pillows. "Yes, I am fine, much better as a matter of fact," Hope said self-consciously. "Thanks."

She swallowed as unobtrusively as possible, feeling the heat of an embarrassed flush spread across her face now that she was on the mend. Of all the places she never would have wanted to be with Chase, number one on her list was her bedroom. "You can go now. Thanks."

Chase started to rise, then evidently thought better of it and stayed where he was. "What brought on the attack?" he asked.

Had he been thinking about that the whole time she was asleep? Hope wondered. Or had he been wondering about something . . . something more intensely private?

"All the pressure lately," she finally said.

"Maybe that should tell you something then," Chase said gently. "Maybe you should consider giving up the presidency of Barrister's. Nothing is worth the ruin of your health, Hope."

She knew he was being kind, not self-serving, but she couldn't help feeling a little insulted that he had so little faith in her in a business sense. She had worked long and hard for the opportunity to run Barrister's in her husband's place. Edmond had wanted her to be at the helm. He had believed in her. She knew in her heart she could not only do her work but manage to make Barrister's thrive again, given half a chance.

She pushed away the afghan, not caring now that her skirt had ridden halfway up her thighs, and swung her legs over the bed, tugging her skirt down as she moved. Impatiently she got to her feet. "I'm fine, Chase," she reassured him tersely, unable to keep the angst completely out of her voice.

She had been weak when she couldn't afford to be weak. She'd been vulnerable around a man who'd seen far too much of what she was thinking and feeling already. "This won't happen again," she announced stubbornly, drawing on every bit of pride and determination she had. I won't let it. She couldn't afford to be weak now, not with Russell back in her life.

Chase followed her to the vanity. He watched while she tugged a brush through her hair and fastened it severely at her nape. "How can you be so sure?" he asked, folding his arms. "The pressure hasn't exactly gone away."

No kidding, Hope thought dryly, and then was unable to suppress a small shiver. I'll give you until Monday, Russell had said. Her hands tightened into fists. Hope braced herself for a return of the pain, but blessedly it didn't come. The migraine-blocking medicine Chase had given her was still doing the trick. She realized she might have to take more of it before this was said and done. Unless she figured out a way to get rid of Russell once and for all. And she couldn't do that while talking to Chase. Deciding a change of subject was in order, she said, "Is Joey home from school yet?"

Chase nodded. "He got home hours ago. Carmelita told him not to disturb you."

"I'd better go see him. He's probably worried."

Thankfully, Chase made no move to stop her. But Hope was aware of his thoughtful gaze, and the questions he still undoubtedly harbored.

HOPE SPENT the next hour eating dinner with Joey and reading the paper. Then she closeted herself in her office for the next half hour, with her mail. Finished with her bills, she realized it was getting late and went in search of her son. If she knew him, he'd lost track of the time, too.

"Joey, isn't it about time for your—" Hope stopped when she confronted his empty bedroom. He had left his computer on, and she could see he was in the middle of one of his games, but he was nowhere in sight.

Figuring he had gone downstairs for a snack, she headed for the kitchen. Again, no Joey. Heart pounding, she retraced her steps, going all the way through the house. Again, she called out Joey's name and got no answer. Joey knew he was supposed to ask permission before he left. That had to mean he was somewhere on the grounds, she reasoned securely.

Still, it was dark now, after eight-thirty. And she was beginning to get scared. Under normal circumstances, Joey would have turned off his computer and put his game away if he were planning to begin another activity, and he would never go out after dark alone. Not even in the yard. Not without clearing it with her first.

Stepping through the doors, she went out into the glass-enclosed swimming pool area. The pool had recently been used. Water was tracked across the concrete from the ladder at the shallow end to the atrium doors exiting the pool area. Beyond, Chase's lights were blazing. Maybe he had seen Joey, she thought. It couldn't hurt to ask.

He answered on the first knock. He was dressed in a thick brown velour robe that was tied loosely at the waist and ended at midcalf. His wet hair was slicked back away from his face. "I bet you're looking for Joey," he said, ushering her into the comfortably messy interior of the two-room guest house.

"Yes." Seeing her son sitting at the breakfast bar, it was all she could do not to collapse with relief. Her worries had been groundless after all. Russell's unexpected appearance in her life again was making her paranoid. She had to get a grip on herself.

"The delivery guy brought the pizza to our front door instead of back here to Chase, so I had to show him where it was," Joey said importantly.

"And then I offered to split it with him," Chase said. He resumed his seat next to Joey, his motions casual and relaxed. His eyes searched hers. "I hope you weren't worried."

She had been. Very. But not wanting to go into that with Chase in front of her son, she said only, "Joey, it's getting late. I think you should hit the shower and get ready for bed."

"Okay, Mom." Joey hopped down from the stool and gave Chase a high five. "Thanks for the grub."

Chase grinned back at her son with genuine warmth. "Thanks for showing the pizza guy where my door is so he'll know next time."

Next time, Hope thought, unwilling to admit to herself how good and how dangerous those two words sounded. Or how safe it made her feel to know there was a man on the premises again.

"You're welcome," Chase replied cheerfully. His face aglow with pleasure, Joey tucked his hands into his pockets and sauntered off.

"I'm sorry. He doesn't always realize when he's intruding. I'll make sure he doesn't bother you again," Hope said apologetically to Chase when Joey was out of earshot. The feeling of intimacy in the room deepened.

Suddenly Chase blinked. His contented expression faded and he regarded her with a worried scowl. "Why do you do that?"

The intensity of his probing gaze made her blush self-consciously. She turned her attention away from him, to the scattered newspapers, the haphazard clothes and shoes lying about and the notes and books. Beyond the open louvered doors that led to his bedroom, the double bed was equally rumpled. He had carted the stereo system from the living room, where it usually was, to the bedroom. Obviously he'd been listening to it a lot because there were at least thirty tapes, records, and CD's scattered on the floor. She tried not to think about a scantily clad Chase lying in bed, listening to music. Or what a luxury that must be for him, after his months of living and working in the jungle. Obviously he had made himself quite at home. And obviously he was in no hurry to leave. Not yet. Not that it was any of her business what he did or did not do over here in his spare time, she thought.

"Why do you do that?" he repeated.

Swallowing, she turned back to face him. "Do what?"

"Assume you know what I'm thinking or feeling." He shook his head in exasperation, a few damp strands of hair fell onto his forehead. He reached for his pitcher of lemonade and topped off his glass. Silently he gestured to her, to see if she wanted a glass.

Mutely she shook her head. "I wasn't trying to do that."

"Oh, no?" he challenged as he swiveled toward her on the stool. He was seated and she still standing; that put them right at eye level with each other. "Then what gave you the idea I resented Joey's presence? Did I say anything or act like I felt he was in the way?"

"No." She backed up slightly, away from the open V of his legs, and knotted her hands together in front of her. Somehow, she managed to keep the defensive note out of her voice. "You were perfectly polite," she admitted with a shrug. "Then again, you were raised by your father to never be anything less to any guest in your home. That doesn't mean Joey should've horned in on your dinner at the last moment."

"If I had wanted to get rid of Joey, I could have," Chase said quietly. He hooked one foot lazily on the rung of the stool.

She was aware of the faint scent of chlorine clinging to his skin, and the bareness of his chest and legs beneath the robe. Edmond, too, had swum or exercised every day. But he had never looked like that, so healthy and virile. Again, guilt assailed her, and again she pushed it away.

"But I didn't get rid of him," Chase continued, "because I enjoy his company." Not only had Hope's palms suddenly started to perspire but she hadn't combed her hair in hours. She tucked a dark strand behind her ear. "Look, Chase, I appreciate your kindness. But I don't want Joey coming to depend on you." Chase's brow lifted in silent discord and Hope plunged on. "He's already suffered enough loss in the past year." And so had she, she thought. But to have Joey think Chase cared about him and then have Chase leave without a backward glance, with nary a letter or a phone call in the future would devastate her son.

"You're projecting again," Chase chided impatiently, draining his lemonade and getting lazily to his feet. He put his empty glass on the navy ceramic-tile countertop with a thud. "First, by assuming I don't want him around. Then, by saying that I'm going to leave."

Her spine stiffened and she took yet another step back, to give them both more breathing room. "Aren't you going to leave?" She clamped both her arms together at her waist.

"Yes," he answered frankly, his gaze holding hers without the slightest hint of apology. "But not for a while."

That was another problem with Chase, Hope thought. He was a bit too footloose. She knew how it was, being around someone like that; her father and mother had been the same way. They hadn't done anything nearly as noble as medical research but like Chase they'd always been looking over the horizon, thinking somewhere else would be better, that the farmland would be richer, the weather better, and their landholders more generous. And so they had moved from tenant farm to tenant farm. Hope and her brothers and sisters had been denied the chance to make any real or permanent ties.

But that part of her life ended when she had married Edmond. And it was going to stay that way. She needed people around her and Joey who she could depend on through thick or thin. And as good as his intentions might be right now, that wasn't Chase. Therefore, she couldn't encourage Joey to spend time with Chase. It was nice Chase had finally noticed Joey was alive, of course, but she feared what would happen when the attention stopped.

She watched Chase pick up the empty pizza box, fold it and then put it into the trash. He carried the dirty plates to the sink.

"You don't trust me, do you?" Chase said.

"I just don't want any trouble." *I don't trust anyone,* Hope thought, *except myself. I learned the hard way I can't afford to do so.* She shut her eyes briefly against his insistent look.

"There won't be."

If only she could believe that, Hope wished fervently, but Russell was back in her life. Hope forced a smile. "I better go. I've got stuff to do at the house."

"I'll see you in the morning."

Hope tried but ignored the promise implicit in those simple words.

"I HOPE YOU'VE HAD your morning coffee," Leigh Olney said. She breezed into Hope's office shortly after nine. "You're going to need it."

"Why? What's going on?"

Leigh slid her coltish figure into a chair and fiddled with the sterling-silver barrette at her nape. "It's Rosemary Barrister. She's called an emergency board meeting for this morning, and two of the six have already arrived."

Hope slowly put down the pen she had been holding. Was there to be no end to the the continual disasters she was facing? "Why wasn't I informed of this?"

Leigh shrugged. "I didn't know about it, either. Neither did Chase, judging from the surprised look on his face when Cassandra Hayes and his mother appeared. Anyway," she said, consulting her watch, "you're due in the boardroom in five minutes, unless you want to miss it."

"I only wish I could miss it," Hope muttered under her breath. "Tell them I'll be right there."

Short moments later, Hope strolled into the boardroom, her leather-bound notepad under her arm. She greeted some people, noticed there were several there she didn't know, then took her seat at the head of the table. She could tell by the victorious look on Rosemary's face that Rosemary thought she'd bested Hope. Hope decided to find out what her nemesis was up to before she spoke, so she'd know what tone to take. She gave the floor to Rosemary.

Not surprisingly, Rosemary took the ball and ran with it. She did her best to make it clear that Hope should be replaced as president, effective immediately, and that she was completely incompetent to boot.

"So you can see," Rosemary concluded haughtily a few minutes later, "my own market research tells us that making Barrister's a less exclusive place to shop is a major mistake. If we do that, our customers will stop shopping in

Barrister's entirely.'' She glared at Hope in a debilitating fashion. ''None of your changes can be made without doing serious damage to the store.''

''Serious damage has already been done,'' Hope countered pragmatically. ''Our old clientele's decreased patronage is exactly why the store is in trouble.''

''She's right,'' Cassandra Hayes, the most hard-nosed member of the board, put in. ''We can't worry exclusively about what old clients think. Change is always hard.''

''We're not a Macy's or a Dillard's,'' Rosemary cried.

''Maybe we should be,'' Chase said, commanding everyone's attention. He looked at Hope, surprising her by giving her his support. ''Maybe then Barrister's would survive.''

Hope did some quick thinking. Edmond had always taught her one picture was worth a thousand words. ''Perhaps it would reassure everyone to see the type of goods we intend to carry.'' Hope pressed the button next to her desk and issued some instructions for Leigh Olney.

Seconds later, Leigh stepped into the room. She was pushing a garment rack. On it were colorful outfits from Children's Wear. She showed the couture children's line the store had been carrying exclusively, then got out an equally attractive line of clothing. ''We'd like to start carrying Esprit, Guess, and Hang Ten for little girls, Polo and Izod for little boys.''

''You'll ruin the store!'' Rosemary wailed.

''I like it,'' Chase said, leaning back into his chair and shoving his hands deep into the pockets of his pants. He looked at Hope, with a very public show of support, then at each of the assembled board members. ''Makes sense to me.''

Hope glowed, from the respect she saw in his eyes as much as the way she had taken control of the meeting.

Rosemary glared at her son as though he was the worst kind of traitor.

"However," Hope continued, addressing the board members gathered around her, "it is a major change."

"Yes, and a rather frightening one at that," Sam Casey said. "Because if the consumers don't like the downgrading of goods, we'll lose them forever."

"Maybe it would make you all feel better if we put together an after-hours cocktail party to introduce our base customers to Barrister's new look," Hope continued. "We could make a real event out of it. Invite the governor, the mayor, anyone and everyone who is someone in this state."

"Sounds good," Chase said. The measure was voted on and passed. Knowing Rosemary was still out to see her fired, Hope took advantage of the opportunity of the meeting and told the group about Russell Morris's offer. To her relief, they were unilaterally opposed to any new business ventures of that sort.

"Too risky," Cassandra Hayes said.

"I agree," Sam Casey added. "Even if the profit margins are high, it would take a while to gain consumer trust. Time we don't have."

Although her face was impassive, inwardly Hope breathed a sigh of relief. The meeting was disbanded. As Hope suspected, Rosemary hung around until everyone else had left but Hope and Chase. She turned to Hope. "You think you've won," she informed her haughtily. "You haven't. I am not going to let you ruin this store."

No, Hope thought, *I am not going to let you ruin it. Nor am I going to let you have the presidency and controlling interest, which you think you so richly deserve.*

Chase might have had some claim to them, if he'd wanted them, but not Rosemary. Whether she had meant to or not, Rosemary had done nothing but make Edmond miserable.

"Mother—" Chase began.

"And you! What in heaven's name possessed you to stand up for this—"

Chase's look narrowed warningly.

"—incompetent person!" Rosemary concluded with a sputter. "Have you forgotten what I told you about her and Edmond in Atlanta?"

At that, Hope felt the blood drain from her face. Although she remained standing, she wanted desperately to sit down. How and when had Rosemary found out about that? And what else did she know?

Seeing the damage was done, Rosemary shook her head in silent admonition. "You owe me more than that, Chase. Much more." She turned on her heel and strode from the room.

The door swung shut behind her. Hope went back to her place at the head of the table. *I have a choice,* she told herself firmly. *I can walk away from this and never know what Rosemary has told him. Or I can have it out with him here and now and risk humiliating myself and his father's memory even further.*

She knew what Edmond would do. He had never run from a battle in his life. He'd confronted each head-on and persevered until he had achieved the best outcome possible. She had learned from him. He had helped her to grow. And she would prove it. Looking up at Chase, she said, "What did your mother mean by all that?"

Chase looked as stricken as she felt. "Don't you know?" he asked woodenly.

"Please. Just tell me," she pleaded softly. *Don't let your mother's half-truths and conjectures stand between us when we're just beginning to be friends.*

Chase turned to her. The support he had shown her in the boardroom was gone, as was the tenderness he had shown her when treating her migraine. All she saw now was tension, and distrust. "All right," he said finally, his jaw set, "but not here. Not where anyone might come in."

"We could go up on the roof," Hope suggested cooperatively, adding, "This time of day no one is on the jogging track." She might not care much what he thought of her, but she cared terribly what he thought about his father. Their relationship had been fragile enough as it was; she wouldn't let Rosemary destroy what few happy thoughts Chase had of Edmond.

"Fine."

The day was sunny and bright with the mild temperature of early spring. The wind was blowing hard. Chase's hair whipped around his face. Once on the roof, he wasted no time with preliminaries. He told her bluntly that he knew she'd checked into an Atlanta hotel for a weekend with his father, just days before Edmond had initiated his divorce from Rosemary. Chase turned to her, the look in his eyes grim. "Hope, I checked the files. There is no business record of the trip. So it had to have been personal."

Extremely personal, Hope thought. "It was," she admitted softly.

Chase's hazel eyes searched her face. "You're still maintaining you didn't break up their marriage?"

"Yes," Hope said, believing it with all her heart and soul. "Edmond told me they hadn't been close for years, that it was an empty union," she said with gut-wrenching honesty.

"And that gave you license to have an affair with him?" he asked sarcastically. "While he was still married?"

Hope lowered her eyes, ashamed that it looked that way. Chase clearly thought she was a tramp. "It wasn't like that."

His patience fled. Chase took her by the shoulders and said gruffly, "Then tell me how it was."

She shook her head. Her eyes full of tears, she twisted out of his grip. *Forgive me, Edmond,* she thought. *I know how this looks and I'm sorry.* "I can't, Chase. I'm sorry. It's too personal."

Chase was silent.

"I'm sorry your mother was hurt by all this," Hope finally said. She was also sorry Rosemary still felt she had to get even.

From a strictly analytical view, she was guilty as hell. The facts said so. Intuitively he felt there was a hell of a lot more.

It frustrated him she wouldn't talk about it. It reminded him of Lucy. She, too, had been beautiful and young and troubled. And she, too, had refused to open up to him. Frustrated beyond speech, he heaved a heavy sigh.

So did Hope. She pursed her lips together briefly, afraid if he pursued this any further she would give in to her growing need to vindicate herself. Knowing she couldn't let the truth tumble from her lips, she switched the subject to more neutral ground. "Listen, thanks for supporting me in the meeting."

Chase was silent, fighting his own welter of conflicting feelings; he wished he could trust Hope implicitly. In terms of the business, he had seen for himself how hard Hope was trying to save Barrister's. And that his mother, despite her sense of self-importance, was about as incompetent as they came in business matters, mostly because she thought with her heart not her head. "It was not an act of chivalry on my part, believe me," he retorted gruffly, his frustration with Hope's silence only slightly abated. He sent her a level look. "Everything you said made sense." Right now, he wanted the store to begin making money, so he could go back to his research with a clear conscience.

Hope nodded gravely, still looking a little tense. "The party and all the attendant publicity should help. If I can pull it off," Hope murmured. She seemed to know that his mother would be working against her every step of the way.

Chase knew that wasn't fair. "Do you need help arranging it?" He heard himself volunteering before he could think. He had to face it: the enforced boredom of not working in research was beginning to make him a little crazy. It was giving him too much time to think about Hope, to speculate and fantasize and try to understand her actions. He'd found himself thinking of her at all hours, especially at night.

Hope studied him suspiciously. Was he anxious to be a henchman for Rosemary? Or just anxious to fix their troubles so that he could leave? "You're offering to be a volunteer?"

"Yes," he said, wondering if he was just going through the motions to be polite. All he knew for sure was that he was beginning to feel stifled again, that there were too many expectations being put upon him. His mother expected him to side with her no matter what. Hope had no positive expectations at all. She looked surprised if he did anything the slightest bit nice. Which only pointed out that he must have been an ogre in the past. But if passion hadn't drawn Hope and Edmond together, then what had it been?

"Why did you put forward the Morris deal when you were so against it initially?" he finally asked.

She turned away, the evasive light back in her eyes. She clamped her arms together, her posture defensive. "I didn't want your mother accusing me of being close-minded."

"Was that the only reason?" he pressed. He had seen firsthand how much she detested Russell Morris; just the mere mention of his name brought out a tenseness in her that was unparalleled and seemed to go far beyond the usual thwarted teenage romance.

No, Hope thought, troubled. With the Monday deadline looming, she had needed to get Russell off her back. Now she could tell him that she had tried—Rosemary could verify that—and it just hadn't worked out. He'd be forced to take his venture elsewhere. She would be rid of him and the danger and the migraines.

Realizing Chase was still waiting for an answer, Hope shrugged and said, "I thought it was only fair. I wanted to test everyone else's opinion, too."

He edged nearer. Glancing up, she held his eyes. He doesn't believe me, she thought. He knows I'm hiding something and he doesn't like it. But she couldn't tell him why she was afraid of Russell Morris, no matter how kind or sympathetic Chase sometimes seemed. She couldn't tell anyone. It was simply too much of a risk.

Chapter Six

"Do we have enough models for the party?" Hope asked.

Chase nodded, from the other side of her desk, and consulted the neatly typed pages he had spread across his lap. "Yes. Ten for every department, with three changes each. They'll circulate among the guests. We're also planning to have live musicians."

"Classical?"

"For the adult sections of the store," he confirmed. "In the teen section on the second floor, we've got a DJ coming in, to spin some records and lend some atmosphere."

"Great. A DJ'll be better than a band, in terms of noise control." Hope smiled, scribbling notes on the pad in front of her. "What about the children's section?"

"We've got Big Bird and other Sesame Street characters."

"The mothers will love that. Maybe they can mill around and hand out discount certificates, too."

Although she had planned to do much of this herself originally, Chase had convinced her to let him handle most of the groundwork, contingent on her approval of course, while she busied herself by checking the new merchandise lines the buyers were ordering.

Seeing Chase in his suit and tie, she was aware of how dashing he looked. He was handsome enough to model clothes in their print ads. And yet beneath the urban pol-

sh, there remained an untamed edge to him, a wildness of
heart and a renegade soul she still found intensely compel-
ing. Unlike his father, Chase wouldn't be an easy man to
ove. But if it was thrills a woman was after, he looked like
he type of man who could provide them.

"What's next?" he asked when he had finished writing.

Hope consulted her own notes. "Invitations." She
glanced up. "When are they going out?"

Chase looked over at her. Being so close to her was hard.
Whenever he was, he kept thinking about all the secrets she
kept locked inside. The evidence didn't matter. She just
didn't seem like the kind of woman who'd set out to steal
someone's husband.

"Chase?" Hope prodded. "The invitations. When are
they going out?"

Chase glanced back down at his list, chagrined. Caught
daydreaming—at his age! Quickly he scanned his timeta-
ble. "First thing Friday."

He was working fast, Hope thought, pleased. That was
good. Advance notice would spark interest among their
customers. "And the caterers?" she continued, forcing
herself to concentrate more closely as she went down her list,
too.

"They've already been contacted. They'll be serving finger sandwiches, petit fours, fruits and cheeses, plus the usual
assortment of beverages."

Unlike Rosemary, Chase never challenged Hope's authority; he was simply there to help. Hence, they'd been able
to work well together.

Finished with his business, Chase stood restlessly. He regarded her with polite deference. "If you don't need me for
anything else, I'll be going."

Hope glanced up, able to see how eager he was to go.
Since he had confronted her about the trip to Atlanta, he'd
been unusually edgy and contemplative. She knew why, of
course. He was upset because she hadn't explained her way
out of the sticky situation or come up with any plausible

excuse that would have allowed her to keep what was left of her reputation. "Fine, Chase," Hope said. She watched him gather his things.

What was she supposed to tell him? That her and Edmond's joint sojourn to Atlanta had been anything but an illicit liaison? That she, distressed by her situation, had been thinking of terminating her pregnancy. And that Edmond, empathizing with her pain and confusion, had gone along to provide moral support for whatever she decided. Then, lauding her decision to bear the child she had never planned for or wanted to have at that young stage of her life, he proposed they marry.

Put like that, it all sounded so cold and calculated. But it hadn't been that way at all. They had been lifelines for each other, best friends at a time in their lives when they'd each been deeply troubled. And they had remained best friends until the day Edmond died.

The phone rang. Thankful for the diversion, Hope picked it up.

Chase watched as the color drained from her face; her hands began to tremble. "I'll be right there," she said. She put the phone down blindly.

Chase felt his own heart race. Instinctively he knew the news was very bad and, just as instinctively, moved forward to help her. He slid a steadying arm around her waist. "What is it?"

"Joey." She swallowed, grateful for his arm around her. "He's been taken to the hospital." She turned to him urgently. "I've got to go."

Chase took one look at her pale face and knew she was in no shape to drive, let alone maneuver the late-afternoon traffic. He helped her get her purse and, his arm still around her, fell into step beside her. "What happened?" he asked. He felt upset, too; they moved briskly toward the elevators.

"He was at an after-school birthday party and had an asthma attack—a bad one. Apparently he didn't have his inhaler with him. They had to call an ambulance to the skating rink where the party was held. One of the parents chaperoning the party went to the hospital with him." Fighting tears, she took a deep breath and wrapped her arms around her waist.

Chase knew how she felt. Seeing how unsteady she looked, he tightened his arm around her as they entered the elevators to the parking garage. "I'll drive you."

Still visibly shaken, she didn't argue.

She didn't look much better when they entered the emergency room and located her son. Joey was resting on a bed, behind a curtained partition. He seemed even smaller and frailer than usual. The pale color of the loose-fitting hospital gown blended into the washed-out look of his skin. "Hey, Mom. Chase," he said weakly. He lifted a hand, trying hard to look dauntless despite the traumatic afternoon he'd had. He looked from one to the other, gauging reactions. "I guess you heard what happened," he said sheepishly, obviously embarrassed.

Hope nodded. "I certainly did." She brushed her lips lightly across his temple. "I'm just glad you're all right."

Chase was, too. In a severe attack, it could easily have gone the other way. "Where was your inhaler?" he asked his half brother gently.

Joey shrugged, looking suddenly very guilty. "I don't know," he mumbled, refusing to look Chase in the face. "I guess I forgot to take it with me."

No, he didn't, Chase thought, watching the telltale play of emotions on his half brother's face.

The mother who had accompanied Joey put her hand to her chest. "It really was awful, Hope. I was never so frightened in my life. One moment he was fine, skating and laughing and racing with the rest of the kids. The next he was sprawled facedown on the floor and turning blue. He couldn't get his breath. None of us knew what to do."

At the chaperone's emotional description of the crisis, Joey paled. He looked as frightened and guilty and upset with himself as Chase felt he ought to look. Hope looked equally discomfitted and alarmed. Recognizing the need to get the woman out of there before she unwittingly did any more damage, Chase took her by the shoulders and guided her out the door, affording Hope and Joey some time alone. By the time he had thanked the woman for escorting Joey to the hospital and paid the cabdriver to take her home, Hope was once again emerging from the curtains around Joey's bed. If possible, she looked even more drained and frightened than before. His heart went out to her. This was not something she or any parent should have to endure alone. And with his father's death, she was very much alone.

He moved to one side of the hall. She joined him. "He's dressing," she reported with a trembling lower lip, trying very hard to keep up a brave front. "The doctor says we can take him home now."

Chase sighed his relief. "That's a good sign," he said. It meant the attack had been a relatively mild one after all. It probably could have been contained had Joey just had his inhaler with him at the rink.

"I know. Oh, Chase, I—" Without warning, tears filled her eyes.

Before he could think, Chase had his arm around her waist and was holding her against him, supporting the softness of her trembling body against his taller, stronger frame. At his touch, she cried all the harder; he automatically gathered her close. And he found there was nothing remotely familial about the way she felt against him. No, she was all woman, he thought.

"Oh, Chase," she whispered. "All the way over here I was so afraid. I get so scared when he—"

"I know." Chase patted her back comfortingly. He had been frightened, too.

Needing simply to be held, she leaned into him, wrapped her arms around his waist and held on tight.

He'd meant only to offer her a shoulder to cry on and that was all. But at her continued closeness, a slow, burning pleasure started in his loins and moved up, until it suffused his entire body.

Not, Chase observed wryly, that it was any great wonder. Slender and feminine, she was everything he had ever physically wanted in a woman. Her breasts were full and soft where they touched against his chest. Her thighs were slim and strong beneath the fabric of her skirt. Her calves curved gently against his. Her hair was fragrant and soft as it spread across his shoulder. Her lips— He cut off the thought.

"Okay?" he asked suddenly. He wished she'd step back now and give *him* some room to recover.

But she didn't. And powerless to prevent it, he felt the traitorous reaction of his body continue to build.

Not that holding her in his arms wasn't the sweetest pleasure. Hell, yes, it was. He wanted to comfort her and wanted to find a way to halt her tears. He just didn't want her to be aware of his body's response. If she backed out of his arms right now, there was a chance, as distraught as she was, that she wouldn't be aware. His mouth was dry as he waited for her to pull herself together, step back and save them both from possible embarrassment.

She only shook her head. Apparently she wasn't yet feeling okay or anywhere near it. Feeling her body shake with those silent sobs that were probably as much for herself and all she had lost as for Joey, evoked a powerful response within him. He wanted to help her channel that wellspring of emotion and devastating loss within her into a cathartic passion that would please them both. As he continued to hold her, it was all he could do *not* to slide his fingers beneath her chin, tilt her face up to his and kiss her, really kiss her. He wanted to taste the softness of her mouth and feel her body respond to his.

Finally, mercifully, her tears slowed. "I'm sorry," she apologized. Embarrassed, she drew back slightly and allowed some space between them, just moments before his own throbbing response became apparent. "I've gotten your jacket all wet," she said.

Chase exhaled slowly. At the moment, a damp jacket was the least of his worries. "It's okay, Hope." Because she seemed to need a reassuring touch, and because he was loath to let her go entirely just yet, he kept his arms loosely around her waist.

"No, it's not okay," Hope argued, her formidable inner strength returning. "And what happened today isn't, either. I'm furious with Joey. How could he be so careless as to leave his inhaler at school? He knows he's supposed to take it with him at all times."

Chase lifted a brow. He was relieved Hope had vented all that pent-up emotion and cried herself out. He was glad to have been able to help her, but he wasn't the one who should be getting this lecture. "Did you read *him* the riot act for forgetting it?" he responded softly but firmly.

"No, of course not." Hope's chin tilted up defiantly, and then she froze, as if fully realizing he was actually holding her, however loosely. She withdrew from the loose circle of his arms. A slightly panicked look on her face, she backed up until her spine touched the mint-green concrete wall behind her. She used her knuckle to dab at the moisture beneath her eyes. "I don't want to upset him even more."

"But you will do so later," Chase ascertained, the words more an order than a question.

But as it happened, to his growing aggravation, she didn't do it later. Not when the nurse came out to tell them Joey was ready to go home, or in the car ride back to River Oaks, or during the light supper Joey ate before falling into bed. And Chase, who felt an obligation to his father to ensure that his half brother retained his health, couldn't understand why she didn't take a harder line with her son.

"You should have scolded him," Chase said, not attempting to hide his mixed feelings of frustration and bewilderment. The two were walking back down the stairs of the home he had grown up in; the house was now Hope's and Joey's in every way, from the redecorated color schemes and the delicate arrangements of flowers to the homey signs of little-boy clutter that graced every elegant room. He just didn't understand this. Hope was so careful and thorough in ever other regard. It wasn't like her to overlook the obvious.

Hope's head lifted. Her eyes glimmered at the implicit censure in his words. "I don't think it's necessary, Chase. I think he learned his lesson. Besides," she shook her head in mute despair, "I don't want to scare him with horror stories of what might happen."

Neither did Chase. But Hope was overly protective when it wasn't necessary, then refused to speak to Joey when there was an emergency. And Chase didn't want to lose him. Unless someone made it crystal clear to Joey that his health was nothing to play around with, that possibility still existed. "He's already scared," Chase countered softly, following Hope into the room. He watched her close the white louvered shutters and turn on several lights against the falling darkness. Carmelita had already left; it was her night off. With Joey upstairs, in bed asleep, the house was inordinately quiet. Keeping his voice low, Chase stepped closer to Hope, continuing to press his point, hoping to talk some sense into her. "That doesn't necessarily mean he's learned anything from this experience except that he managed to come out of it relatively unscathed. This time, anyway."

Hope shut her eyes in silent prayer. "Thank God for that," she whispered, a clenched hand pressed to her throat, the other tucked tightly against her waist.

"But he could have died," Chase continued urgently. He was desperate to get through to Hope now in a way he hadn't before. He knew she was vulnerable, too. He felt angry with himself for not knowing how to help her.

"Don't say that." She put her hands up, as if to ward off his words.

He went to her, cupped his hand over hers, brought her hands down and turned her face to him. Joey wasn't the only one who was hiding from the truth. And Chase cared about Hope too much to let her play the deadly game of hiding, too.

"Why not?" he asserted softly, his eyes challenging the denial in hers. "It's true." Hope paled. Knowing it was what his father would've wanted, Chase held on to her hands tightly and pressed his advantage, "You've got to stop protecting Joey, Hope. You've got to level with him, tell him that what he did was a very stupid thing. If you're angry, let him know you're angry, and why. Respect him enough to be frank with him and stop treating him with kid gloves. That, right there, is a big part of your problem with him. And his problem with himself."

Her jaw clenched and she shot him a harassed look. She appreciated Chase's help. She had needed someone to drive her to the hospital. For a short while anyway, when exposed to the tender caring side of him, she had felt very close to him. It had been wonderful, being held in his arms, knowing she could lean on him that way, when she had needed a strong shoulder so badly. But there were limits to the amount of help she was willing to take from him. "No," she said stubbornly. "He's been through enough."

Chase bit down on his exasperation and returned, "He'll go through even more unless you see that he does what he is supposed to. Like carry his inhaler with him."

And she'd thought Edmond was persistent! She saw now he had nothing on his son. "I've already done that," she countered reasonably. "He'll be fine by tomorrow. Trust me."

Chase wasn't so sure Joey would be fine. Small for his age, slightly built, he seemed to be constantly trying to prove himself. It was okay for him to want to be healthy; it wasn't okay for him to be taking unnecessary risks. Chase had a hunch, from the guilty look on Joey's face this afternoon, that forgetting his inhaler had been no mere accident. It was an attempt to deny his illness. Hope didn't want to believe that, of course. But her refusal to see the situation for what it was wasn't helping any, either. Right now Hope and Joey weren't listening to each other. He was telling her he felt singled out and hated it. And she was trying to tell him if they hid long enough it would all go away, as if by magic. If his father were here, Chase knew it would have been different. Edmond could have made her see reason. But he wasn't his father. And Joey wasn't his son. This didn't have to be his problem. But it was. And it had been ever since he'd been back.

Chase sighed. He knew they'd said all there was to say. It wasn't as if he hadn't been in situations similar to this before. He had, especially with Lucy. He'd tried to talk some sense into her, too. Only she hadn't listened, either. Just like Hope wasn't listening. And he had learned the hard way it was impossible to help someone if they didn't want to be helped. "I hope you know what you're doing," he said, still staring at Hope.

"Everything is going to be fine, Chase," Hope said, trying her best to convince him.

Chase yearned for that to be true. Because if anything did happen to Joey, Chase knew he'd never get over the guilty feeling that he'd somehow let them all down.

"MORE FRENCH TOAST, Joey?" Carmelita asked the following morning. "Half a piece."

Joey eyed the plate hungrily, trying to gauge the limits of his appetite. "Half a piece."

"What about you, Mr. Chase?" Carmelita said as Chase entered the kitchen via the back route. "Would you like some breakfast?"

"I just came over for a cup of coffee," he said. He looked at Joey; he was pleased to see he had his old color back and looked none the worse from his traumatic experience the day before. "Going to school, I guess."

"Yes, sir. I have a spelling test today." Joey made a face. "I hate making up tests."

"Good morning, Chase," Hope said from the other end of the kitchen table.

Carmelita handed Chase a steaming cup of coffee. He smiled his thanks, then turned back to Hope. If she was still mad at him for speaking his mind, she wasn't showing it. "Morning."

Looking fresh and rested in a navy Anne Klein suit, she smiled at him over the rim of her own cup. "Joey looks good this morning, doesn't he?"

Knowing a loaded question when he heard one, Chase nodded. He reached out and ruffled Joey's hair. "He sure does. Keep eating that way, slugger, and you're going to be an iron man before we know it."

Joey grinned. "Sounds good to me."

Hope gave Chase a smug smile and went back to her paper. Okay, he thought, so maybe in this instance Joey's mother did know best. Maybe he was letting his imagination run away from him. Unfortunately, his gut feeling wasn't concurrent. His gut feeling told him that like it or not this was a situation that had to be dealt with more fully. He knew Edmond would've wanted him to intervene, in his absence, and that there was no one else who could do so. He also knew Hope wasn't likely to appreciate his efforts, now or at anytime in the future.

"Hey, Chase," Joey said breaking into his ruminations. "Do you think I could ride in your Jeep sometime, with the top down?"

Hope opened her mouth to protest.

Chase shrugged evasively. "I don't know. We'll see. All right, buddy?"

Joey's small shoulders slumped beneath the tailored school blazer. "Okay," he said, visibly depressed, obviously thinking it was his asthma getting in the way again. And since it was, Chase didn't know what to say.

Hope gathered the papers she had been studying and stuffed them into her briefcase. Consulting her watch, she said, "Hurry up and finish your French toast, hon. We've got to go. I don't want you to be late."

"Okay, Mom."

Her mood pleasant but aloof, Hope passed Chase in a cloud of perfume that would haunt him for the rest of the day. By the time five o'clock rolled around and he received a person-to-person call from Costa Rica, he was ready for a break. "Chase, old buddy, how are you?" his co-worker shouted through the staticky lines.

Bored, Chase thought. Fenced in. "Anxious to be back to work," he said. *My real work.* He kicked back and put his feet up on the corner of his desk. Swiveling his chair, he glanced out at the blue Texas sky outside his office window. It was pretty, but not nearly as entrancing as the beautiful, mysterious rain forest. Aware of what this call must be costing his friend, he shouted back clearly and loudly, "How's it going out there?"

"Couldn't be better! I got the last of the samples we needed today. I'm shipping them back to the National Cancer Institute for testing and I'm heading home."

Chase felt a moment's regret that he hadn't been there to see the project through to the end, then pushed it aside. He had family responsibilities here. In the past, it was the kind of thing he had generally tried to duck, but with his father gone, he had to fill in. That decision had been made; he wouldn't waste time feeling sorry for himself. "Are you going to be able to go to New Zealand with me in July?" his partner asked.

Chase knew he couldn't leave until absolutely everything was in order here. He also knew he'd work like crazy to see that it was. "Probably," he answered, confident he could clear up every problem in that amount of time, including Hope's unnecessary coddling of Joey. "What's up?"

"The NCI has a lead on a possible cure for arthritis. I thought it might bear checking out."

"Sounds good," Chase said, willing to go just about anywhere, for any length of time, in the name of medical research. "The only problem is funds. I haven't got any." And it generally took months and months of red tape to get a grant.

"Well, you know I don't, either. You're the only one of us who's filthy rich." His partner paused. "Any chance you can raise funds by then?"

Chase sighed and immediately thought of Rosemary. This was precisely the sort of thing she loved, and she was very good at raising money. That might get her mind off the store and her vendetta against Hope. "I don't know. I can try," Chase said.

"OF COURSE I'd be happy to help you raise funds for your research, darling," Rosemary said when Chase approached her, later the same afternoon. She was in her office, busily trying to find fault with the plans he and Hope had set up for the after-hours party. "You'll have to be there in person, though," Rosemary warned. She examined a faint chip on one rose-colored nail. "You'll have to wine and dine the possible contributors."

"It won't be a problem," Chase assured his mother. He could live through one more black-tie event if it meant he could get back to the rain forests in July.

"Will you bring a date or shall I get you one?" Rosemary asked cagily. She pulled out a bottle of polish from her purse and began repairing the slight imperfection in the veneer.

Knowing the kind of woman his mother was liable to fix him up with—beautiful, empty-headed and filthy rich—Chase passed on the matchmaking. "I think I can find someone to go with me, thanks," he said dryly.

"I know you *can,* darling. The problem is you usually *don't.*" She paused. "Have you been seeing anyone since you got back?"

No one except Hope, Chase thought as he left his mother's office. He'd been seeing Hope with alarming frequency. At work, at the estate. In the past, he'd had no problem avoiding her even when he stayed in the guest house. Maybe because his father had been there to handle anything that came up, like Joey's trip to the emergency room. Chase didn't want to be Hope's savior. Hell, considering her past and all she still wouldn't tell him, he wasn't even sure he should trust her at all. But more and more he found himself being cast in that role. More and more he found himself thinking of her as a woman. When he'd held her in his arms and felt her soft body pressed up against his, he had known without a doubt it could be very good between them. It still bothered him that she had been married to his dad, but he also knew his father was gone now. And Edmond wouldn't want Hope to be alone. Not for the rest of her life. He would want Hope to be happy, to be loved again.

If his father was all that was standing in the way of them, maybe in time it all could have worked out. But he wasn't. Chase knew that unless Hope opened up to him and trusted him enough to tell him everything, that nothing more would ever be possible. And that thought made him feel depressed and dejected as hell.

Chase sighed and raked a hand though his hair, tired of fighting his feelings and tired of continually wrestling with his sense of what was right and wrong. His partner was right. He had to get back to the rain forest. He had to go to New Zealand and do his real work. And the sooner the better.

"YOU DISAPPOINT ME, Hope," Russell said over drinks at Maxim's. It was Monday evening, after work. Russell regarded her with a smug, insinuating look that made the muscles in her neck stiffen with tension. "You've turned into a fine businesswoman. You *should* have been able to sell the deal I'm proposing."

"I tried," Hope said with as much calm as she could muster, trying hard to ignore the cloying smell of his aftershave and the disturbing memories it evoked. She remembered Edmond's advice, to always treat her enemies with as much courtesy as her friends. "You can ask Rosemary," she said pleasantly.

"I didn't have to ask her," Russell continued in his slick, insincere voice. His soulless blue eyes fastened on her face. "She called me as soon as the meeting was over. She said you mentioned the deal but you did *not* stand behind it."

Sweat gathered between her breasts and under her arms but Hope faced him equally. "I let the Board of Directors make up their own minds."

His expression turned ugly. He lifted his Scotch to his lips and drank deeply. "They would've bought it if you had persevered." He set his glass down on the tablecloth with a thud.

Unable to look at him a second longer, Hope focused on the plush red interior of the restaurant. "I don't think so," she said calmly.

"Well, we'll never know now will we?" he asked sarcastically, his displeasure evident in the cruel twist of his lips. He lifted his glass and took another lengthy sip.

The way he savored the taste of the expensive liquor brought back a lot of memories, too. Please, she said in silent prayer, not another migraine. "Look, I'm sorry it didn't work out," she lied. "But now that it hasn't, maybe you can sell your proposal to someone else."

"And maybe," he said, in a voice that was both soft and harsh, "you'll just have to figure out another way to appease me."

Something in Hope went very cold and very still. "What do you mean?" she whispered hoarsely. "I've done what you asked."

"No, you pretended to do what I asked because you didn't see any other way around it." His blue eyes narrowed.

Unable to contain her anger now, Hope clenched her hands together on her lap and snarled, "Did you really expect me to help you? After what you did to me, the way you ruined my life?"

"I didn't ruin anything, Hope. You did."

"That's a lie." Hope felt the blood begin to rush to her face.

"Things could have been so easy for you, so sweet, if you had only gone along—"

She got up so suddenly she jarred the table. Blindly she headed for the exit. Russell caught up with her and closed his hand around her upper arm. He exerted pressure, unmindful of the fact they were in a very public place. "Sit down, Hope," he said behind a fixed, deadly smile. "We haven't finished."

People at the bar were beginning to stare. Russell smiled even more broadly and made a loud, flirtatious joke for the benefit of their audience, making it look as if they were in the midst of a lover's quarrel.

"Sit down," Russell prodded softly, beneath his breath, "or I'll have no choice but to bring up how we knew one another before."

Knowing she had no other choice if she didn't want a very ugly scene, very public scene, Hope reined in her quaking fury, returned to the table and sat down.

"You owe me, Hope," Russell said cordially, as soon as they were seated again. "I thought I made that very clear."

Two could play this game, she thought as she met his gaze courageously. "And I thought I had made it clear I can't help you." She spat out the words like shards of glass.

His look hardened. "Maybe not in business. But fortunately for you, I am *not* a picky man. I will accept cold hard cash."

She stared at him in shock. "You're crazy," she whispered disbelievingly.

He leaned forward, rested both elbows on the table, and spoke in the arrogant, amoral tone she detested. "No, just blunt. I want two hundred and fifty thousand dollars, Hope. Within the next few weeks."

"I won't—"

"Oh, I think you will, that is if you don't want our secret past leaked to every gossip columnist in town. It'd be interesting, wouldn't it, to see how your son would react to the news of what his mother was really like." He sat back smugly.

The thought of Russell anywhere near her son made her skin crawl. Unable to bear looking at his face a second longer, Hope fastened on the open collar of his silk shirt. Seeing a glimpse of his darkly tanned skin, she shifted her gaze again. "You bastard."

"I thought you'd see it my way." Satisfied he'd done all the damage he could, he tossed a bill on the table and stood up. "I'll be in touch." And then, with a smile, he walked away.

Hope sat there for several minutes, feeling sick and shaken. The waiter came back and asked her solicitously if she were feeling all right. She nodded and said yes, but as soon as he left she reached for her purse and removed a small brown vial. In it, was her migraine medicine. She'd had the foresight to get it from her family doctor before her meeting with Russell. Now, with her vision beginning to blur and her head beginning to pound, she was glad she had it.

She swallowed the pill, and then put the bottle away. She knew from bitter experience that taking a pill during the onset of an attack often was enough to prevent a full-blown migraine. All she had to do was sit here, and wait for the medicine to take effect. The only problem was she couldn't drive after taking the medication, as it made her drowsy.

CHASE WAS OUT BACK, playing catch with Joey. He and Joey were both surprised to see Hope emerge from a cab.

"I wonder where her car is," Joey said, pushing his Astro's cap back on his head.

"I don't know," Chase said, absently thumping his mitt. Hope didn't exactly punch a clock with him. But all day today she seemed a little distant, troubled. He had tried to talk to her once, to fill her in on the invitation list for the cocktail party, but had given up and just left a typed list for her because she was so distracted.

"Maybe she had car trouble," Joey said.

"Maybe," Chase agreed slowly. And maybe, Chase thought suspiciously, something else was up, something she didn't want him to know about. After catching the grounder Joey had sent his way, he closed the distance between them. "I think that's about enough for tonight," he informed his half brother genially.

"Okay. I gotta go in and watch *The Cosby Show* at six-thirty anyway," Joey said. "Thanks for playing ball with me, Chase."

"Anytime," Chase murmured. He handed over his mitt and the ball. He watched Joey run off, their gear cradled in his arms, and then headed for the front of the house. Hope was in the living room when he entered. She had put down her briefcase and was sitting in the fading light; her hands were knitted together in her lap and she was just staring ahead of her. He knew at once that she was in some sort of distress. It was impossible to tell whether it was physical or emotional.

"Hope?" he said softly, watching her turn slowly to face him. She didn't look as if she wanted to see him or anyone else. "Everything all right?"

She blinked, still looking a bit stunned. "Yes," she said quietly. "Everything's fine."

She didn't look fine, Chase thought. If she was so fine, why had she come home in a cab when she had driven to work? He knew she'd left early for an outside appointment—with whom or where, he didn't know. Was that outside appointment responsible for her upset state? Or was something else bothering her? He was tired of Hope's lying.

He stepped closer, able to see how pale her face was. He'd never been able to resist helping a person in need, and right now she had never looked more vulnerable. "I saw the cab outside. So did Joey." Unable to help himself, he took a closer look at her shuttered expression. "Are you all right?"

And then it hit him, he knew by the faint waxy look of her skin. "Are you having another headache?"

For a moment he thought she was going to deny it. She swallowed as if in great pain. "Yes, but it's all right," she answered, her voice low and irritable. "I've already taken some medicine. I'll be fine. I just need to lie down for a while."

Her bad temper didn't alienate or offend him; he was grumpy, too, when ill. He regarded her carefully. He was still ready, willing and able to help. "You're sure?"

She turned and took a deep breath. "Yes," she said flatly, her patience for conversation exhausted. "I'm sure." She touched a trembling hand to her temple, doing her best to keep up the barriers. "Have you seen Joey?" She wouldn't look at him directly.

Hurt that she wouldn't let him help her, Chase said, a bit miffed, "He was going up to watch *The Cosby Show*—"

"Oh, of course. Thanks." She moved past him now, still looking as white and scared as if she'd seen a ghost. She still looked unwilling to talk to him or be with him.

He didn't want her to feel like that. More importantly, he knew it was partially his fault. He hadn't exactly been friendly to her the past few days. He'd been keeping his distance, too.

"Hope," he said, when she reached the bottom of the stairs. She looked so damn helpless, so stricken, so scared and distressed that he couldn't bear it. "If there's anything I can do—" he offered. Not so much for his father's sake, this time, or even for Joey's, but his own. Because strangely enough, he still found himself wanting to help her, wanting to get past the barriers, to find out what was really going on with her.

She shook her head firmly, not about to share whatever trouble she was in. "No. Thanks anyway." And to Chase's disappointment, on that note she climbed the stairs and didn't look back.

Chapter Seven

Hope waited until Joey was fast asleep that night before going to the safe in her bedroom and removing her jewelry case. She carried it over to her bed. Sitting cross-legged in the middle of it, she began laying the pieces out, inspecting them one by one. Every piece she owned had been a gift from Edmond. Every piece was very valuable. And aside from the stock she owned in Barrister's, it was the only liquid asset she had. She would have to sell it. All of it.

Leaning back against the pillows, she closed her eyes. She could hardly believe she was actually considering giving in to blackmail. Russell wanted two hundred and fifty thousand dollars. The man was insane. But if she didn't give in to him he was just evil enough to do what he had threatened, to tell Joey, and she couldn't bear that. Joey would never learn about her sordid past or Russell's part in the scandal that had ruined her former life, torn her apart from her whole family, and almost destroyed her emotionally.

No, she had to get rid of Russell, the sooner the better. The jewelry was a small price to pay. So first thing tomorrow morning, she would see about cashing it in.

Her decision made, Hope met the owner of the River Oaks jewelry store at eight the next morning. She laid out all the pieces. She had no idea what the pieces were worth collectively. It was time she found out.

"This is a beautiful set," Mr. Fitzgerald murmured. "I remember selling it to your husband. It was right after you were first married, wasn't it?"

Hope nodded, her gaze falling on the garnet necklace and earrings. That set in particular had deep emotional significance for her. She could still remember Edmond fastening the necklace around her neck on the eve of their wedding. "I can't promise you forever," he had said. "Only that I'll take care of you as long as we're together." And he had. He had loved her until the day he'd died. And she had loved him.

Surely, she thought, Edmond would understand why I'm doing this. He would want me to protect Joey.

"Twenty-five thousand," Mr. Fitzgerald said.

Hope felt herself begin to panic. This was by far the most valuable set she owned, in her opinion. She had a long way to go before reaching the two hundred and fifty thousand Russell was demanding. "That's all?" she asked, trying hard not to conceal her mounting panic.

Mr. Fitzgerald smiled comfortingly. "I can see you have attached great sentimental value to the set, but, I promise you, Hope, that's all it is worth."

She knew he wouldn't try to cheat her. If anything, because of the business the Barristers had done with the River Oaks store over the years and because she was Edmond's widow, he would give her a slightly inflated price.

Hope looked at the beautiful sapphire and diamond ring and matching bracelet Edmond had given her for their first anniversary. She tried to swallow the tears that clogged the back of her throat. "What about these?"

"Twenty thousand."

Hope swallowed. "The aquamarine necklace?" Given to her to celebrate Joey's birth.

"Ten thousand."

And so it went. By the time she had added up the value of all the pieces she owned, she was still far short of her goal. Worse, she had nothing else of value to offer, Hope thought dispiritedly, except one thing. She looked down at her hands. Her diamond wedding and anniversary rings.

Slowly, she took them off her hand. She gave them to Mr. Fitzgerald. "What about these?"

He looked as stricken as she felt. "Hope, you don't—"

"Yes," she interrupted, feeling dangerously near tears, "I do." She had to sell them. She had to sell everything. And she would do it with no regrets, too. She would do anything to protect Joey.

Mr. Fitzgerald bent down to examine the rings. Hope was still numb as he quoted the final price. "When can you have a check for me?" she asked. She was in a hurry to leave now that the deed was done.

He frowned, not liking her haste, but too much of a gentleman to inquire deeply into the reasons behind it. "The end of the week." He paused and then added gently, "But only if you're sure this is what you want to do."

It was, Hope thought grimly. She had no choice.

UNFORTUNATELY for Hope, her day did not get any easier. "What do you mean you're planning to close the store for a few days at the end of the month?" Rosemary complained, storming in on Hope and Chase about ten o'clock. She waved the memo Hope had instructed her secretary to distribute.

Hope's secretary appeared behind Rosemary, gesturing helplessly and rolling her eyes. "I'm sorry, Hope. She saw them while I was still preparing them."

"Are you crazy?" Rosemary continued, advancing farther into the room. She thrust the stolen memo at Chase, who, after accepting it, silently began perusing the print.

I don't need this, Hope thought. Not after the morning I had. To Rosemary, she countered with a calm only Chase seemed able to appreciate, "I'm just being practical."

"Practical!" Rosemary echoed with a huff.

"Our first shipments of the new merchandise will be in by then. We can't mix couture and ready-to-wear in the same departments," Hope retorted evenly.

"So what are you planning to do?" Rosemary countered sarcastically, her beringed hands on her fashionably slim hips. "Rearrange the whole store?"

Hope lifted her chin a notch higher, daring Rosemary to challenge her. "As a matter of fact, I am," she enunciated plainly, feeling her temper flare in response to the other woman's continued harassment.

"What?" Rosemary gasped in shock. "Chase, do something," she pleaded, turning to her son.

Chase sent Hope a questioning glance, looking just as disturbed as his mother. In an effort to reassure him, Hope patiently explained her plans. "I'm going to put all couture on the third floor. It will be available for viewing by appointment only. The first floor will be cosmetics, jewelry, and adult ready-to-wear. The second floor will remain as it is, with furniture, bedding, linens, china and the children's departments."

"That will require quite a bit of upheaval." Chase frowned.

"I know. Which is why we are going to have to close the store for a few days." Hope got up and brought back the plans she'd commissioned an architect to draw up. "As you can see it will involve several new sections of sheet rock being put up, some replastering and painting—"

"Absurd." Rosemary paced back and forth. "This whole revamping is crazy."

"No," Hope countered, "it is not. These changes are necessary if Barrister's is to survive in the nineties."

"You'd know a lot about surviving," Rosemary said bitterly.

"Mother," Chase intervened, "let's not get personal here."

"Oh? Am I supposed to overlook what this—this idiot— is doing to our family store? She's going to drive away all our loyal customers and if you don't see that, Chase, then you're a blind fool!''

"Our loyal customers will remain loyal," Hope said calmly.

Rosemary snorted and Chase gave her a chastising look. "I'm sorry," Rosemary said to her son, "but loyalty is something Hope obviously knows nothing about. All you have to do is examine her past to know that. Look at how quickly she turned her back on her own people, for heaven's sake. No sooner had she married rich than she all but disowned them!''

Rosemary was right in so far as the facts went, Hope thought with a debilitating mixture of shame, guilt and remembered hurt. She *had* walked away from her own family. But her doing so had nothing to do with who she had married. Or why, even now, she had no desire to be in contact with them again.

Chase stood, putting the plans for the renovation carefully on Hope's desk. "Mother, that's enough," he ordered sternly.

"Siding with her again?" Rosemary turned to Hope and gave her an ugly look. "You'll pay for this," she swore, and stormed from the room.

The door slammed behind her. For a moment, Chase was silent. Head bent, he gave Hope a long-suffering look that silently begged her forgiveness. Then he ran a hand through his dark gold hair.

Although she was still very angry with Rosemary, Hope's heart went out to Chase. She knew firsthand how frustrated he felt. She had suffered similar problems when trying to deal with her mother, too. She could still remember how much it had hurt, how betrayed she had felt, in the days before she had left her family for good. She could remember the way her mother had looked at her, accusing her silently, telling her it was all her fault, that she'd brought the traumatic scandal on herself.

That still hurt her unbearably. She had expected her own family to back her up. But they hadn't. And consequently, Russell and his family had won. They'd triumphed in the whole ugly mess. But that was in the past, she reminded herself firmly. And thanks to the sacrifices she was making now it would stay there. "It's okay, Chase. I understand. I know firsthand how unreasonable mothers can be sometimes."

He glanced up. His gratitude faded gradually and was replaced by curiosity. "Is that why you left home the way you did?" he asked, his voice soft.

Hope said, evasively, "We were never a close-knit family. Large, yes, but it was every person for his or herself."

He strolled nearer, seating himself on the edge of her desk. "And yet you're so devoted to Joey."

Hope shrugged off his praise. "I didn't want him growing up the way I did, with no parental support or attention." Wanting him to understand that much about her, she lifted her eyes to his. "My parents thought that if they put food on the table and clothes on our backs it was enough. As soon as a child could walk, a door was opened and he or she was sent out to play."

Chase moved closer. "Is that why you had only one child, to be sure you had enough time to devote to Joey?"

Caught off guard by the unexpected intimacy of his question, Hope drew in a quick breath. "Why would you think that?"

"Because I know for a fact my dad always wanted to have more children."

Hope would've liked to have had more children, too, but she couldn't tell Chase why they had never done so, not without possibly revealing everything she and Edmond had agreed must be kept secret from the rest of the world.

"You being so young, so obviously maternal—" Chase continued casually "—I just wondered, that's all. But I can see it's none of my business, so forget I asked."

Hope knew no harm was meant by his impulsive questioning. He was just trying to understand her, on every level. She knew because part of her wanted that, too. Chase would be hurt if he knew the truth, that Edmond had kept secrets from him, too.

"We better get back to work," she said, averting her glance.

"Yes." Chase nodded slowly, looking momentarily as lonely and disappointed as she felt, "I guess we'd better."

"I KNOW SOME of these pieces have been in your family for generations," Mr. Fitzgerald said the following morning. "I wasn't sure how you'd feel about Hope selling them. I wanted to be sure you knew."

"I didn't know. Thanks." Chase paused, bewildered and upset by this latest revelation about his stepmother. "Did Hope tell you why she'd decided to sell them?"

"No," Mr. Fitzgerald answered, sounding as inwardly troubled as Chase felt. "Only that she wanted it done right away and to get the best price possible for her."

Chase struggled with himself. Although he was overwhelmed with curiosity, he also knew this was none of his business. If Hope wanted to sell her jewelry, certainly she was allowed to do so. She didn't have to consult him. But why was she selling it? And not just a piece or two but everything, even her wedding rings? Was Hope simply after the money and hence as greedy and uncaring as Rosemary kept asserting Hope was? Or was she in some sort of trouble, as his gut feeling kept telling him she was? And if so, wasn't it his duty as Edmond's son to help her?

He found her in the cold-storage room, checking the furs that were going to be offered at reduced price. They were alone and weren't likely to be disturbed; still, he didn't know how to broach the subject without offending her. Finally he just said it. "Mr. Fitzgerald called me a little while ago. He heard I was in town. He thought I ought to know what was going on."

"I see." Hope's reaction was subdued. Careful, she ran a hand over a balmacaan mink, checking tactically for any flaws. Finding none, she wrote the tag number down on the clipboard. The cold air of the vault had brought a rosy color to her cheeks. When she looked at Chase the color deepened even more. "You're angry with me for selling the pieces?" She kept her voice neutral with effort.

"No," Chase said, refusing to turn his glance away from her lowered gaze, "I know they're yours to do with what you wish."

Her relief about that was visible, but she let it pass without comment. Still not looking at him, she moved down, to the next fur on the rack. "You see," Hope said touching the sleeve of a beautiful mink and changing the subject, "this is what I was talking about." She turned to him, her expression all business. "Ten years ago at this time of year, we would have had maybe ten coats left to put on sale. This year we're stuck with thirty-five of the original forty we ordered. And we have almost no chance of selling these unless we mark them down to fifty percent off. Even then it won't be easy. Which, as you know, reduces our profit margin on the coats to nothing. All we have to show for it is the prestige of carrying the coats, and the electric bill for the cold-storage room."

And prestige, nice as it was, Chase thought, didn't begin to pay the rent. Chase smiled, beginning to feel a bit chilly himself. Clamping his arms over his chest, he drew nearer to her and said, "Weather-wise, there's not much reason to wear mink in Houston."

Hope grinned and countered dryly, "Women in Houston don't wear furs because they're cold."

No, Chase thought, discomfitted, they wore furs, like they wore jewels, because they were filthy rich and wanted everyone to know it. Which brought him back to the original reason he had tracked her down. Was the poor performance of the store the reason she was putting her jewelry up for sale? Was she in personal financial jeopardy as well, fearful of losing her house? That was the only reason he could figure that would motivate her to sell the jewels. He was sure Hope knew that Edmond would've wanted the jewelry to stay in the family if at all possible, for sentimental reasons. If possible, Hope would have honored that wish. But if that were the case, why wouldn't she just tell him so? he wondered. He was frustrated anew at the way she'd cut him off.

Hope confessed quietly, "I wish Mr. Fitzgerald hadn't called you."

Chase didn't think he could stand to see her looking so sad. He watched as she went through the sensual process of inspecting the next coat. Her slender hand moved over the silky fur with sure, sweeping motions and he found himself wondering what it would be like to have that same hand on his skin. Or better yet, to have Hope naked, wrapped in one of those furs. Had she ever vamped like that for his father? Would she do it for him?

His throat dry, he said, "Mr. Fitzgerald knows some of the pieces are heirlooms, and he wanted to give me the first shot at them." Without warning, the coat slid off the heavy hanger. Hope was left awkwardly juggling the coat, clipboard and pen. Chase stepped forward to rescue the coat before it fell to the floor, and as he put it back on the hanger, asked gently, "Hope, are you sure you want to sell everything?" More than ever, he wished it wasn't greed that motivated her.

Hope's chin tensed stubbornly. "Yes."

Chase could tell she resented his intrusion, although she was doing her best to cover it. And maybe that was fair. Still, he didn't like her secretiveness.

"I just thought you might want to save a piece or two for Joey and his wife someday. The emerald pendant, for instance."

The one that had belonged to his grandmother, Hope thought. She faced him awkwardly. "I don't know what to say, Chase." Obviously, she thought, he felt she was being a little bit callous being able to sell the jewels at all. But she could hardly tell him that she had no choice but to give in to Russell Morris's blackmail. Then Chase would know the truth about her marriage to his father. He'd know Edmond wasn't the strong, virile man he had pretended to be, and that he had kept secrets from Chase. If Chase knew that, he would be hurt. Worse, his view of his father would be changed forever. Lessened. She couldn't have that. Especially now that Edmond was no longer here to defend himself or explain his actions to his son.

"Hope, are you in some kind of trouble I don't know about?" Chase asked.

"No," Hope denied promptly, turning back to her task of inventorying the unsold minks.

Chase knew he was pushing it, but he had to ask. "Then why are you selling the jewelry, Hope?" He followed her over to the next rack. She tried to keep him from being able to see her face, but he positioned himself so she had no choice but to be aware of him. "Why now?" he persisted. He was aware they were close enough for him to see the warm vapor of her breath against the chill of the room; her nipples had tightened visibly, too. He felt an answering pull in his own body. Before he could think, he was moving toward her, watching her dark blue eyes widen, her lips part. She was so sweet and so near he could almost taste the kiss. And though he sensed she wouldn't, couldn't resist such a move on his part, at least not initially, he drew back.

Chase swallowed hard and forced his mind back to the jewelry. "Why sell all of it?" he asked abruptly, trying not to notice how relieved Hope looked when he took a second step back, away from her.

She shrugged, the evasive motion drawing his eyes to her slender shoulders, and away from the fullness of her breasts. "I thought it was time I moved on with my life."

She still wasn't looking at him directly. Except for her slowly growing closeness to him, he hadn't noticed her warming up to any other men, or dating again. But then, maybe this was just the first step, a step that would get her out of mourning. While the pragmatist in him applauded that, another side of him was deeply jealous. Telling himself he didn't want her doing anything she would regret later, he probed, "And you don't want to keep any of it for sentimental value, if not for Joey and his wife, for yourself?"

Briefly, a look of pain crossed her face and was quickly masked. "I have my memories of my life with your father, Chase," she said, all the love she'd felt for Edmond reflected in the inherent tenderness of her voice. "That's all the memento I need."

Looking at the serenity on her face as she finished, Chase could see that was true. And knowing how she'd been brought up, in relative poverty, perhaps that was to be expected; she would value cold, hard cash in the bank over any pretty baubles in the safe. Nevertheless, he couldn't help feeling disappointed. He had expected her to be more sentimental. And maybe she would have been, he reasoned further, had she the luxury.

"Are you worried about the fate of your job with the store?" he asked gently. Was that what was behind her sudden actions? Was that what was giving her the murderous migraine headaches?

At his question, her expression changed, becoming defensive and irritated again. "Your mother is gunning pretty hard to have me fired. Or hadn't you noticed?" she queried dryly.

"Oh, I noticed. I also noticed she doesn't seem to be succeeding."

Hope lifted a dissenting brow. "The night is young yet, as they say." She sighed.

But Hope was strong, Chase thought, and smart and determined. Rosemary, as much as he loved her, was all selfishness and hot air. The other board members knew it, too, which was probably why no one was paying particular attention to her. They knew, long-range, they'd never be able to count on her sustained interest in the store. No, once

Rosemary had plenty of money to spend again, she'd be off to Europe.

Hope studied Chase. The cool air in the room had brought out color on his cheeks. "I know you don't understand about the jewelry." Briefly she searched for the words to explain. "I'll just feel better if I'm a little more solvent, with assets I can get to if I need them."

And, Chase thought, maybe it was time she got on with her life, even if she was unable to say that to him, for fear it would sound as if she were demeaning her marriage. Suddenly, despite the unexpected surge of jealousy, he wanted that for her, too. He wanted her to go on, to have a new and fulfilled life, to find a husband for herself, a father for Joey. She was still young. She deserved to have everything. "You'd call on me if you needed help, wouldn't you?"

"Yes, I would call on you," she said, her eyes meeting his frankly. "But only if I had no alternative."

He nodded, accepting that, too. He had clearly overreacted. It was just his imagination going into overdrive. She wasn't in any sort of trouble. She was just taking healthy, normal steps to try to sort out her life. Her moving on reassured him. Still, he felt jealous and unsettled and he disliked that almost as much as the way she kept holding him at bay.

HOPE STAYED where she was long after Chase left the coldstorage room. That had been close, she thought, feeling the sticky perspiration beneath her arms. His questions had been far too close for comfort. If they hadn't been in the cold-storage room, he would have seen her sweating. And he would've known...

Why hadn't she realized Chase would find out about the jewelry? She was lucky Rosemary hadn't heard about it and used the information to further discredit her. Maybe she should have gone to New York or Los Angeles to sell them but that would have raised suspicion, too. People would have wondered how she could leave town when the store was in the midst of a crucial transition.

She had to stay on and see this through, for her sake and for Edmond's. She wanted people to know he had been right to trust her, and that she not only could and would do a good job but that she cared deeply about Barrister's.

As for Russell, well, she'd get rid of him soon, as she had gotten rid of him before. And when that happened, she would no longer have to be so excruciatingly careful. Maybe then she could let down her guard a little with Chase. She hoped so because he was a nicer, more generous man then she had ever realized. And she needed strong, caring people like him in her life.

If Edmond were alive, maybe it would've been possible to think of Chase only as her stepson. But he wasn't. And she knew now they would never have the kind of familial regard for each other Edmond had wished for them, nor could she in all honesty imagine them being just friends. Because every time they were together in an even remotely intimate setting, their fledgling feelings of camaraderie and understanding invariably led to something else, something sexy, something she was afraid, once started, would not be able to be stopped. The truth was she wanted Chase. And he was beginning to want her, too. The near-kiss in the vault proved it.

Heat flooded her face as she imagined how she might have responded to him if he had ignored all common sense and reason and kissed her. Just thinking about his lips moving slowly, sensually over hers made her limp with longing. Hope thought of Edmond then and felt somewhat guilty.

Still, it had been so long since she had been really kissed, Hope thought, beginning to tremble with a mixture of thwarted anticipation and nerves. And she'd never been kissed by a man as sexy and indomitable and as ruggedly good-looking as Chase. Would it be as wonderful as her heart promised, as deeply fulfilling? Sadly, she thought, that path was forbidden to them both.

She sighed, fighting the depth of her disappointment. No one had ever told her life was fair, but there were times, like now, when the hand of fate seemed almost too cruel to be borne.

Chapter Eight

"What's the matter, slugger?"

Joey kicked at a tuft of grass in the manicured lawn and tucked his hands even further into the pockets of his grass-stained jeans. "Nothing," he muttered, never looking up.

"Doesn't look like nothing to me," Chase said gently. Mindful of the fact Joey'd just returned from Little League practice, Chase continued, "Rough practice?"

Although he had never thought of himself as the paternal type, he found it remarkably natural and easy to take over that role with his half brother, and not just for his father's sake, but for his own. Joey was a great kid. It gave Chase a lot of satisfaction to be close to him, to be his pal. And right now Joey looked like he needed a pal.

"No rougher than usual." Joey shrugged.

"What happened?" When no answer was forthcoming, he prodded again. "Did the coach yell at you?" Chase knew how intense some grown-ups could be.

"The coach didn't yell at me. I screwed up during batting practice again."

"And?"

"And the Bateman twins made fun of me. They started calling me Four Eyes and said I couldn't hit the side of a barn if I was standing right beside it. The coach made 'em stop but not before everyone else on the team started laughing." He looked up at Chase in abject misery. "I might

as well face it,'' he lamented passionately. ''I'm never go
ing to be any good.''

''Sure you will,'' Chase soothed, ruffling Joey's dark
hair. His hair was like his mother's: it felt soft and thick and
springy beneath his fingertips. ''It just takes time to de-
velop batting skill. How long have you been playing?''

''This is my third year.'' Joey blinked up at him hope-
fully from behind the thick lenses of his glasses. ''You really think I'm gonna improve, Chase?''

''We'll never know unless you practice, will we? Run up
and get your bat and ball and we'll give it a go, okay?''

''Okay.'' Looking noticeably happier, Joey sprinted off
toward the house.

At nearly seven, the back lawn was quiet and peaceful. A
high white brick wall kept it private. An abundance of
flowers and shrubbery kept it beautiful. Much of the land-
scaping was new, put in by Hope. Like her, the lawn was
beautiful and delicate looking, but hardy underneath.

Gazing at it, Chase's thoughts turned to Hope. It was
hard to believe how much everything had changed since he
had been home. He'd never thought he would be close to
her, or that he'd want to be close. To his frustration, she still
kept putting up walls between them, at the least expected
times. She wanted to be close to him, for Joey's sake. She
didn't want his help when it came to handling her own personal stress. Maybe that was the way it should be, he sighed.
And maybe it wasn't. All he knew was that he wanted more
from a woman than just a cursory relationship at her con-
venience. He'd had that before, with Lucy. It hadn't
worked. Hope would either have to let him into her life, or
step back, and let him out. She couldn't have it both ways.
It was simply too disappointing.

The back door slammed. Jerked from his reverie, Chase
turned to see Joey trotting out, a bewildered but compliant
Hope in tow. ''Mom's gonna catch!'' Joey said, pointing to
the mask and mitt in Hope's hand.

Chase smiled and strode forward to join them. This wasn't what he had counted on, either, but now that it was happening he wasn't so opposed. "Where'd you get all that stuff?" he asked genially, referring to the protective chest gear designed specifically for catchers. It hadn't been around when he was growing up.

"Dad bought it for me," Joey said confidently. "He used to help me work on my batting sometimes. He'd pitch and Mom would catch."

Conjuring up the mental image of that, Chase felt a moment's envy. It all sounded so nice and normal and happy, so unlike his own childhood. Then the house had been more like an armed camp than a home. His admiration for Hope grew. And he felt bad, for misjudging her all these years. She'd not only made his dad happy, but she'd also given him a real sense of family.

Hope looked at him questioningly, clearly wondering why he was so quiet. "Did you want to catch?"

Joey rolled his eyes and let out an exasperated breath. "Don't let her pitch," Joey put in quickly, turning to Chase man-to-man. "She can't pitch worth a darn. Sorry, Mom." He cast her an apologetic look over his shoulder. "But it's the truth."

"Just call me Wild Thing," Hope retorted dryly with a mockingly put-upon look that let them both know she hadn't really take offense.

Chase slid on his glove. He had a feeling it was going to be harder than usual to keep his mind focused on what he was doing. "Batter up," he said. He sauntered to the "mound" and Hope, slipping on her catcher's gear, hunkered down behind "home plate." She had caught her hair at the back of her neck, and her face was obscured by the mask. There was still something very sexy about the way she looked in her faded, straight-legged jeans, oversize hunter-green-and-navy-blue rugby shirt, and sweat socks and high-topped sneakers.

Realizing he was thinking about her like a woman he'd very much like to have in his bed, Chase felt a renewed surge of guilt. He forced his mind back to the game.

Batting practice lasted an hour. Darkness fell and they had to turn on the floodlights to see but that only made it all the more fun. Chase would've liked to think they'd made eons of progress in Joey's ability to hit, but it simply wasn' true. Improving Joey's batting noticeably and permanently would take a lot of time and effort on his part, and maybe that was something he could do for Joey before he left again.

"I'm hungry," Joey announced as they gathered up the gear. He turned to Hope. "What can I have to eat?"

Hope looked amenable to anything. "What do you want?"

Joey thought long and hard. "A cheeseburger, fries, and a shake."

Though Carmelita was off for the night, Hope didn't blink. "What kind of shake?"

"Chocolate."

She grinned as if she should have known. "Of course," she said dryly. "Chase. What about you? Did all that pitching and fielding work up an appetite?"

Don't accept, a small voice inside Chase said. You're already far too attached to her already. But out loud he heard himself saying, "A cheeseburger sounds terrific."

"Better hit the shower," Hope said to Joey, as they entered the house; it was nearly eight-thirty. "Then you can come down and eat."

"Okay, Mom," Joey said.

Chase settled across from Hope at the kitchen table, while she went to work putting hamburger patties on to fry. He noticed the exertion had put color into her cheeks and a relaxed sparkle into her eyes that hadn't been there for days; he was glad Joey had thought to include her. He was glad she was such a good sport.

"Thanks for working with him tonight," she said as she salted frozen fries and put them into the oven. "He misses his dad. Sometimes I forget how much."

Then, as if realizing what she'd just said, she touched a hand to her soft, unglossed lips, and added, "I'm sorry. That was thoughtless of me." She sent Chase an apologetic look. "He was your father, too. You must miss him."

Touched by her concern for his feelings, Chase took a long pull on his soda. The can was damp with condensation. He rubbed his wet palm on his jeans. "Yeah, I do miss him. But not as much as Joey. As much as it pains me to admit it," he continued sadly, "Dad and I weren't all that close."

Hope didn't deny Edmond had felt that way, too; rather she looked as if this were old news to her. Apparently his father had confided his frustration about their lack of father-son closeness. Chase liked the fact that Hope was ready and willing to listen to him; he hadn't had much of that in his life. But he hated the fact that she already knew all the negative about him. She didn't know his side of things.

"Why weren't you close?" Hope asked gently, looking for a moment as if she needed and wanted to get to know and understand him as much as he did her. "I know he loved you."

Chase shrugged. Restless, he put his soda aside and got up to roam the room. Seeing the hamburgers needed turning, he picked up the spatula and obliged. "Maybe it goes back to the relationship between my parents. They were always fighting. I didn't want to take sides in any of their battles and if I got too close to either one, that's what it felt like I was doing. What about you? Do you miss Dad?"

Hope got out the Dutch-chocolate ice cream and began ladling scoops into the blender. "Yes, I do miss him," she said quietly, pausing long enough to meet his gaze. "I miss him terribly. But it's not as bad for me as it is for Joey." She turned away and got out the milk from the refrigerator, adding with an absent sigh, "Maybe because I always knew it was coming."

Chase stared at her in shock, the sizzling hamburgers forgotten. "What do you mean?" he asked hoarsely. His father had had a sudden, massive coronary on the tennis courts. "Did you know he had a bad heart?" If so, Chase thought, she had been the only one.

Briefly Hope looked stricken, as if she had inadvertently said something she shouldn't have. She recovered quickly, saying, "No. We had no warning about a possible heart attack. It was...the age thing, I guess, that made me think that way." Lowering her gaze to her task, she picked and chose her words carefully. "He was so much older than I was. He used to worry about not being around until Joey grew up. And I worried about that, too. Because he was worried." Grimness crept into her tone briefly before she forced herself to lighten up. "But he took very good care of himself and he gave Joey a lot of memories and a lot of love, so—"

"No regrets?" Chase asked softly.

"No regrets." She looked at him, relieved he understood. "About Joey." She wet her lips. "I'm glad you're here for him, too, Chase. He needs a man in his life." She paused. "All little boys do."

Footsteps on the back stairs signaled Joey's impending arrival. It saved them from the intimacy of the moment, for Chase found himself wondering what it would be like to be here every night, sharing Joey's ups and downs and sharing Hope's. Before, the idea of being in one place had seemed confining. In many ways it still did, but for the first time in his life Chase was beginning to understand the lure of home and family. At its best, it meant love and stability and warmth, problems that could be shared and solved together. And for the first time, he was achingly aware of all he had missed both growing up and now.

"YOU SURPRISE ME, Hope," Russell said. "I give you two weeks and you got back to me in what, three days?"

It wasn't a willingness to be blackmailed, or a spirit of cooperation, Hope thought grimly. It was the fierce urge to be rid of him. She knew she would never have a moment's peace until he was gone. Only then would she feel that she and Joey were safe.

Aware her nerves were jangling, she handed him the envelope. "This is all I could get."

He gave the flat envelope a discerning look, not deigning to open it himself. "How much?"

She swallowed. Now was the tough part. "One hundred thousand dollars."

His look turned even uglier before he adopted that smooth, falsely soothing, aristocratic tone she hated. "I trust that you're kidding, Hope." He drummed his fingers on the white linen tablecloth. "You know one hundred thousand dollars is far, far less than what I asked for or need. And you also know I don't like to be played with."

A chill went down her spine at the grim reminder. Russell Morris was the kind of man who always got precisely what he wanted, no matter who he had to hurt, or what he had to do. "I am not playing with you," she whispered. "It's all I could get. I sold everything. Even my wedding rings, for God's sake."

"Yes." His glance raked her slender fingers. "I see that you did. But that doesn't solve our problem, does it, Hope?" He sipped his Scotch calmly.

Hope watched him in frustration, angry as well as sickened. She balled her hands into fists. "I don't know what you want from me," she admonished impatiently.

He smiled. "Try another one hundred and fifty thousand dollars."

Reminding herself of his utter lack of conscience and her equally strong need to remain calm, she retorted matter-of-factly, "I don't have it."

"Then get it."

"No," she said firmly, her mind made up about that much. If she did that, this would never end. "I won't. I've done far too much in terms of giving in to your demands as it is. I did so to get rid of you but if you continue to harass me, Russell, I swear I will go to the police.''

"And tell them what? That I'm extorting money from you?" He sat back, unimpressed. "They won't believe you. It'll be your word against mine."

Like it had been in the past, Hope thought. Steadying herself with a sip of her mineral water, Hope reminded him pointedly, "I'm a Barrister now—"

"A Barrister with an unsavory past," he interrupted cruelly. "Or need I remind you?"

No, she thought, he didn't have to remind her. "I repeat, Russell. This is all you're going to get."

"Perhaps you'd prefer to pay me in human terms." He grinned evilly.

The sick feeling in her middle intensified. "I don't know what you mean." She hated this cat-and-mouse game, but it was one he was well versed in.

"Oh, I think you do. I think if you search that pretty little mind of yours you'll be able to come up with what I want. What was owed me all these years. I don't think a court would take too kindly to that, do you, Hope? The way you cheated me out of what was rightfully mine?"

"I don't—"

"The hell you don't." He leaned forward urgently and his eyes fixed on hers with murderous intent. "Let's cut the bull. I know about your sin of omission, and I have known for years. But until Edmond Barrister died there was really no point in confronting you. Once you inherited, though, it was very different." He straightened smugly. "Now you have money. You have power. And you owe me, Hope."

He couldn't know what she'd done, Hope thought. But one look into his eyes told her that he knew everything. "What are you saying?" she asked hoarsely, fighting a panic that was almost debilitating in its intensity. She and Edmond had both feared this might happen someday. As the years had passed, they'd been lulled into a false security. And now she was paying for it.

His voice lowered dangerously. "You have a choice. Either you give me back what is mine or lots and lots of cash. Enough to put my company back on the road. I'm a generous person, so I'll leave that decision up to you." He paused then spoke heavily, "You can give me whatever you wish, as long as you satisfy me."

"I don't have any more cash," she whispered miserably, feeling a fear more intense than any she had ever known. Finding out about her past and her involvement with Russell would destroy her son.

Russell lifted a shoulder in an indifferent shrug, oblivious to the pain he was causing her. "You *are* in a quandary, aren't you, dear Hope?" He pushed his glass away and picked up the envelope containing the money. He slid it into the inner pocket of his bright orange blazer. "I'll give you two more weeks to come up with the additional one hundred and fifty thou. Two weeks, Hope. Or I see you in court."

He didn't have to explain. She knew precisely what he meant.

"WHY CAN'T I have a pet?" Hope's son demanded petulantly.

"Joey, we've been all through this," Hope said, realizing from the hurt, stubborn look on his face that he wasn't about to listen to anything she had to say. "Animal dander will aggravate your asthma."

Joey stabbed at the chicken Parmesan on his plate. "How do you know that?" he challenged.

Was it her imagination or did he look a little wan? Hope wondered. "Because the doctor told me."

Color flooded Joey's face. "Well, he's wrong. I was around a puppy all afternoon and I didn't have one bit of trouble!"

She stared at him, hardly able to believe he'd been so foolish.

"Aw, Mom, come on, don't get mad," he said, before she had a chance to say a word. "I had my inhaler with me, but I didn't even need it. I was fine the whole time. And that puppy was so cute, Mom." His appeal was straight from the heart. He was so in love with the little animal it made her heart break just to hear him talk about it. "It was a little cocker spaniel, the buff-colored kind," Joey continued earnestly, while Hope sat and let her own dinner get cold. "The lady who breeds them still has some for sale. But if you like another kind of dog that'd be okay, too," Joey hurried to reassure her. "I wouldn't mind. Big or small it wouldn't matter. It wouldn't even have to be a puppy. It could be older and already housebroken. And I'd take care of it all by myself. You wouldn't have to do a thing."

How well she knew that. Feeling like the cruelest mother in the history of the earth, Hope put down her fork slowly. "Joey, it's not the work and you know it."

He let out an impatient breath, ignoring her compassionately issued statement. "I told you. I was around a puppy all afternoon and my asthma was fine."

Hope sighed. His breaking the rules was another issue, one they'd have to go into later. Right now they had to settle the question of a pet, once and for all. "I'm sorry, Joey."

"You're sorry! Think about how I feel! You won't let me do anything," Joey accused. He stood, his eyes bright with tears. "I can't go camping with my friends or have a pet or anything. I hate having asthma! I hate it!"

He bolted from the room and ran up the stairs. The door slammed behind him, exacerbating the silence of the big, empty house. Hope remained where she was, her heart heavy with despair. As much as she yearned to go after Joey, she knew he needed time to cool off and accept her decision. Then she would go and try to make him understand she wasn't refusing him an animal to be mean. She just loved him and wanted him to stay healthy.

She picked up the work she had brought home from the office but found herself unable to concentrate on anything but the broken-hearted little boy upstairs. She put it back down again.

Thinking there might be something for her to do in the kitchen, she made her way to the rear of the big house. It was as spotless as Carmelita had left it. Going over to the window above the kitchen sink, Hope noticed that the guest house windows were completely dark. Chase's Jeep was gone. She wondered where he was, what he was doing and who he was with. Not that it should matter to her, she chastised herself firmly. He was a free man, able to do as he pleased. And, after her meeting with Russell, she had spent most of the day avoiding him, afraid he would be able to see that something was wrong.

At the same time she had yearned to talk to him and pour out her troubles. If anyone would understand how much she loved Joey, and would do anything to protect him, it would be Chase. Restless, she moved toward the front hall. Without warning, Joey was at the top of the stairs. He had his hands to his throat and a terrified look on his face. He was wheezing audibly and his chest pinched in with every harsh, rapid breath. Her own heart pounding, she ran toward her son.

THE LIGHTS in the big house were blazing when Chase pulled into the driveway at 2:00 a.m. Wondering why, he parked beside the guest house and made his way across the lawn. As he approached the back door, he could see Hope standing at the kitchen counter. She was in a robe and slippers. She looked distressed. Knowing she'd probably heard his Jeep, he rapped on the glass. She walked over to let him in.

"Everything okay over here?" he asked.

Her eyes bright with emotion, Hope nodded. "Yes. Joey had an asthma attack tonight."

Unwilling to acknowledge, even to himself, how much that news disturbed him, Chase shut the door behind him and asked calmly, ''Is he okay?''

Hope nodded again. Aware her coffee had stopped brewing, she went to pour herself a cup. ''Want some?''

Chase nodded; it was all he could do to stop himself from pulling her into his arms and holding her close. ''How long did the attack last?'' he asked.

''A couple of hours.'' Hope answered his question with a sigh. ''We were able to control it with his bronchilator, but it shook him up just the same. He's pretty low.''

''Is he awake?'' Chase asked softly. He didn't want to disturb the little boy; he did want to see him.

Hope hesitated, and unconsciously tightened the belt on her robe; it was a long fluffy white terry-cloth thing with blue satin piping. Like Chase, Hope seemed suddenly acutely aware of her nighttime apparel, modest as it was. ''I don't know.''

''Would you mind if I looked in on him?'' Chase asked.

Hope shook her head, signaling it was okay, but kept her hands clasped protectively against her, one at her throat, the other at her waist. Watching her, Chase wondered at her unexpected prudency. It seemed so at odds with the self-assurance she exuded during the day. But then, maybe this, too, was to be expected, he thought pragmatically. After all, they were both single people of the opposite sex. She'd been widowed for some time. The were approximately the same age. He knew damn well he was attracted to her and that she felt the same about him.

Hope wished she were still fully dressed. It was awkward being with him when all she had on was a nightgown and robe. Forcing herself to let go of the stranglehold she held on the belt to her robe, she followed him up the back stairs and down the long hall to Joey's room. Joey was curled up on his side, his battered teddy bear in his arms. What he really would have preferred, Hope knew, was a puppy sleeping at the foot of his bed. But he couldn't have that.

Considering what had happened earlier tonight, she couldn't think of giving in.

Joey looked up as he heard Chase come in. "Hi, buddy," Chase said, sitting down beside him on the bed.

Joey fingered the black silk tie that hung over Chase's pleated white tuxedo shirt. "Where you been?" he asked sleepily.

"At a boring party."

"If it was boring, why'd you go?" Joey asked.

Chase grinned. "Because I was the guest of honor and it would have been rude of me not to show up." His eyes darkened with regret as he looked at Hope. "I'm sorry I couldn't have invited you. There were some people, medical researchers and friends of mine. You would've enjoyed meeting them."

"It's okay," she said, glad he hadn't slighted her deliberately. "I realize you weren't the host."

"So what were you doing there?" Joey asked.

Chase turned back to her son. "I was trying to raise some funds for my next project."

Joey perked up at the hint of adventure. "Are you going back to the rain forest?"

Chase nodded. Realizing Chase would be leaving them again in the process, Joey's face fell. Hope knew exactly how her son felt; thinking about it, she was disappointed, too. She kept fantasizing Chase would decide to stay on here, even though she knew that was unlikely in the extreme.

Chase smoothed back Joey's hair. He noticed, as did Hope, that Joey still held his inhaler tight in his hand.

"Well, we better let you get some sleep," Chase said softly. "But I'll be here the rest of the night if you need me," Chase continued.

"Okay. Thanks, Chase." Joey sighed. Curling on his side, he closed his eyes.

Hope kissed Joey good-night and they left the room. As they walked down the hall, Chase asked, "Can you hear him from the kitchen?"

Hope nodded. "I've got the intercom turned on in his room, so I can listen in."

All scientist, Chase asked, "Any idea what brought this attack on?"

Hope gestured to a seat at the kitchen table. "He disobeyed the rules and went to see a friend's new puppy this afternoon." Hope shook her head unhappily as she poured them both a fresh cup of coffee and got out the cream and sugar. "You should have heard him tonight, Chase. He wants a puppy in the worst way. I feel like Simon Legree, being unable to give him one."

Chase made an emphatic sound as he lifted the coffee cup to his lips and blew on the steaming liquid before taking a first sip. "Poor kid. I know how he feels. I wasn't allowed to have a pet when I was a kid, either, for completely different reasons. My mother thought animals in the house were déclassé and if left outside, they tore up the yard."

"What did your father say?" Hope couldn't imagine the softhearted Edmond refusing Chase a pet for those reasons.

"I never asked him."

Hope looked up in surprise.

Chase shrugged and eased out of his tuxedo jacket, hanging it on the chair behind him. "I knew he'd probably say yes. That would've made my mother furious and put me in the middle of World War III. I had no desire to go through that, so I contented myself by seeing other friend's pets. And now I can't have one, of course, because he'd have to be in a kennel at least half the time." He sat back in the chair, stretching his long legs out in front of him. "What about you?" he asked lazily. "Did you have a pet?"

Hope smiled, dwelling on the one part of her childhood that had brought her nothing but happiness. "Lots of them, as it happened. We lived in the country and people were always dumping animals out there. So we always had a number of dogs and several farm cats.'' She rested her chin on her upturned hand, her voice softening contentedly. ''I loved those animals. Which, of course, makes it all the harder for me now.'' She straightened and as she did so, her robe gaped open slightly, revealing the V-neck of her lace-edged blue cotton gown. All too aware Chase had just had a good look at the shadowy cleft between her breasts, she drew the edges of the robe together self-consciously. ''I really wish I could give Joey a puppy.''

With effort, Chase kept his eyes trained on her face, and not what he had just inadvertently seen. ''But you can't.''

''No,'' Hope said, still holding on to her robe with one hand. ''And he resents me for it.''

Trying not to notice the color in her face, or wonder if her thoughts were as voluptuous and ill directed as his own, Chase soothed pragmatically, ''He'll get over it.''

Hope thought about that a minute. She got up restlessly and walked over to freshen first her coffee, then his. ''I don't know, Chase,'' she confessed as her eyes filled with tears. ''You didn't see him earlier tonight. He was so upset.''

''And that's when he had the attack, after the two of you argued?'' Chase asked.

Hope nodded. Looking somewhat relieved, she admitted shakily, ''Fortunately it was over pretty quickly.''

She sat down across from him again, aware of the restless feeling deep inside her that was wholly unrelated to the asthma attack.

Beneath his surface calm, Chase looked edgy, too. ''You planning to stay up all night?'' Chase asked practically after a moment.

As strung out as she was, Hope knew she couldn't sleep. She ran a hand through her dark hair, sweeping it back away from her face. ''I think I should, in case he has another attack.''

Chase's gaze darkened sympathetically. "You look ex hausted," he said softly. "Why don't you let me stay with him? I'll go up and sit with him in his room."

"You wouldn't mind?"

"Not at all," Chase reassured her with an easy smile "Just don't expect to see me at the store before noon."

Hope returned his grin. "If you stay up all night, I don' expect to see you there at all," she qualified.

"You've got a deal on that," he said. Together, they headed up the stairs.

Chapter Nine

Hope awakened to see early-morning sunlight streaming in her windows and Carmelita carrying a tray into her room. "Breakfast in bed?" she commented bewilderedly. That wasn't part of the morning ritual and never had been. Wealthy or not, she and Edmond had always had breakfast together in the dining room.

"Mr. Chase says you need it. You were up very late last night," Carmelita said, fitting the tray across Hope's lap.

Hope asked worriedly, "How is Joey this morning?" She wasn't used to having anyone else care for Joey during these times. Even when Edmond was alive, she had always been the one who sat up nights with Joey.

"Joey is still asleep. Mr. Chase sends you a message. He says not to worry, Joey is fine."

"Thank heavens for that," Hope said. Her limbs felt heavy and uncooperative, and she struggled to sit up against the pillows.

"Now, is there anything else you need?" Carmelita asked. She removed the stainless-steel covers on a steaming Denver omelet and fluffy buttermilk biscuits with fresh strawberry jam and real butter. Juice and coffee rounded out the meal.

"No," Hope said, taking her first heavenly sip of caffeine. "Just make sure Chase has a good breakfast, too."

Carmelita grinned. "I already have. He had a Denver omelet, too." She paused. "He said to let Joey sleep as late as possible. Is that okay with you?"

Hope nodded. "I think he's going to have to skip school today."

Carmelita took the news in stride, which made Hope wonder if she was the only one, besides her son, who had trouble coping with Joey's asthma. "What about you?" Carmelita continued officiously. "Are you going in to the office?"

"Probably later, after Joey is up." But right now, she thought, still feeling groggy and exhausted, there was no hurry.

To Hope's relief, her morning went much more smoothly than the previous evening. Joey woke up cranky but fine. Considering all he had been through and the disappointment he was dealing with, Hope considered that status quo. She phoned the school and picked up his assignments. Chase was in her son's room when she walked in. He was wearing jeans and a Rice University sweatshirt. His jaw was freshly shaven and bore the traces of a brisk after-shave. His layered blond hair curled damply around his collar.

"Well, you all are busy," she said, looking down at the playing cards they held in their hands. She too had taken the time to shower and dress in a favorite navy suit and silk blouse. Joey was still in his pajamas, sitting propped up against the pillows. He was pale and washed-out, but like Chase, had a devilish glint in his eyes. The kind little boys got when they were up to a harmless bit of mischief and knew it.

"I'm teaching him how to play poker, a skill no man should be without," Chase said with comically exaggerated seriousness. He gave her son a discerning glance and placed a firm hand on Joey's thin shoulder. "This boy has a lot of potential, Hope. A lot of potential," he stressed.

Hope rolled her eyes. "Thanks, heaps, Chase."

He ducked his head modestly, as if accepting the highest praises. "Oh, anytime."

Hope dumped Joey's book bag on the bed. "Your homework, sire." She turned serious. "I told your teacher I thought you'd be back in school tomorrow."

Joey nodded, his expression turning glum. Chase soothed, "Sitting in a classroom is that bad, huh?"

Joey shook his head, the gaiety of moments before forgotten. He shuffled the cards in his hand. "It's not that."

"Then what is it?" Chase asked gently.

"It's the stupid asthma." Joey's chin trembled and he refused to meet either of their eyes. "I'm never going to be able to do anything! I can't have a pet! I can't play ball worth a darn. I can't go camping. I—"

"Whoa, whoa!" Chase held up a hand. "There is nothing stopping you from being an A-number-one athlete, kiddo."

"What do you mean? You know I can't even run all the bases without getting out of breath."

"Yeah, but that's typical of a lot of kids your age," Chase said. Joey sent him a pained look. "Okay," Chase conceded on a slightly less optimistic note, "so they don't all have to use an inhaler. But there are plenty of people who have succeeded athletically who do have to use an inhaler."

Joey folded his arms across his thin chest and sent Chase a challenging glare. "Name one."

"I'll name two. Baseball pitcher Jim 'Catfish' Hunter."

Joey did a double take. "He has asthma?"

"Not only does he have asthma, he's pitched in the World Series," Chase affirmed. "And then there's Olympic track star Jackie Joyner Kersee. She has asthma but she didn't let it stop her. You can have a normal life, Joey, a good life, but you've got to work for it and stop feeling sorry for yourself. Now, I know you're disappointed about not having a pet, and I'm sorry about that, but things could be worse, you know."

"Yes, they could be," Hope chimed in softly, glad Chase was talking so honestly with her son. Times like this, she needed someone to back her up, both emotionally and verbally, where Joey was concerned. And Chase, bless him, was doing just that.

Briefly Joey looked ashamed for his temperamental attitude. He hung his head and drew a design on his bedspread with his fingertip. "I know. I could be homeless, or not have a mom or any toys or anything."

"That's right," Chase said. "And instead, you have a wonderful home and a great mom." He reached behind him and taking Hope's hand in his own larger, warmer one, pulled her forward. "If you ask me, pal, you have a lot to be thankful for."

Chastened, Joey gave a little sigh, this one accepting. He still wasn't happy but he wasn't nearly so unhappy, either. He looked from Hope to Chase, and seeing the mingled forgiveness and empathy in their eyes, said, "I guess I better get started on my homework."

"I think that's a great idea," Hope said. Chase, all easy grace and sinewy strength, dropped his hold on her hand and got laconically to his feet. Trying not to notice how empty her hand felt now that he was no longer holding it, Hope continued tongue in cheek, "Not that poker playing isn't a much needed skill."

"But." Chase leaned forward and tapped Joey's math book. "You gotta learn how to add up all those winning points, first."

Joey grinned. "Yeah, right," he drawled in the same comically exaggerated tone.

Hope and Chase left Joey's room together. "You going into the office?" he asked, his attitude suddenly becoming businesslike.

She nodded, trying not to feel disappointed. She wasn't as close as her son was to Chase. She gave him a direct, appreciative look. "Thanks for spending the night and giving

Joey the pep talk." She shrugged. "I tell him the same things but he doesn't seem to hear me."

"Of course not." Chase agreed, as if that were the most natural thing in the world. He laced a comforting arm around her shoulders. "You're his mother. Who ever listens to their mother?"

At that, Hope had to smile. She hadn't listened to her mother, either. They reached the front hall and he dropped the casual hand he had laced around her shoulders.

Chase stuffed both hands into the pockets of his jeans. "I had an idea last night about how to make Joey feel better."

"I'm all for that," Hope said tiredly.

"I think part of his problem is that he doesn't feel enough like a regular guy. And he had a point about the camping—"

"He can't go to the mountains with his friends, Chase."

"I agree with you there. But he could rough it somewhere here in Texas. Say down in Galveston or Padre Island or up in the state park in Bastrop."

Hope's expression grew apprehensive. "What if he has an attack?"

"There are hospitals close by," he soothed. "And I'd be there," Chase continued. "As far as his medical condition goes, we'd talk to his doctor first. Make sure we had everything we needed in terms of medications, peak flow meters, nebulizers, and so forth. You could even go with us if it'd make you feel better."

Hope knew Chase was more than qualified to handle any problems that came up, medical or otherwise. Still, it was hard for her to let go; Chase saw that.

"You don't have to give me an answer right away," he interjected gently, touching the back of his hand to her face. "Just think about it for a few days, okay?" Exerting the tiniest pressure, he lifted her face to his, continuing softly in the same velvet-edged tone, "Consider how much this would mean to Joey and how much better it would make him feel about himself, how much more normal. Think about how much fun he'd have cooking his meals over an open fire and tromping through the woods. And then give me your answer.''

She knew he was right. Joey would have a blast. She sighed, still feeling torn. Her intellect said to let him go, her mother's instinct said to keep him home. Chase wasn't making it easy for her to say no.

''I AGREE with your stepson, Mrs. Barrister,'' Joey's physician said later the same day. ''A camping trip of the sort Chase has in mind sounds like excellent therapy for Joey.''

Hope paced back and forth nervously, the telephone receiver pressed to her face. ''What about the pollen?''

''We can put him on some medication, short-term, to help lessen his potential reaction to any pollens he encounters. And you can take his peak flow meter and inhaler. With Chase there with you, you shouldn't have any problems. And even if you do, he'll know what to do.''

That wasn't what was bothering her, Hope admitted to herself after she thanked the doctor, and hung up the phone. It was the idea of being in the wilderness with Chase and Joey for three or four days.

She was just too aware of Chase, as a man. She couldn't get rid of the image of how he had looked last night, coming through her back door, in his black tuxedo. Or how fresh he had looked this morning, despite his lack of sleep. She couldn't forget the way he laced a companionable arm around her shoulders or how gently he touched her face. He made her feel like a woman again; he made her feel vulnerable. He made her aware of how acutely alone she had been, the past year.

But that wasn't all. He had been so sweet when he had talked to Joey last night, so caring. So sympathetic to her, too. And then so boyishly mischievous when he had been caught playing poker with Joey. There was so much life to Chase, so much energy, and so much fun. The more she saw

im, the more she yearned to be close to him, and not in any
vay remotely connected with their current familial ties.

No, she wanted to get to know him the way a woman gets
o know a man she's interested in. And that couldn't hap-
en. Chase was a man who wanted the truth from a woman,
he whole truth. He had demonstrated as much by his an-
ry, frustrated reaction to her meetings with Russell Mor-
is. He had expected her to confide in him, and when she
adn't, he'd been deeply hurt.

She knew all she would have to do is level with him. If she
old him the whole ugly story, he would understand her re-
uctance to confide in him. But she couldn't do that, either,
ot without destroying all he held near and dear about his
ather. Not without destroying his image of her. No, she had
romised Edmond his secret was one she would carry with
er to her grave. It was a promise she still had to keep.

'COME ON, Joey! Get a hit for us!'' Joey's teammates
elled two days later as he stepped up at bat for what was to
e the first game of the season.

In the stands, Hope sat tensely. Beside her, Chase seemed
just as anxious for Joey.

Glancing over his shoulder at the two of them and then
his coach, a white-faced Joey choked up on the bat as he had
been told to do. He faced the pitcher determinedly. To
Hope's silent lament, the first pitch was a strike. So was the
second.

"Oh, man!" one of the Bateman twins yelled at Joey
from the bench. "Can't we get a pinch hitter for that nerd?"

At the words, Hope's jaw clenched, and it was all she
could do to stay in her place. Chase, who seemed to be
handling the rude heckling better than Hope, touched her
arm lightly. "Relax. He's doing okay," he murmured.

Her son *was* handling the twins better than she was. Hope
took a deep breath and forced herself to calm down as the
pitcher wound up and threw the third pitch. There was no
reason this should be getting to her the way it was, she

thought. Determined to maintain control of her erupting temper, she concentrated on the pitch. It was too low and Joey didn't swing. "Ball one," the umpire cried.

"See," Chase said triumphantly, every bit as proud of Joey as Hope was. He reached over and briefly squeezed her hand. "He knows what to do, Hope."

Hope relaxed slightly. Somehow, it was easier sitting through this with Chase at her side.

The next pitch came. Joey swung, and a solid cracking sound filled the air as the wooden bat made contact with the ball. A cheer went up from Joey's team. He tossed down the bat and trotted off to first, long before the ground ball was returned. "Way to go, Joey!" Chase shouted.

Next up to bat was a Bateman twin. "Let's see how he does," Hope murmured, hoping rather mean-spiritedly that the obnoxious twin wouldn't do nearly as well as her son.

The twin missed the first pitch but recovered and hit the second, sending the ball flying out into left field. As Bateman sped toward first, he already had his eye on second. The opposing team's outfielder had the ball seconds after it hit the ground, but Bateman, determined to make this a double, was already flying toward second base, waving and yelling at Joey. "Go, go!" he shouted.

Joey took a trembling look at third, at the outfielder, and at Bateman, then did the only thing he could. He took off for third; he had an impossible task ahead of him. Bateman should have stayed on first instead of trying to hotdog it.

Nevertheless, knowing his team was depending on him, Joey gave it all he had, running forward as fast as he could, and sliding headfirst into third. The ball hit the third base-man's glove an agonizing split second before Joey hit the base. "You're out," the umpire called, pointing at Joey.

"Oh, man, did you see that!" The other Bateman twin shouted from the bench to his brother. "You sissy!" he called to Joey. A disappointed Joey got to his feet and headed, slump-shouldered, back toward the dugout.

"You cost us a run." The other twin continued his ha-
assment loudly. "You sick little wimp!"

The cruel words lit a fuse underneath Hope. "That does
t," Hope said. She'd had enough of the lack of good
portsmanship. She'd be damned if she'd sit there all sea-
on and listen to this, or be forced to take Joey off the team
because the league officials couldn't handle the boys.

"Hope—" Chase cautioned.

But she was already halfway down the bleachers. She
marched past a sea of surprised parents and onto the diamond. She approached the umpire behind home plate, who
promptly held up his hands in the time-out sight. "You're
not supposed to be here," he disciplined Hope firmly. "No
parents are allowed on the field."

Tipping her chin up, she said, "I wouldn't have to be if
you would see that the teams adhere to league rules. Those
twins—" she pointed to the Batemans "—owe my son an
apology." And she was staying right where she was until
they delivered it.

Mr. Bateman yelled, "Oh, for Pete's sake, ump! Get the
broad off the field and get on with the game."

Broad? Hope thought in raging disbelief. He had called
her a broad? How dare he!

Seething, Hope turned to face the barrel-chested Mr.
Bateman. He was making his way down to stand beside the
umpire and Hope. The coaches from both sides were coming out onto the field. The crowd was quiet, for the most
part, waiting to see what was going to happen next.

"Need I remind anyone how much I donate to the league
every year, to see the boys get uniforms and to maintain the
playing fields?" Mr. Bateman spoke in a voice only the
people gathered on the field could hear. Looking at Hope
with a sniff of disapproval, he continued disparagingly, "I
don't see the Barristers donating any money."

His lack of tact made the coaches visibly uncomfortable
and made Hope see red. It reminded her of the worst time
of her life, a time when Russell Morris's family had treated

her in the same unjust manner. Only then she'd had no one to stick up for her. Well, that wasn't the case now. Joey had Hope to defend and protect him, even if he didn't have Edmond.

"You," she said, pointing to Mr. Bateman, "are as rude and cruel as your sons. It's no wonder they've turned out the way they have."

The senior Bateman turned beet red. He was president of his own oil company; no one talked to him like that. "Just a minute—"

"Hold it! Both of you!" the umpire said, stepping between Hope and Mr. Bateman. He tugged at his collar nervously. "Let's not let this get personal."

"It's already personal," Hope said, pointing to Mr. Bateman. "He and his sons just made it so by the continual verbal insults they sling at my son."

"So let him quit," Mr. Bateman advised cruelly. "I wouldn't miss you or your pansy son, who, by the way, has no business playing ball. He's an invalid."

"He is not an invalid. He does have asthma," Chase intervened quietly. He stepped reluctantly in to join the melee, with a deadly look at Mr. Bateman. "I agree with Joey's mother. The twins do owe Joey an apology. Either that, or they should be thrown out of the game." Chase looked at the umpire, pressuring him for an immediate decision.

The coaches exchanged looks, then called Joey and the twins over to the bench. Prompted by glares from Hope and Chase, and other fair-minded adults in the crowd, they publicly reprimanded the twins and made them apologize to Joey. Joey looked even more crushed and embarrassed than the twins. And he stayed that way the rest of the game.

"Just say it. You're angry with me," Hope said to her son en route home, unable to take his resentful silence anymore. She turned around to look at Joey, who was sitting directly behind her, in the back of Chase's Jeep.

He glared back at her and then at Chase, who was busy driving them home. "Well, cripes, what'd you expect?"

oey countered, the angry words spilling out before he could think. "You embarrassed me worse than the twins ever did!" He shook his head, his jaw taut. "I should've made it to third, Mom."

"No, Bateman should have stayed on first," Hope said.

"I agree with your mother on that, sport," Chase said, casting Joey a glance in the rearview mirror. "Bateman should have stayed on first, but he didn't and you gave it a hell of a courageous try. As for the other—" he shrugged as he concentrated on the traffic once again "—what your mother did took a lot of guts, too. Not many people would be unafraid to stand up in front of a group of people that way and take a position. I also have a feeling what she did is going to make a difference for all the teams the rest of the season."

Joey hung his head. Chase continued, "You don't want other kids heckled the way the Bateman twins heckle you, do you?"

"Well, no," Joey said, squirming in his seat.

"Okay. Your mother did her best to stop it. Not just for you but for everyone else. I think you owe her an apology."

Chastened, Joey looked up at Hope.

"I am sorry I embarrassed you," she said gently. "I didn't mean to do that. I just lost my temper."

Joey nodded. "I'm sorry, too," he mumbled, "but I still wish it never would've happened."

"He'll get over it," Chase said as he walked Hope into the house. Joey ran on ahead and up the stairs.

"I don't know. I was pretty out of control." She shook her head, feeling herself flush fiercely. She hugged her crossed arms closer to her chest. "I guess he had a right to be embarrassed."

Chase shrugged indifferently. "You were protecting your son."

"It was more than that," Hope admitted reluctantly. "It was the flaunting of wealth and power that got to me." It reminded her so much of Russell Morris's family. They'd used every advantage to ruin her life. They'd bought local officials and created a whole campaign against her, insisting she was lying.

Aware Chase was watching her and waiting for her to go on, Hope said, "I think people in our position have a responsibility to use our influence wisely. We shouldn't mow down the less fortunate, whether it is someone who is poorer or less athletically inclined."

"I agree."

"But it didn't push any hot buttons with you."

He thought about that for a moment. "It made me angry. Like you, I planned to talk to someone, but I was going to wait until after the game and do it then, privately."

"Without causing a scene."

He grinned and acknowledged with a wicked drawl, "Come to think of it, maybe causing a scene was the way to go. It certainly got fast results."

It had done that, Hope conceded silently. She offered him a small smile.

Chase was still studying her. "Were you bullied as a kid?"

Again, Hope felt the frustration of not being able to tell Chase everything, of not being able to be open with him. But there *were* things she could talk about, she realized slowly, things that had nothing to do with Russell. "I can't remember a time when I wasn't bullied. The way I grew up—I was always the new kid in town, struggling to fit in. And there was always someone who couldn't wait to take advantage of that, someone who resented me."

Chase didn't wonder at that. Hope was very beautiful. No doubt her very presence had created a stir wherever she went. Other girls, especially those who were not as fortunate in the looks department, would have resented her for that reason.

Hope sighed. "No sooner would we get settled than my parents would decide to try their luck someplace else, so we'd all pack up and move on. Soybeans, wheat, cotton, oranges, grapefruit, tomatoes, lettuce. I think they grew it all.''

Still, Chase thought, her reaction tonight had been unusually fierce. As if she were reacting not to a lifetime of general oppression and occasional slights, but of something specific that had hurt her deeply, something she wasn't quite over yet. "How did you handle it?"

Hope shrugged. "I don't really remember. I don't think I ever did anything specific except try to blend in and not be so noticeable, you know?"

He nodded. He had tried that, too, though for very different reasons.

"But I never had the right clothes or anything," Hope continued with a heartfelt sigh. "Mostly, I just wanted to get away."

From the stigma of being a tenant farmer's daughter, he wondered, or the childhood years of poverty and neglect she had hinted at? "Is that why you went to work in Barrister's?" Chase asked casually. He was hungry to know more about her, to know everything, and yet at the same time, he was excruciatingly aware that drawing information from her was like locating a stack of scattered pins in a haystack.

Hope grinned. "I went to work in Barrister's because it was the only job I could get." She lifted her eyes to his and admitted with a candidness he yearned to see more of, "I only had a high-school education. No money for college."

But she had been beautiful enough to sell cosmetics, Chase thought. Every woman wanted to look the way Hope did. Sensual, vulnerable and beautiful. If they thought they could buy those qualities in a bottle, they would. It was no wonder Barrister's had hired her, and no wonder Edmond had fallen in love with her.

She walked over to a framed picture of Joey and touched it lovingly. He could see she was still hurting over the discord with her son and embarrassed by what had happened at the game.

Without warning, an idea came to him. He knew how to make it better. Fast. For all of them. Because he, too, was wishing he could just get away from all the stress and pressure and scrutiny they had been under the past few weeks. He wanted to spend more unfettered time with Hope. "Hope, about letting Joey go camping. Have you given it any more thought?" He wanted to comfort her, but couldn't risk having that turn into something else. Something as sensual as her elemental beauty.

Putting a firm damper on his erotic thoughts, Chase said softly, "I promise you, I'd take good care of him. I wouldn't let anything happen to him. And I meant what I said when I first issued the invitation. You're welcome to go along, too." He wanted her to go along, but didn't want to appear overly anxious.

Giving Joey permission to go camping would make up for the scene she had caused at the ball diamond tonight, Hope knew. With Chase leaving again in July, there wouldn't be many more opportunities for Joey. Still, she had no intention of letting her son embark on something so potentially exciting and dangerous without her.

She looked at Chase thoughtfully, appreciating how ruggedly handsome and at ease he looked in the jeans and rumpled long-sleeved cotton shirt. He had done so much for them since he had been back. She no longer knew how she would manage without him. But he had also come very close to kissing her once, in the fur vault. And she'd come very close to kissing him back. She took a deep bolstering breath. "You said something about Bastrop?" She could handle this. She could handle him.

Chase nodded, his smile alight with anticipation at being in the wild again. "They have a nice state park there. I've got some pediatrician friends in the area. We could leave Friday and be back early Sunday afternoon. It's not long, Hope, but I promise you, it will do Joey a world of good to get away."

Me, too, she thought, trying to ignore the close and continual proximity to Chase such an outing would entail. Hope said simply, ''You're on. It's a threesome for this weekend. Shall I tell Joey or would you like to?''

Chapter Ten

"Chase, you've got to do something," Rosemary began early the following morning. "Customers are complaining right and left about the renovation."

"It'll be completed in another week."

"And until then, everyone is inconvenienced. The whole store smells like new paint. Customers are tripping over drop cloths and stepladders. And that filmy plastic Hope hung up to section off the areas under renovation looks tacky as hell."

Chase put down the camping supply catalog. His mind was full of thoughts of Hope and Joey and the fund-raising efforts for his research. The last thing he wanted to think about was the store. "I know it's a pain, Mom, everyone does, but it'll be done in another week."

"So? Our customers are unhappy now." He followed Rosemary from his office. At her insistence, they went down to the second floor together, where what had once been a glitzy novelty area for grown-ups was now being transformed into children's clothing department. It was hard for Chase to imagine that the customers wouldn't be delighted with the finished area.

They continued their tour, going down to the first floor, where similar renovations were also taking place. Behind the plastic curtains, it was just as cluttered as the second floor with workmen, ladders and buckets of paint. Able to see it was a problem, although not the huge one his mother deemed it to be, he turned to Rosemary. "What are you suggesting we do? Shut down the store entirely?"

"No, of course not. That would be even worse." Rosemary picked up a demonstrator bottle of Christian Dior's Poison from the cosmetics counter and spritzed herself with perfume. She continued to rant. "Not that Hope is ever here to see any of it or be inconvenienced herself. No, she is far too busy with her clandestine love life to properly supervise much of anything, never mind something as complicated as this!"

Although he knew Rosemary was baiting him deliberately, Chase latched on to the words and couldn't let go. He followed his mother to the Lancôme counter. "What love life?"

Rosemary turned in surprise. "Didn't you know? Hope has been seen with Russell Morris twice recently, at Maxim's. If you don't believe me, call them. I'm sure they'd be happy to confirm it."

"Why would I want to do that?" Chase asked, bracing himself for the commentary on his growing closeness to Hope.

"I don't know." She walked over to needlessly straighten a display of Clinique moisturizer. She gave an eloquent shrug. "I just thought you might be interested. I know I am. I'm determined to find out what is going on between that little tramp and Russell Morris."

Chase had no doubt what his mother had told him was true. When it came to social matters, her sources were unflaggingly correct. Determined not to let her gossip get to him, he said, "So she's had drinks with him. Why should you care?"

Rosemary whirled, her expression indignant. "I care because she lied! And because she is mercurial and inconsistent. Or had you forgotten the way she behaved when Russell first came to see her here? One minute she won't give him the time of day and refuses to do business with him, and then the next she takes off work to meet him on the sly. That kind of behavior doesn't make sense to me.''

Nor did it to Chase.

''But then as close as you seem to be getting to Hope,'' she continued slyly, ''I suppose you already know all about their meetings.''

No, he hadn't known about them and it bothered him that he hadn't. Not wanting his mother to see the hurt and betrayal he felt, he turned away from her, ostensibly to study the new Estee Lauder line for men. ''No, I didn't know.'' Turning back to her, he girded himself for battle. ''Not that it's any of your business if it is social, as you suspect. Hope's a grown woman, free to do as she pleases.'' He shouldn't give a damn, either. But he did.

His mother regarded him smugly. ''Her calendar for those meetings was marked 'outside business appointment.'''

Chase struggled between his curiosity and fury. His mother was dogging Hope's every move. Wasn't it enough that Rosemary was at the store every day, stirring up trouble? How much further did she think she had to go to make Hope's life, and inadvertently his own, miserable? ''How do you know that?'' he asked. His calm voice betrayed none of his inner turmoil.

Rosemary smiled smugly and touched a hand to her impeccably coiffed hair. ''The same way I know everything about her,'' she countered in absolute triumph. ''I checked.''

Chase sighed. He hated these cat-and-mouse games his mother liked to play. So had his father, if memory served him correctly. ''What is your point?''

''My point is,'' Rosemary countered, ''that she might be working out a deal with him on the sly. A deal that will earn them both money and leave Barrister's out in the cold.''

Or maybe, Chase thought as all the little details he had seen came together, she was being blackmailed. That would explain Hope suddenly selling her jewelry. Then again, maybe he was making too much of this. Maybe she was

seeing Russell because she wanted to, because they'd rekin-
dled whatever they'd had.

Rosemary paced back over to the Lancôme lipstick display. Examining it critically, she said, "Regardless, I know
something unsavory is going on there and I'm going to find
out what it is." She started in the direction of her office, her
detailed examination of the cosmetics all but forgotten.

Chase followed her to the elevator and stopped her with
a touch on her arm. "What are you doing?"

"Going back to my office so I can call a private investigator, of course."

He stepped in front of her, his tone firm. "No. You've got
no right to invade her privacy that way."

Rosemary tried, unsuccessfully, to push him aside. "I do
if I have evidence she's trying to defraud our store."

"Which you don't—"

"Yet." Rosemary paused. "But I will get it. I'm going to
find out what she's hiding. I'm going to find out about her
past and expose her for what she is if it's the last thing I do."

"No," Chase said. He knew there was only one way to
put a stop to his mother's interference, underhanded and
despicable as it was. "I will."

HOURS LATER, Chase still didn't know why he'd volunteered to act as supersleuth. It wasn't like him to want to pry,
but his mother was right. There was too much about Hope's
recent actions that didn't make sense. Her rift with her
family, for instance. He didn't buy her lame excuses. Maybe
there was a rift but it should be mended. Otherwise, she'd
feel the same deep lament and irrevocable loss and shame he
had when his father died. And yet he knew because of the
circumstances such a feat wouldn't be easy. Something very
serious had torn her family apart if it had caused a rift that
had continued for over a decade.

And as for the rest of the mystery... he had seen the way
she looked at Russell Morris with utter loathing, fear and
distrust. Yet according to Rosemary's sources, which were

unfailingly accurate, the two were now meeting on the sly.
If Russell was holding something over Hope it had to be
because of something that had happened in the past, when
she'd known him years ago.

But what could that be? He had no answers. But Hope
knew and so did Russell and probably so did her family.
Part of him wanted to let it go. But he knew if he didn't un-
earth the mystery and put the pieces of the puzzle together
first, his mother's lackeys would. There was no doubt in his
mind she would use whatever negative information she was
able to uncover to hurt Hope, in the most public way possible.

UNFORTUNATELY, his meeting with Hope's mother, Louise,
proved anything but uplifting. She met him at the screen
door of their small ranch house. In a gingham shirt and
slacks, her faded beauty was evident, but she had none of
Hope's inner generosity or warmth.

Trying hard not to make any premature judgments, Chase
stepped inside the cluttered, unkempt house. "I had hoped
to talk to you and Mr. Curtis about Hope—"

"As far as Hope's concerned, Henry hasn't got a daughter," Louise said sourly. She motioned for him to take a seat
on the lumpy plaid sofa next to the door. Like everything
else in the house, it had seen better days. "I only agreed to
see you when you telephoned," Louise continued in the
same pained tone, "because I figured you wouldn't leave us
alone until you did."

She was right about that, Chase thought. Now that he'd
seen this much, he had to know more. "About Hope—"

"I know she married some rich man." Louise sank into
an armchair opposite him.

"My father," Chase admitted.

"And he died."

"Yes."

Louise squinted at him suspiciously. "You trying to take
her money away from her?"

No, but my mother is, he thought. So far his first emotional reaction to Louise Curtis's home had been identical to Hope's—to get the hell out and never look back. Chase twined his hands loosely together and let them rest between his spread knees. He had come this far; he might as well go the whole nine yards. "I'm here because I think Hope might be in some sort of trouble." This information neither surprised nor fazed Louise. Encouraged by her lack of immediate comment, Chase went on carefully, "There's a man she used to know, years ago. His name is Russell Morris."

Louise shut her eyes and looked ill. She got up, ran both hands agitatedly through her gray hair and paced the length of the room. "Doesn't that girl ever learn?" Although she revealed nothing more to him, she seemed very angry and upset.

With effort, Chase remained in his seat on the sofa. "What was her relationship with him?"

Louise narrowed her gaze suspiciously. "Didn't she tell you?"

Chase only wished she were that open. "She won't talk about it," he admitted honestly.

Louise harumphed. "Doesn't surprise me," she muttered. "Well, I don't want to talk about it, either." She moved toward the door, as if ready to show him out.

Desperate to know more, Chase took his time about getting up from his place on the sofa. "Was he a threat to her?"

"More like the other way around." Louise's lips thinned unpleasantly. "But Hope's scheme to ruin his family didn't work. Instead, it ruined us. And I'll never forgive her for that." She turned to Chase, her eyes blazing. "We got thrown off their tenant farm in the middle of the growing season because of Hope. Lost darn near everything we had. And why? Because that stupid, money-grabbing girl of ours didn't have enough sense to stay away from those rich boys." Louise shook her head disparagingly. "She always did want more than we could give. I guess she finally found it.'' Louise looked sharply at him. ''That is if she can hang on to it,'' she said astutely.

Chase moved slowly toward the door, more aware than ever his time there was severely limited. The Hope Louise was describing was nothing like the Hope he knew. Was it possible he had misjudged her all this time? Was it possible she had changed over the years? Or simply that they had never known and understood their daughter the way he was beginning to? ''What do you mean, scheme?'' Chase asked.

Louise held up her hands to ward off further questions. ''I've said enough.''

''Wait. Do you have any interest in seeing her?'' Chase asked as she pushed open the screen. To his mounting horror and disappointment, he saw no love or traces of lingering affection in Louise's eyes. Just cold contempt.

''I think you'd better go,'' Louise said gruffly. And this time she did show him the door.

The meeting with Hope's mother haunted Chase. He understood now why she'd cut her ties with her family and moved on. They didn't love her, didn't even care enough to ask how she was. Such indifference was foreign to him. Despite their difficulties, he had always known he could talk to both parents, that they would welcome him if he went home. He had always known they loved him. For Hope, that obviously wasn't the case. He doubted she would be welcome there, for even five minutes. And she had Joey's feelings to consider. She wouldn't want to expose him to her mother's bitterness and her father's indifference. So she kept her distance from her folks. But at what cost? What were she and Russell discussing so clandestinely?

He wanted to talk to Hope about what he had learned. Even if he drove straight through, he wouldn't arrive in Houston until Thursday evening, and it would be far too late to approach her. And he didn't particularly want to get into any of this with his mother before he set off on a camping trip with Hope. For that reason, he would have to avoid his mother entirely, at least until after he returned from his camping trip with Hope and Joey.

That presented yet another problem, he thought as he pulled off the freeway and guided his car into the parking lot of a Holiday Inn. They were supposed to leave on Friday afternoon to go camping, and he hadn't even begun to pack or get provisions.

He could make it, of course, if he got up early. He walked into the hotel lobby and arranged for a room. Staying here for the night would buy him a reprieve from his mother's questions. It would also give him time to consider how to approach Hope about what he had discovered. One way or another he would get his answers. He only hoped she would forgive him for looking into her past.

HOPE PULLED into the driveway shortly after 2:00 p.m. Friday afternoon. The garage doors were open. Chase was kneeling just inside them, securing the ties on a rolled-up tent. In jeans and a soft blue cotton shirt, with a red bandanna knotted into a sweatband on his forehead, he looked much like he did when he'd first come back from Costa Rica.

Her heart pounding, her briefcase in hand, she got out of her car. There was no reason to feel so on edge, she told herself firmly, but as she looked into his eyes, she felt her awareness of him go up another notch. She struggled for control of her voice. "Your mother was looking for you."

Chase glanced up, his dark blond brows lifting a disgruntled notch.

Hope's chest tightened, making it harder to draw a breath. "She wondered why you hadn't come to the office today."

"What'd you tell her?"

Nothing that had satisfied her, Hope thought. Both hands still clenching the handle, Hope held her briefcase in front of her knees like a shield. "Only that I hadn't seen you since early yesterday morning.'' I neglected to mention you were out all night and this morning, she thought.

''And?'' Chase looked at her expectantly.

Hope shrugged and shifted her briefcase unnecessarily, glad she had something solid to hang on to. ''That seemed to satisfy her.'' Her gaze lingered on his and she admitted to herself she understood Rosemary's actions in this regard. Hope was as hungry for information as to his previous whereabouts as his mother seemed to be. ''But she still wanted to know if I knew where you were,'' Hope continued flatly.

''And you didn't.''

''No.'' Hope paused. One adult to another, she felt Chase was entitled to a private life. No questions asked, no answers given. Nevertheless, his absence had unnerved her. He had left the office rather suddenly, without explaining to anyone where he was going. He'd been out all night, he hadn't bothered to go to the office, and hadn't called. Prior to this, he had seemed interested in helping her get Barrister's back on an even keel. His disinterest was all too reminiscent of the Chase she had known in the past, the Chase that wanted no part of his father's legacy. That being the case, she'd begun to wonder if he had changed his mind about the camping trip and his commitment to helping her and Joey as well.

It was a relief to find him here again, busy packing up camping gear. Still, she was surprised by the tumultuous depth of her feelings. She wasn't used to being concerned about the nocturnal comings and going of any man, especially her stepson. So what if he had stayed out all night? It wasn't her concern.

Chase stood slowly and wiped off his hands with a rag. Tell her, an inner voice demanded. Tell her and get it over with. Don't start this trip with a lie between you. Deciding to get it all out in the open, he rubbed his hand over the aching muscles in his neck and said, ''There's something we need to talk about.''

This sounded ominous, Hope thought, reading his reluctant expression. "Okay," she said.

"Not here," Chase said. "Somewhere private. The sun room?"

Hope nodded her agreement. Aware of him close behind her, she led the way. They didn't speak again until they were ensconced in the glass-walled room, with the spring sunlight streaming in around them. Chase gestured to one of the wicker chairs and she sank obediently into the plump floral cushions.

"There's no easy way to say this," he began, "so I'm just going to say it right out. My mother found out you've been meeting with Russell Morris." Chase watched as all color promptly drained from Hope's face. Forcing himself to go on, he said, "She told me yesterday she was going to hire a private investigator to dig into your past and find out what went on between the two of you."

Hope remained very still, looking both sickened and angry.

Chase rushed on, his brusque voice giving no clue as to the inner turmoil he felt. "I didn't want anyone nosing around in your business. So I offered to do it for her."

Hope bolted from her chair. She glared at him incredulously. "And now what, Chase? Am I supposed to thank you for this?"

Maybe, Chase thought, when you've had time to think about it, you'll want to do just that. "Right now I just want you to listen." She spun around. He caught her arm, preventing her escape. She wasn't leaving until she had heard him out. "Hope, I talked to your mother yesterday. That's where I was."

"Why?" she whispered. "Why would you do such a thing to me?"

"Because I didn't want to see you hurt," he said gruffly. "We both know anything Rosemary learned would be used against you."

She took a moment to contemplate that, then asked woodenly, with mute terror on her face, "What did you learn?"

Studying her, Chase wondered what it was she didn't want him to know. He answered her in a soft, compassionate voice. "I learned that you must have had a very unhappy childhood." *That you weren't loved.* "I'm sorry, Hope." Aware of her closeness and his ardent reaction to it, he swallowed and let her go. "I'm sorry if I hurt you but I had to do what I felt was best."

Distressed, she ran a hand through her upswept hair, the careless motion knocking down a third of the elaborately pinned dark strands. "You said you saw my mother?" she repeated, as if in shock. "What did she say about me?" Hope took a tiny breath and after a moment dared to look at him. "About Russell."

Chase shrugged, more aware than ever of how little information he had gotten out of Louise. And how much more he still wanted to know about Hope, how much he wanted her to feel she could confide in him. "She didn't want to talk about it. She seemed very bitter."

Briefly Hope seemed to relax. She sighed and shook her head in mute regret. "She always was," she admitted softly, her huge eyes glimmering with an inner sadness that made his own heart ache. Hope looked up, searching his face. "What are you going to tell your mother?"

Chase held her insistent gaze honestly. "That there was nothing to find out," he said. "That you dated Russell briefly and were, from what little I could discern, considered out of his league socially and monetarily. It ended. Your family left the area."

Hope's mouth twisted bitterly. "She told you they got kicked off the tenant farm because of me, didn't she?"

Yes, Chase thought, she had. And their anger at Hope over that seemed out of proportion for what she'd done. The Curtises had moved frequently anyway. Moving again shouldn't have been such a big deal to them, even if Hope's brief dating relationship with Russell were the reason. It shouldn't have prompted them to *permanently* disown Hope. Something more had to have gone on. The question was what. Did it have anything to do with the "scheme" Louise had hinted at, or with her estimation of Hope's need from an early age to have more than they could give her? He had never been poor, so he couldn't really imagine what it must be like to grow up that way, but right now, Hope looked more victim than perpetrator, and that puzzled him, too.

Hope buried her face in her hands and took a deep, ragged breath. "They never forgave me for that, either of them." Her voice broke. "I don't think they ever will."

Wanting only to comfort her, Chase moved forward and took her in his arms. Where she had swept her hand through her hair, it was falling down in loose, unkempt strands around her pale face. Her eyes were huge and wet...and angry.

"Damn you," she whispered hoarsely. "Damn you for dredging this all up." As if unable to bear the sight of him, she wrenched herself out of his arms. She moved away from him and stood with her arms clenched tightly at her waist. She stared out at the lawn. Uniformed men were cutting and trimming and sweeping away the last remnants of winter.

"Hope—" Chase began. Jaw set, she whirled to face him. And suddenly he couldn't go on. He didn't know what else to say that would make her understand, not now, not when she was still so upset and angry. "About the camping trip—"

Hope glanced at her watch. She expelled a weary breath. "We'll go," she said tersely, lifting her gaze to his. "We promised him. And he's already been through too much to even consider reneging on that promise."

But that was the only reason she was still going with him. She'd made that very clear, Chase realized, disappointed. The only reason.

Chapter Eleven

"Hand me the hammer please, will you, Mom?" Joey asked.

Hope picked it up and walked over to where Joey was kneeling beside the half-erected tent. The trip she had been looking forward to had turned out to be agony; she tried to keep her tumultuous emotions hidden from her son. Fortunately he was so hyped up about the fact they were actually going to rough it at long last, he hadn't noticed much of anything except the beauty of the rolling central Texas countryside and the tall fragrant pines that populated much of the Bastrop area. Chase shot her a concerned look from time to time when Joey wasn't looking, but he had disguised whatever he was feeling as well. He was some trooper, her Chase. He was able to go behind her back one moment, and then be her and her son's camping buddy the next. She didn't know how he felt but she was so mixed up she could hardly see straight.

"Pull that rope a little tighter before we stake it." Chase instructed her son genially from the other side of the tent, where he, too was, holding on to a couple of stakes.

"Okay." His glasses falling askew on his nose, Joey yanked on the rope, pulling it as tight as he was able.

"Now, Hope, set that stake at an angle and hammer it down firmly into the ground," Chase continued.

Their eyes met and again she felt that sharp sense of betrayal. She didn't know who he was or what he was thinking or feeling. And though part of her wanted to know everything, the other part of her wanted only to be kept in the dark, away from any further hurt.

I can get through this, Hope told herself firmly. I just have to concentrate on setting up the campsite. That was much easier if she didn't look at Chase directly, or let him get a good look at her. Feeling like a fish out of water, Hope knelt and did exactly as Chase instructed.

Chase gave her and Joey a grin of approval when she'd finished. "Now that wasn't so difficult, was it?" he asked.

"Nope, it was easy!" Joey said. He turned to Hope and gave her an impulsive hug. "Thanks for letting me go camping, Mom," he said.

Hope hugged her son back tightly. It did her heart good to see him so happy. Right now she needed a hug, too. "You're welcome," she said.

"And thanks for talking her into it," Joey continued, coming forward to embrace Chase in an awkward hug. Chase put his arms around Joey, too. It was the first time Chase had ever embraced his half brother.

Hope turned away. She didn't want to see the two of them becoming closer. Not now. Not when it was all about to come tumbling down. She had known from the beginning that Rosemary would be a threat to her. She just hadn't wanted to think about that threat becoming a reality. And she hadn't wanted Chase to be unwittingly drawn into the mess she had once made of her life. But it was happening, and as hard as she was trying to keep the situation under control, she was powerless, it seemed, to prevent her past from slowly unraveling and from becoming Joey's nightmare...

"What's the other tent for?" Joey asked curiously, when Chase began unrolling the second aqua canvas.

"Your mom." Chase glanced at Hope as if to gauge her reaction to that.

She blushed with a mixture of apprehension and embarrassment. She was suddenly acutely aware that in their rush to go camping they hadn't discussed sleeping arrangements once.

His eyes on hers, Chase continued matter-of-factly, "I figured she'd want a little privacy."

He was right about that much, Hope thought fervently. More to the point, she wished she had never agreed to come. Not just because she was angry with Chase, but because it was already even more awkward than she had anticipated. They were in the woods alone, and they had only been here a little over an hour. This early in March, when the night temperatures dipped into the lower sixties and upper fifties, the state park was still relatively deserted. Consequently they'd been able to get a campsite that was both beautiful and very private. The only sounds were those of their voices, and the whisper of the wind through the pines.

She felt vulnerable, physically and emotionally, as dinnertime approached. She couldn't imagine how she would begin to feel when the sun went down and darkness fell, and they had nothing to distract them from each other. Maybe she would keep Joey up later than usual, she thought a little desperately, or use him as a shield to keep the conversation from becoming too personal between her and Chase. Maybe Chase would be tired, from all his spying, she thought, and frowned.

"Am I going to sleep with you?" Joey asked curiously, his brows knitting together. With his index finger, he pushed his glasses a little farther up his nose.

Chase shrugged, as if it made little difference. "Wherever you want, sport, with your mom or with me. The tents are the same size. They both sleep four, so there's plenty of room either place."

"I'm sleeping with you, then," Joey said, deepening his voice deliberately and physically aligning himself with Chase's taller form. "Us guys need our privacy, too."

The grown-up sound of her son's voice and his attempt to be macho and fearless, coaxed a reluctant smile from Hope. No matter how difficult this was for her, it was very good for Joey. And she would weather anything that would benefit her son.

"How soon is dinner?" Joey asked. "I'm getting hungry."

"Dinner won't be for a while, but there are some granola bars and canned juice in my backpack," Chase said. "Help yourself to a snack."

When Joey went off, Chase straightened slowly and looked at Hope. "Thank God he doesn't realize anything's wrong," Chase murmured."

A chill ran down her spine at the dissatisfied look in Chase's eyes. "Let's keep it that way," Hope said, just as softly. Although she could see he wanted to sit down and talk, she didn't want to discuss his visit with her mother. She didn't want to discuss her meetings with Russell Morris, or his mother's attempts to discredit and ruin her. She wanted to leave that all behind, for just a little while. She just wasn't sure he would let her.

CHASE ENDURED Hope's silence through their meal preparations, dinner and dishes. He knew she was ticked off at him, and maybe she had a right to be, but he'd be damned if he would endure the withering glances she gave him whenever her son's back was turned.

"How long are you going to stay mad at me?" Chase asked, after a thoroughly exhausted Joey had finally gone to sleep. Hope was standing next to the picnic table, her hands immersed to the elbow in the small dishpan of soapy water. Used to seeing her mostly in suits and blouses, it was disconcerting to see her in a simple yellow cotton turtleneck sweater and cords. Her windswept hair hung down around her face, and her cheeks filled with a color generated by the cool night air. Chase had the feeling she didn't let herself relax very often, and as he watched her, he saw she was a long way from tranquillity despite their serene surroundings. Her back and shoulders stiff, she scrubbed vigorously at the aluminum plate in her hand.

"I don't know," she said tightly. She slid the clean plate into the small tub of clear water next to it.

Chase picked it up and began to dry it.

"Probably a while," Hope admitted.

At the depth of her fury, Chase felt his own temper begin to fray around the edges. "A while or all weekend?" When she didn't answer, he said, "All month? Until I leave again? How long, Hope?"

She turned to face him so swiftly that water splashed out of the tub, soaking them both at the waist. "You want the truth?" she snarled in an exasperated whisper, inching forward until they stood nose to nose. "I will probably be mad at you forever. Dammit, you betrayed me, going to see my mother like that, asking all those questions."

"I explained to you why I had to do it."

"No, Chase," she countered, "you rationalized why you had to do it. There's a big difference."

He closed his eyes and counted to ten. He never had been able to understand why people feared the truth. It was the lies and deceptions that ended up really hurting. He opened his eyes to find her still glaring at him. "I didn't have to tell you anything," he pointed out reasonably.

"Why did you?" She held his glance until doing so became uncomfortable for both of them, then turned her attention back to the stack of camping dishes.

"Because I didn't want a lie between us."

"Bull," she said, slamming both sudsy hands quietly down on either side of the dishpan. She faced him fiercely. "You just couldn't deal with feeling guilty about what you'd done and thought by confessing your misdeed you would be exonerated in some fundamental way." Her statement hit its target.

The heat of regret filled his face. "Maybe I did feel guilty," Chase admitted reluctantly after a moment. He tried hard not to notice how the lamplight illuminated the fragile beauty of her face and brought out the shadows beneath her eyes, and the vulnerable trembling of her mouth and its softness. "I don't like dealing with people that way."

"Then maybe that's a clue not to do it again in the future," Hope countered stiffly, resuming her dishwashing with unnecessary force.

Again, water surged over the rim of the small plastic dishpan, this time dampening both their thighs. Tears sparkled against her lashes, but fell no farther. Desperate to mend the rift between them, Chase grabbed her shoulders and turned her to face him. He held her there when she would have bolted. "Hope, I was trying to protect you." In her heart, he felt she knew that.

She gave a bitter little laugh, and looked even more distressed. "If you cared about my feelings you would never have gone there," she whispered hoarsely. Her wet hands inched up to try to pry his fingers from her shoulders. "Ever! Damn you!"

Afraid she would wake Joey if her escalating emotions remained unchecked, he cupped a hand beneath her elbow and half dragged, half led her farther away from the tents, not stopping until they were standing at the far edge of the campsite, in a stand of trees.

"I'm sorry, okay?" He knew he'd had no right to go snooping around like that, but he also knew instinctively that she was in some sort of trouble. Russell Morris was a part of that trouble, even if she wouldn't yet admit it to him. "But at least I was honest," he continued when she pushed away from him and leaned her back against the spreading base of a live oak. "At least I leveled with you."

She shook her head in exasperation and tilted her head up to his. "Is that oh-so-noble gesture supposed to win you my admiration?" she questioned sarcastically. "Is that supposed to get you off the hook with me?"

Yes, dammit, Chase thought, it was. He had expected her to be open to reason with the passage of this much time; the fact that she wasn't was both frustrating and annoying. "I said it before. I'll say it again. I'm sorry if I hurt you," he repeated tightly.

"Well, sorry doesn't cut it," she snapped. She tried to step around him. "Not in this case. You lied to me, Chase." And that she wouldn't sanction. She'd been played for the fool once. It would never happen again.

He stopped her from fleeing by planting a hand on either side of her. She had run from too much already—from her past, her home, her parents, and Russell Morris. She wasn't going to run from him, too. "And you're not lying? Pretending you have no feelings for Russell Morris, then meeting him on the sly."

The thought of her with Morris made him furious. Dammit, she knew the guy was a sleazy jerk! Yet she was spending time with him again! Why? Were they back to her need for money again? Was she part of one of Russell's schemes?

Hope was aware how close they were, how damp and clinging the midsections of their clothing, and how very much she wanted him to hold her in his arms. "I don't have any feelings for Russell." The idea that she could was ludicrous! She hated Russell Morris. It was Chase she cared about, Chase who she didn't want to think badly of her. Chase who, if he found out the truth, undoubtedly would think her a fool and a coward and maybe even a tramp. And she couldn't bear that. She couldn't bear it if he, too, looked at her with the same disdain as her parents and all the people she had once known. They hadn't believed her story, either.

Chase's glance narrowed. "Then why were you meeting with him?" he asked in disbelief.

Hope pushed at his shoulders, and found them immovable. Dropping her hands, she leaned back against the cold, rough bark. Although they weren't touching, she was acutely aware of his body and of the energy seething between them. Turning her head to the side, she ignored his nearness. "I only saw Russell for one reason. I was trying to get rid of him!"

His arms flexing slightly, he studied her. "You're not still carrying a torch for him?" he asked roughly.

"No." Just the thought of him made her ill and brought on the awful migraines. She closed her eyes briefly, unable to deal with Chase's penetrating gaze, or her need to vindicate herself in his eyes. She feared she would inadvertently reveal too much, and cause an even bigger mess than the tangled web of lies and half-truths they were already in. "I hate the man!"

He waited until she opened her eyes again before he spoke. "Because of what he did to your family?" Chase watched as she wet her lips.

"Yes," Hope answered hoarsely. Part of her wished he would let her go, the other part wished he would find out everything now, so they could just get it over with. Then he could think her a fool like everyone else. He would walk away before they became any closer. She knew now how very wrong they were for each other. Chase thought they should tell everything, risk everything. Only she knew how very much the truth could hurt.

The moments drew out and the embattled silence continued. Whatever had happened back then had scarred Hope irrevocably and made her afraid to trust, Chase thought. He wanted to help her, but in order to do that he had to get her to talk.

Realizing abruptly how shaky she looked, he dropped his hands from either side of her and laced one around her waist. "What happened back then, Hope?" he asked gently, pulling her against him. "Why did your family get thrown off the tenant farm after you and Russell stopped dating?"

Again, misery filled her face. Her arms pressed tightly against her waist, Hope slipped from the warm circle of his arm and stalked further back into the trees. "Russell Mor-

ris told a lot of lies about me. He insinuated I was after him
because of his money and everyone believed him.''

Her words had the ring of truth. And yet, he knew instinctively, there was still so much she wasn't saying, so
much she was afraid to say. Only harsh questions would
make her angry enough to forget her inhibitions and speak
her mind. ''*Were* you interested in him because he was
rich?'' Chase asked, deliberately letting a lazy, faintly insinuating tone creep into his voice.

Hope whirled to face him and sent him an aggrieved look.
''I dated him exactly twice,'' she enunciated clearly, pushing the words through her teeth, ''because I was very young
and very naive and too inexperienced to see through his
surface charm. I couldn't have cared less about whether or
not he had money! I went out with him because I thought
he *liked* me.''

Looking into her eyes, Chase could believe that. He also
recalled what Louise had said about Hope and her schemes.
There was something more here that Hope didn't want him
to know. ''Then you didn't try to extort money from the
Morrises?''

Hurt flickered in her eyes. ''Is that what my mother told
you?'' Hope asked. If so, it didn't surprise her.

Ignoring her question, he deftly closed the distance between them. ''Is it true?'' He knew he had hit on something here, from the tense, wary expression in Hope's eyes.

Her shoulders slumped with defeat. ''All I wanted from
the Morrises,'' Hope began tiredly, running a hand through
her hair, ''was for them to be fair, to tell the truth, to admit
they were wrong about me.'' But she knew that would never
happen. They had sided with their son, against her, and they
always would. Her family had sided against her, too. And
Chase might, if he found out the truth. It wasn't a chance
she was willing to take. She'd rather he know nothing and
resent her for her secrecy than have him find out the truth
and despise her for the naive fool she had once been.

Feeling more trapped and desperate than ever, she moved blindly away from him. If they kept this up she'd have a throbbing migraine by morning. "I can't talk about this with you," she said in an anguished voice. She wouldn't. It was just too painful. He was too important to her.

Having come close to getting at the truth, to getting close to Hope, and then having it all slip away was more than he could bear. Aware he was losing control but helpless to do anything to prevent it, Chase went after her. It took three steps, maybe four, and they were even. Another for him to cut her off. Catching her implacably by the arm, he swung her around to face him. "What are you so afraid of?" The depth of his frustration oozed from every pore.

Trying to steady herself, Hope took a deep breath. "I'm not afraid."

"The hell you're not!" he retorted, his low voice intense.

The silence drew out between them and their gazes collided, held. She knew he wanted her; she knew she wanted him, and that the passion they felt was dangerous. But as time suspended and they stood there facing each other in the moonlight, none of that seemed to matter. No matter how firmly she told herself to move, to get away from him now while she still had the chance, she couldn't seem to drop her gaze. Nor could he. "Hope," Chase said hoarsely.

The next thing she knew he was stepping closer, anchoring an arm around her waist. His head was slanting, lowering, and then the barest second later his mouth was on hers.

She fought him at first, her arms coming up between them, to splay against the rock solidness of his chest and push him away. She didn't want this. She didn't want him. Not when she was still so very angry. But as the seconds ticked out, her hurt and her sense of betrayal began to fade. The passion she felt for him overrode her anger completely. She was entranced by the feel of his warm, smooth lips on hers.

She hadn't known it could be like this, so soft and warm and enticing. So gentle, yet so provocative. He made her feel

as though she was something precious, like this was something precious. And it was. And she wanted more of it,
wanted more of him. Only she didn't know quite what to do,
or how to act, or what he wanted from her. But that didn't
seem to matter, either. She followed her instinct, opened her
lips slightly, and his tongue slid inside her mouth. Gingerly
she touched her tongue to his, and felt an answering shiver
deep inside her. He tasted of mint and coffee and man.

So this was passion, she thought, stunned, as her arms
and legs, indeed her whole body, tightened. The arm he had
anchored at her waist pulled her even nearer. She felt the
strength of his desire pulsing against her. She felt the same
strong yearning pulsing within her. But she wasn't afraid.
Not at all. Not this time. And that was such an incredible,
awesome relief.

I SHOULDN'T HAVE done that, Chase thought, hours later,
when he was lying in his sleeping bag, with his hands folded
behind his neck. Joey slumbered peacefully beside him. He
shouldn't have kissed her. But he'd been unable to help
himself. She'd looked so beautiful and fragile standing there
in the moonlight. She'd been so frightened and so much in
need of someone to love her. He'd acted on impulse and
gotten the surprise of his life. She kissed like a virgin, ten-
tatively and shyly. And that, combined with her smolder-
ing, come-hither beauty was sexy as hell.

Maybe that was her turn-on, he speculated guiltily. Maybe
that was how she drove men insane. Maybe that was how
she'd gotten his father to marry her so quickly. God knew
it had worked on him against all common sense and familial loyalty.

The really strange thing was that her shyness hadn't felt
like a put-on. It had seemed very real to him. So real, in fact,
that he'd had a heck of a time stopping with just the one
long, soul-shattering kiss. But somehow he had stopped and
they'd stepped back from each other.

If she had slapped him, he would've felt better. She adn't. Instead, she had looked at him as though he was ome sort of marauding angel. At that point, he'd had a vi-ion of his father. Edmond wasn't angry exactly, but he vasn't exactly pleased, either.

Chase rolled over on his side, thinking again of how Hope ad looked after the kiss, so stunned, as if that had never appened to her before. Certainly she'd been kissed before. he'd been married to his father for ten years, for cripes ake. Surely, Edmond'd—

No, he didn't want to think about that, Chase repri-nanded himself grimly. If he did he'd be dreaming about his ather all night. Thinking about Hope and Edmond to-ether, even in the most obscure, scientific fashion possi-le, was just too kinky for Chase's taste. He had to put that ut of his mind entirely. He didn't want to know what had appened in his father's bedroom, ever. Even if Hope *had* een there.

He also had to stop agonizing over the kiss if he were ever oing to get through the rest of this weekend. So what if Iope had once been married to his father? So what if he'd issed her once? It wasn't as if she were still married. She vas single, a widow. His dad had been gone a year. Hell, eing the generous soul he was, his dad would probably vant Hope to have a life and maybe even get married again. ust probably not to him, Chase conceded on a weary sigh.

He knew if he and Hope hadn't been previously related by narriage, he would have given in to desire and kissed her ong ago. And considering how Hope had responded to him y going all soft and cuddly and weak-kneed, she probably vould have kissed him back. And it was just a kiss. One iss! He had no reason to feel guilty. He shouldn't let this other him. So why was he still feeling so torn up, so bad bout the whole thing?

Because of his dad? Or because Hope had yet to com-letely open up to him? He felt, in his heart, she might never o that, no matter how long they were together. He knew if he *did* get together with Hope there would be plenty of talk. And though he might be up to weathering it emotionally, he wasn't sure either Hope or Joey was. Not to mention the fight they'd have to put up with from his mother.

Rosemary was already harassing Hope night and day. If she were to get wind of a possible romance between Hope and himself, there was no telling what she might do. And he knew it wasn't fair to make Hope walk through fire again. She had already done that once, when she married his father. To ask her to do it again by getting involved with him, especially when she now had Joey to consider, too, was uncaring and selfish in the extreme. So what if he'd never felt one-tenth the passion for another woman that he felt for Hope? So what if she kissed like an angel? She was still his father's wife.

He turned on his side, away from the slumbering Joey. Maybe the solution was to simply keep his distance. He'd try not to do anything else rash, like kissing Hope again. Maybe they both just needed time, to think this through, to figure out if letting their relationship take a passionate detour was going to be worth it in the end. Right now it wasn't too late. They both still had time to back out and to leave things as they were. He knew in his heart, everything considered, perhaps that was the best choice of all. Certainly it would be the path of the least resistance.

HOPE, too, was unable to sleep. Chase's kiss had come out of nowhere, and although she had fantasized about an embrace, having him actually take her into his arms and hold her against him, length to length, had left her speechless and shaking and drained of every ounce of strength. She had wanted him in a way she had never wanted any man, not even Edmond. And that scared her. She didn't like the feeling that her passion for Chase was stronger than her common sense. Tonight that had indeed been the case. Worse, she was scared it could easily happen again. All he would have to do was touch her.

No. She couldn't think about that. Not when there was
ill so much at stake. Chase knew something was going on
etween her and Russell. Both curious and concerned, he
ought he could help her. She knew he couldn't. And he
uld never know both she and Edmond had lied to him
bout the facts surrounding their marriage or that she was
ill lying to him to this day. She knew how Chase felt about
e truth. It was everything to him. Everything.

Having been betrayed by her parents, she knew how much
hurt. She couldn't, knowingly, put Chase through an
qually debilitating trauma. Especially when it might not be
ecessary. After all, she had paid off Russell. She'd given
im everything she had. He wasn't happy now with what
e'd been able to raise, but he would accept it sooner or
ter and find someone else to milk for cash. Knowing him,
e thought, shuddering, there were probably plenty of
ther potential victims.

She climbed into her sleeping bag and zipped it to her
hin. The ground was rough beneath her, and no matter
hich way she twisted or turned she couldn't seem to get
omfortable. Nor could she seem to sleep. She just kept re-
embering Chase asking her why she had dated Russell in
e first place. Looking back, it seemed so unreal, like it had
ll happened to another person, in another lifetime. Of
ourse, they had changed. Back then, Russell had been fit
nd healthy. With his deep blue eyes and charming, very
ristocratic, very Southern manner, he had been different
om any boy she had ever known and he'd seemed deter-
ined to sweep her off her feet.

She sighed, folding her arms behind her head. Maybe it
ad been the money that had drawn her. Maybe Chase was
ght. If Russell hadn't sent her that first big bouquet of
ses or the second or the third, and if he hadn't insisted
pon taking her to the most expensive restaurant in town on
e first date and treated her like such a queen, she would
ever have gone dancing with him on the second.

Was it her fault that he had started drinking heavily tha night? She didn't want to think so. She knew she hadn' suggested the tequila sunrises or indulged in even a sip of th one he had ordered for her. But she also knew, for fear o making a scene and calling attention to herself, that sh hadn't prevailed hard enough to get him to stop drinkin once he had started. She hadn't walked out on him at th first sign of trouble, or insisted she telephone her parents fo a ride.

Louise and Henry would only have been furious tha Hope inconvenienced them and humiliated their landlord' son. She had decided to handle the situation alone. Stone cold sober, she had insisted she drive them the fifty-fiv miles back to the Morris ranch. And that's when the rea trouble had started, when she insulted Russell's manhood.

Shuddering, she put the thoughts of that evening aside It wouldn't help to remember the crash on the lonely coun try road or what had happened afterward. It wouldn't hel to remember the looks on her parents' faces when she ha straggled in, bruised and battered, shortly after dawn. O the days of screaming accusations and raging disbelief tha had followed.

She had to concentrate on the present, on getting throug this weekend. She wouldn't be able to do that if she contin ued to hold on to her anger. Or let herself give in to he passion. Yes, Chase had betrayed her in going to see he mother, but he had been trying to help. He had made thing worse, but she couldn't continue to fault him for that. Hi heart had been in the right place.

She had to go on. She had to be civil to him, more tha civil. She had to make him think the past didn't matter t her any longer. And she had to make sure he didn't kiss he again.

Chapter Twelve

Hope was already up, frying bacon in the black iron skillet when Chase and Joey emerged from their tent Saturday morning. She had done her best to clean up, washing her face and hands in water they had brought, but she still felt grubby and ill kempt. It didn't matter that she had tied her hair back with a neat ribbon, or put on clean clothes. She wanted her usual morning shower, with plenty of soap and shampoo and water for rinsing.

She also wanted a reprieve from the sexy, indomitable Chase.

"Good morning," he said in a careful, neutral tone.

He's thinking about the way we kissed, too, Hope realized uncomfortably, working hard to hide a blush. "Morning." Keeping her eyes on her task, Hope lifted the crisp bacon from the pan and broke eggs into the skillet.

"Biscuits, too?" Joey asked, looking at a square metal pan on the other side of the grill.

"You bet," Hope told her son cheerfully.

Chase headed for the supply chest, his expression remote. "I'll put some coffee on," he offered, keeping his back to Hope.

"And I'll make the powdered orange juice," Joey said, noticing nothing amiss between the two adults.

Thanks mostly to her son's nonstop chattering, breakfast was easy enough. Immediately afterward, they did the dishes and then set off on a nature hike. Chase took the lead, Hope the rear. The conversation was dominated by a barrage of curious questions from her son. Joey listened raptly as Chase pointed out types of flowers and explained to Joey how the forest they were in was different from the rain forests he liked to explore.

"I wish I could go with you, to see a rain forest," Joey said wistfully, after a while.

Chase grinned and placed his hand on Joey's shoulder. "Tell you what," he promised warmly. "If you still want to go when you're grown up, I'll take you."

Joey absorbed that news happily, but for Hope, the conversation just served to remind her how soon Chase would be leaving again. Last night, in a brief moment of passion, she had allowed herself to forget all the things that kept them apart. She'd been drawn into his spell. She couldn't allow herself to make that mistake again. Joey needed a full-time father. Maybe it was corny and unliberated, but she wanted to be married again. She wanted a husband to live with and love. It would have to be someone who wouldn't badger her with questions about the past, or make her feel disloyal to Edmond in the bargain. That just wasn't Chase, she realized sadly.

"Poor kid," Chase said later that evening, after he and Hope had tucked Joey in. "I think we've worn him out."

"No wonder, with the hiking this morning and the canoeing this afternoon." She'd hardly had time to catch her breath, either, which perhaps was also for the best.

Chase got up to pour himself some more coffee from the battered metal pot. "Don't forget our mutual hair washing in a basin this afternoon. He enjoyed that, too."

So had Hope. Despite her pique with Chase, there had been something very sensual about having Chase rinse her hair after she had washed it. Forcing her mind back to the practical, she commented, "I was surprised you brought shampoo."

His eyes met hers over the rim of his cup. "I would have dragged it out first thing this morning had it been warm enough." Instead, baths had been relegated to late afternoon, when it was the warmest, and carried out individually within the privacy of the tents.

Hope had to admit she did feel better now that her hair was clean again. Chase's blond locks weren't too shabby, either. Soft and clean, they gleamed gold in the firelight. "Is that what you do when you're in the rain forest?"

Chase nodded. "Generally, yeah, we get by on hand baths and wash our hair in a basin. At least here we were able to get our water from a pump. Out there we have to carry it in buckets and sterilize it."

"Sounds like a lot of work."

"It is."

Hope studied him curiously. "How do you stand it?"

He shrugged noncommittally, his eyes still holding hers. "It's for a good cause." He paused as if that said it all, then shrugged. "Joey didn't seem to mind the hardship."

"No, he didn't." Hope smiled. "In fact, I'm sure he'll remember this trip for the rest of his life." As will I, she thought. She felt a little sad, for Joey's sake, because such a trip wasn't likely to be repeated anytime soon. Determined to keep her own thoughts from turning maudlin, she put her coffee cup to her lips. The brew had cooled to lukewarm, but she sipped it anyway, to keep her mind off Chase and the possible repeat of last night's kiss.

The awkward silence between them continued. It was only nine-thirty. Neither of them were sleepy enough to head for the tents. With no television or radio, they had nothing else to do but talk. "It's peaceful here," Chase said.

"Yes." Hope plucked at the crease on her Liz Claiborne jeans. Although fresh from the laundry this morning, they were now speckled with mud and grass stains. Still, Chase continued to look at her as if she were clad in the most resplendent of evening gowns.

"Nothing like being out under an open sky."

His attempts to make small talk were turning deliberately comical. Hope shot him a droll look. "Yes," she agreed.

"But you're not thinking about how nice it is to be here," he continued, baiting her.

"No?" she asked. No, she was hoping he wouldn't try to kiss her again.

"No," he drawled, looking very smug. His teasing demeanor was breaking the tension that had built between them all day and intensified sharply once they found themselves alone. "You're still thinking about how tiresome it was to wash up before dinner in that little washbasin in the tent. You're wishing you had a way to shower and watch TV—"

"Now wait a minute," Hope countered. She wasn't about to be pigeonholed as some citified prima donna. After all, she had done without a lot of things as a kid and still turned out nicely. "I like the peace and quiet out here."

He mulled that over. "Well, you've got a point. No one from Barrister's can bother you way out here."

Nor could Russell. But she didn't want to think about that. Nor did she want Chase asking her anything personal again, so she said, "Tell me more about your research."

"What's to tell?"

That you're tired of it, she wished fervently, that you don't want to do it anymore, and that you want to stay here in the States and be closer to me and to Joey. "Do you really think you're going to find cures out there?" she asked, managing to keep her tone noncommittal with effort.

He shrugged, promising nothing. "I've only been at it a couple of years but already we've come very close to finding a possible new treatment for arthritis." He paused reflectively. "It's strange, visiting with people from such different cultures. There's so much that's different, and so much the same. Families are still families. People still love each other and fight and make up."

As she watched the play of emotions on his face, she sensed he was talking about more than just different cultures here. "Do you regret not patching things up better between you and your dad before he died?"

A flicker of pain moved across his face. Chase nodded. His eyes on hers, he said with that trademark honesty of his, "Yeah, I do. I regret it all the time." His voice roughened and he shook his head in obvious regret. "Looking back, it all seems so senseless. If I'd only gone to him and talked to him—but I didn't. Instead I avoided him like the plague. In essence, I ruined what could have been the best years of our lives together."

"Is that why you're spending so much time with Joey?" she asked quietly. "To make it up to Edmond?"

He looked her straight in the eye. "Maybe. In the beginning. I do it now because I'm fond of him." He gauged her reaction carefully. "Is that okay with you?"

Feeling the conversation had once again turned too intimate for comfort, she got up to pour herself more of his industrial-strength coffee. "Why wouldn't it be okay with me? Unless, of course, you insist that his next camping trip be in the rain forest."

Chase grinned. "Wimping out on me?"

"You bet." Hope resumed her seat. "I have no desire whatsoever to be out with the snakes and the scorpions and the tarantulas."

"There are snakes and scorpions and tarantulas around here, too," he pointed out knowingly. "I haven't noticed you being bothered by them. Or did I miss you screaming hysterically at some point?"

"Very funny," Hope said.

Chase merely lifted a brow. Suddenly, she knew he wasn't teasing, that he had seen and ignored what she hadn't even bothered to look for. She looked around nervously, then got up to move restlessly around the campfire. A shiver moved down her spine and she tucked her hand in the pocket of her jeans. She looked back at where she had been sitting. Was that her imagination or was there a spider hanging from a nearby tree?

She took another step and nearly tripped over Chase'
outstretched leg. He reached up to catch her. "Hey," he saic
softly, his skin warm where it was pressed against hers, "]
didn't mean to upset you. You're not in any danger."

"I know." That didn't change the fact that this was a
natural setting; there *were* crawly things out there. Hope hac
lived on farms long enough to know that was true. She
shuddered again, feeling nervous and on edge. Deciding she
was behaving like a fool, she sat down next to Chase,
thought she felt something crawling up her back and immediately got back up again.

Chase stood, too. "You really are jumpy tonight."

She lifted her chin and enunciated plainly, "Not at all."

He grinned, taunting openly, "Liar."

She blushed and her eyes still on his, held her ground.
Reminded of the previous night's embrace, she felt an answering wave of desire. You're not going to kiss him again,
she told herself firmly. You know it wouldn't be wise. But
she wanted to kiss him. Very much. It didn't matter he was
her stepson.

Suddenly Chase stepped back. "You really hate it out
here, don't you?" Chase slid a marshmallow onto the
pointed end of a stick. He sat again and stretched his long
legs out in front of him. He aimed the stick in the direction
of the flames and held it there.

Hope lifted her shoulders expressively. "Hate's a strong
word, but yes, you're right, I do despise the lack of facili-
ties." She met his gaze equably.

"Why?" The end of his marshmallow began to smoke.
He lifted it quickly, and turned it so the uncooked edge was
down, facing the flames.

Hope reached for a marshmallow, trying not to let unhappy memories get her down. She poked it on the end of
her long-handled cooking fork and positioned it a good
distance from his. "Maybe because this reminds me of some
of the places we lived while I was growing up. Places without central heat or air or even indoor plumbing."

Chase leaned back against the log behind him and studied Hope. Having met her mother, he realized what a tough time she'd had growing up. It surprised him she had turned out as well adjusted as she had. So many would have become bitter or selfish. She was neither of those things. She was a very loving mother, who was extremely sensitive to her son's needs. And to his, too, if he were honest. Today she had gone out of her way to make sure he felt comfortable around her. He appreciated her willingness to try to get along, and his mingled feelings of respect and gratitude had intensified as the day wore on. Now he found himself almost behaving normally again. Still, there was that edge of tension and unresolved conflict between them, and that edge of passion. He knew it could flare quickly out of control.

"But I suppose I'll have to get used to roughing it for Joey's sake," Hope continued in a deliberate, conversational tone. She turned her toasting marshmallow so it would brown evenly.

"Joey has liked it, especially the fishing this afternoon."

"I know." Hope ruminated softly, sending him a genuinely grateful look. "I haven't seen him this happy in a long time."

Chase grinned. Unable to resist, he teased, "Macho activity will do that for a guy."

At the exaggerated authority in his voice, Hope rolled her eyes. "Only a man would consider living without every conceivable luxury having a good time, Chase." Having lived this way because she had to, she saw no reason to seek it out. Then again, maybe that was precisely the appeal for Chase, Hope thought. He wanted a change of pace from the luxuriant way *he'd* grown up. He wanted simplicity. She wanted comfort.

She went to the supplies and brought back a container of graham crackers and an unopened box of Hershey bars.

Chase watched as she made herself a S'more. Earlier in the day, she had still looked tense, despite her deliberately buoyant mood. The lines in her face had softened as the

hours had passed. Now, with her hair drawn into a berib-
boned ponytail at the back of her neck, and her face framed
in the gentle light of the campfire, she was more beautiful
than ever. He felt an ache start deep inside him. It was an
ache that had to be quenched, not by activity, but by diversion, he decided firmly.

"Joey's not the only one with a good appetite," he teased.
Moving to sit beside her, he reached for the graham crackers and chocolate. If he were busy eating, he wouldn't be so
aware of her. Unfortunately, as he moved, the marshmallow he had so carefully roasted slipped off the end of his
stick and landed in the dirt. He swore, roundly. Hope gig-
gled at the distressed expression on his face.

"Don't laugh," he warned soberly. He slanted her a
quelling look, "It might happen to you next."

"I don't think so," Hope said loftily.

"Why not?"

"Because I know how to hold on to what I have," she
continued grandly. The playful words were out before she
could think. Too late, she realized her bald statement could
be construed to include her position and power at Barrister's, her child, or the lovely River Oaks home Edmond had
left her. It was true though. She would fight to the last
breath to hold on to what was hers.

"I guess you do at that," Chase replied softly.

She couldn't tell if he approved of that or not; she only
knew a rapid change of subject was in order. "Back to Joey,
though," she continued, steadying her voice with effort,
trying hard not to be so aware of the thoughtful look in
Chase's hazel eyes, "I had expected him to be having an
asthmatic episode by now."

At the mention of her son, Chase exhaled slowly. "I half
expected it, too," he admitted, frowning. "I'm glad he
hasn't run into any triggers out here."

"So far," she added cautiously, almost afraid to hope.

He studied her, looking serious and concerned. "When
exactly did you find out about Joey's asthma?" Chase

.sked softly. He leaned forward to stir the fire. "I remem-
er Dad telling me," he said. "I just can't recall any of the
letails. It's been so long."

Nor would he have wanted to recall them, considering
ow he had distanced himself from his father's new family,
Hope thought. But perhaps that, too, was understandable.
t would be hard for any guy to see his father start his life
over again, just as he himself reached adulthood.

Wrapping her arms around her bent knees to ward off the
hill of the night, she answered Chase's question in a quiet,
reflective voice, "It was when he was four. He had a cold he
ust couldn't seem to recover from. He eventually ended up
n the hospital because he was having trouble breathing.
That's when he was diagnosed." She closed her eyes, un-
villingly remembering that stressful, fear-filled time. "At
irst I kept thinking there had to be a mistake." She met
Chase's eyes and saw he not only understood but empa-
hized with her denial. "But our doctor helped us understand what to do." She released a long breath. "That was
he easy part. The hard part has been dealing with other
people's reactions to him. Sometimes kids are so cruel."

"Like the Bateman twins," Chase empathized softly.

"And their father," Hope added.

Not wanting to talk about that, she got up and carried the
bag of marshmallows back to the metal supply chest in the
ruck. Chase followed her. "I'm sorry," he said penitently,
rom behind her. "I didn't mean to upset you, bringing that
up."

"You didn't," Hope reassured. It was just that talking
vith Chase this way made her feel so vulnerable and close
o him. That disturbed her. She wanted to see him as Edmond's son. She didn't want to be attracted to him. She
didn't want to yearn to reach out to him or feel as if she was
under his spell.

"This trip wasn't just for Joey, you know," Chase said
gruffly. "I wanted you to have a good time, too. I know how
much stress you've been under. And—" he took a deep,

ragged breath, as if it pained him to admit it "—I know I'v
been the cause of part of it." Apology radiated in his eyes
"I'm sorry." Most of all, he thought, he was sorry for th
way he'd come on to her the previous night.

Caught off guard, Hope flushed. Was he talking abou
her work at Barrister's? Or was he really talking about th
passionate way he had kissed her? "Chase, you don't hav
to apologize—"

"I think I do," he said gruffly. "So, will you forgive m
for going to see your mother?" *And for kissing you the way
I did, with no holds barred, as if you had never been mar
ried to my father.*

Twenty-four hours before, Hope hadn't thought it pos
sible. Now, having spent the day with him, she knew it was
"I think it's already happened," she said shyly. But fo
Joey's sake and her own peace of mind, she intended to
hang onto this unofficial truce they had called. Anything
was better than risking another angry flare-up between
them, or worse, another ardent kiss.

"Good, because I've discovered something," he said
softly. His eyes held hers for a brief, honest second. "I don'
like having you mad at me."

Hope didn't like being mad at him, either. And that, too
was a revelation.

Chapter Thirteen

"Where have you been?" Rosemary demanded first thing Monday afternoon. "I've been trying to get you all weekend. Well, say something," she demanded impatiently. "What did you find out about Hope and Russell Morris?"

It felt strange to be back in a suit and tie after spending all weekend in jeans and Chase fought the urge to loosen the knot of his tie. Knowing he had to tell his mother something, he said finally, "I met her mother."

"And?" Rosemary waited for details with bated breath.

Talking about Hope made him feel disloyal. However, he realized if he didn't give enough detail, that Rosemary would go looking for Hope's mother herself. His only way out of it would be to offer what information he could without doing serious damage to Hope, while still satisfying his mother.

Recalling his visit with Louise, Chase summed up her character dryly, "Hope's mother wasn't exactly warm or maternal. She doesn't seem to have any love for her daughter and her father didn't even care enough to be there. From what little I saw, it's no wonder Hope doesn't keep in touch with her family."

Rosemary looked briefly disappointed. Wafting forward in a cloud of Poison, she sat down in a chair and crossed her legs at the knee. "What about Russell Morris?"

Chase shrugged. There, unfortunately, he was still sty-mied. And not because he hadn't tried. He wondered if Hope would ever be able to confide in him. And how he would feel if she couldn't. At the moment, her continued silence on the subject hurt like hell. "Apparently there was, as Russell Morris hinted, some sort of romance or relation-ship between the two," Chase admitted, working to keep his tone pragmatic, emotionally uninvolved.

"And?" Rosemary waved her hands impatiently.

"The result was Hope's family got thrown off the tenant farm in midseason."

Leaning forward, her petite figure swallowed up by the high-backed chair, Rosemary ate up every delicious detail. "Why?" she asked, her eyes glimmering with malicious delight.

Chase sighed. "It's not hard to guess," he said, making his impatience known. "There was a romance going on."

Rosemary nodded knowingly, "The Morrises wouldn't have approved."

"Probably not," Chase agreed. In fact, having met Rus-sell, he would imagine the Morrises were livid.

Before he could say anything else, there was a knock on the door. Not waiting for him to answer, Hope stuck her head in. Like him, she had rushed to shower and change the moment they got home. She had twisted her dark hair into its usual topknot, but he could still remember the way it looked falling down around her shoulders in loose waves. He could still remember how leggy and slim and curva-ceous she had looked in her cotton sweaters and jeans.

"Chase?" Hope grinned energetically, before rushing on. "About the weekend. I just wanted to tell you you were great with Joey and I—" She broke off abruptly, her face ashen as her gaze rested on his mother. "Rosemary." Real-izing her impetuous words had been overheard, Hope looked as if she wanted to fall through the floor. Chase knew exactly how she felt. Hope's timing was incredibly bad today.

Rosemary turned to Chase. "Darling?" She spoke as if underlining every word. "What was going on over the weekend? Something I should know about?"

Not if he'd been able to help it, Chase thought. Ashamed of his cowardice, yet wishing their camping trip could have remained private, instead of fodder for the cosmetic counter gossip, Chase met his mother's astonished look. "I took Joey camping."

Rosemary's expression went from surprised to aghast. "You. Chase, why?" she breathed.

Irritated, he spelled it out for her. "Because I wanted to, that's why." And the trip had nothing to do with his familial ties to Joey, he'd realized belatedly, but everything to do with his increasingly fond feelings for Hope.

Sensing the storm clouds up ahead, Hope backed out the door. "I can see this isn't a good time. I'm sorry I interrupted." As quickly as she had come, she was gone, the door closing behind her.

Chase sighed. In the awkward, heavy silence that fell, Rosemary looked at Chase. "I think," she said slowly, "you had better explain."

HOPE WAS GOING over the ads for the All New Barrister's sale when Rosemary marched in and delivered an ominous warning. "I don't know what you think you're up to, but I am warning you right now it is *not* going to work."

"I don't know what you're talking about," Hope said, getting up from her desk and crossing the room to get a glass of water. Nor was she sure she cared.

"I'm talking about that little camping trip you machinated."

And what about the search-and-destroy mission you machinated? Hope thought. But not about to sink to Rosemary's level, she kept her thoughts to herself.

"How pathetic, to have to stoop to using your child to gain a man's attention," Rosemary continued.

Hope felt angry color rise from her neck to her face. Insults to herself she could take, but the mere mention of Joey's name was off limits to the vindictive socialite. "I have never done that," she asserted flatly, sending Rosemary a warning look.

"Oh, no?" Rosemary's brow rose. "Then why did you ask Chase to step in as a big brother to him?"

"First of all, Rosemary, I didn't ask. Chase volunteered. Second of all, he is his half brother."

"Not so anyone could have told, not at least until recently, until Edmond died! The two of them were like strangers!"

The thought that Rosemary might try to step in and destroy the new relationship between Joey and Chase made Hope resent the vengeful woman even more. "What exactly are you trying to imply?" she asked tightly.

"You're after my son," Rosemary retorted with complete confidence.

"After?" Hope repeated incredulously, unable to believe her ears.

"And let me tell you something, your attempts to steal my son are not going to work because I'm going to tell him the truth!"

Hope froze. Here it was. The threat she had been dreading from Rosemary all along.

"Do you think I don't know how you hoodwinked Edmond? How you poisoned his mind against me and our marriage?"

"I never said anything against you!" Hope asserted hotly.

"No?" Rosemary quirked a dissenting brow. "Perhaps you didn't have to. Perhaps all you had to do was play the helpless female, and make him think he was doing something supremely noble by marrying you because you were pregnant!"

"That isn't true," Hope said feebly, both hurt and shaken by the extent of Rosemary's knowledge. "He loved me!" That was why they had married.

Rosemary laughed bitterly and shook her head in patent disbelief. "Right. And who did you love? Certainly not a man old enough to be your father."

Hope clenched her hands until the knuckles turned white. "I loved Edmond with all my heart."

"You must really think I'm gullible if you expect me to believe that," Rosemary said.

"No," Hope countered, "you must think I'm gullible if you think I don't know that even if I hadn't come along, Edmond would have divorced you." He had told her so many times. "So don't come to me with this holier-than-thou attitude. I happen to know the truth," Hope finished.

Rosemary reeled as if she had been slapped. "You may have stolen my husband from me but you are not going to steal my son! Do you hear me?" Her face was white with fury. "You are *not* going to steal my son!"

"What the hell is going on in here?" Chase asked roughly, storming in. He shut the door behind him, then advanced furiously, until he was standing between the two women. He looked as if he wanted to throttle them both. "You can hear the two of you shouting all the way down the hall."

Rosemary glared at Hope, the threat implicit. "I've said what I had to say," she said calmly. She tossed her head. Then to Hope, she added icily, "You've been warned. Stay away from him. And keep your illegitimately conceived son away from him, too!"

Pivoting on her heel, Rosemary slammed out of the office. Chase turned to Hope impatiently. "You want to tell me what that was all about?"

Hope suddenly felt tired. "She disapproves of our friendship. And under the circumstances, Chase, maybe she's right. People *will* talk if they see us together. They'll make all sorts of remarks about the fact that I was married to your father."

His jaw took on a stubborn tilt. Looking handsome and indomitable in his suit and tie, he folded his arms across his chest. "That's no reason to do or not do anything."

If it were just herself, Hope wouldn't care, either, but she wasn't like Chase, footloose and fancy-free. "I have Joey to consider," she said stubbornly. "I don't want Joey hurt."

"Neither do I."

Hope sighed. "Your mother would hurt him, Chase."

To her relief, he didn't argue that point with her, but he did seem to think the problem was something that could be managed. "I'll handle Rosemary," he said firmly. He turned to go, as if it were all just that simple, when sadly, Hope knew it was not.

"Chase—" She wished she had his courage. She wished she could pour out her heart to him, regardless of the consequences, regardless of how her confession might affect their future relationship. But she couldn't. She wasn't that brave. Her throat dry, Hope worked to mask her growing feelings for him and continued nervously, "Maybe your mother is right. Maybe we are getting too close."

No, Chase thought, the problem was they weren't close enough. And considering the way Hope kept putting up walls between them, they probably never would be.

NOT SURPRISINGLY, Chase kept his distance from Hope the next few days. He was there to help with the cocktail party and the transition of the store. He spent time with Joey. He attended another fund-raiser thrown by his mother to underwrite his research. And he helped out at the store in countless ways, his most valuable contribution being the fact that he kept Rosemary so busy and so far away from Hope that the two women didn't have a chance to get into another fight.

Hope should have been relieved he had done as she asked and given them both time to reconsider the wisdom of their actions. She wasn't. By the time their preopening party began the following Sunday evening, she missed him so much she ached. As she stepped to the front doors of the store, where their fabulously dressed guests were emerging from black limousines, all she wanted was the chance to see and speak to Chase alone again, even if it was only for a minute.

"So glad you could be with us this evening, Governor," Hope said, greeting the distinguished politician and his wife at the door. Born wealthy, and considered two of the prime movers in the state, both politically and socially, their support was considered critical.

He looked around, clearly impressed. "This is quite a party."

Yes, Hope thought with satisfaction, it was, through no small effort of her entire staff. Waiters circulated with sterling-silver trays of finger sandwiches, Godiva chocolates, and champagne. Musicians played on nearly every floor. The formally attired crowd was busy inspecting the new layout of the store. But Chase, bless him, was nowhere in sight.

Board of Directors member, Cassandra Hayes, joined Hope and the governor and his wife.

"We're very hopeful about the changes," Hope continued, wishing Chase would appear so she could at least get a glimpse of him.

"Yes, well..." the governor's wife, never one to mince words, said, "The new merchandise is lovely, Hope, but it's rather pedestrian, don't you think?"

No, Hope didn't think so. Trying hard not to take offense, she informed them brightly, "Our couture lines are all on the third floor now."

The governor's wife lifted a penciled-in brow. "Won't that be a little crowded?"

"Why don't you go up and see for yourself," Hope suggested.

Cassandra frowned after the couple had left. "The consensus seems to be you've dedicated too much of the store's floor space to ready-to-wear."

Calmly Hope reminded her, "We expected this sort of reaction from all our old base customers. What happens when we open tomorrow at ten to the general public is my main concern."

"The ads in today's papers were well placed, eye-catching," Cassandra murmured approvingly before her brow furrowed worriedly once again. "We'll just have to see what happens tomorrow."

In other words, Hope thought, if the sale's a disaster I will probably be run out of town on a rail.

Cassandra walked away. Rosemary appeared at Hope's side, her black silk gown as outrageously sexy as Hope's was demure. "I told you this was a mistake," she hissed. "Tomorrow is going to be a disaster."

Hope smoothed the pleated skirt of her long-sleeved rose silk gown and smiled out at the crowd. "Let's not continue with the doom and gloom speech, okay?" she said beneath her breath, her patience exhausted. "I've heard it before."

"And obviously paid no attention."

Not wanting a public scene, Hope walked briskly to the elevator, a smiling Rosemary snipping at her heels. The two of them stepped inside. Hope punched a button. If there was to be a scene, she wanted it on the executive floor.

"You just don't want to face reality. First you ruin my marriage—" Rosemary continued as the elevator sped upward and lurched to a halt "—and now Barrister's, too."

Hope had taken a lot from Rosemary the past few weeks. But this was the last straw. Her temper snapped as the doors slid open and they stepped out onto the floor.

"First of all, Rosemary, let's get this straight. I did not ruin your marriage."

"Like hell you didn't."

Hope continued flatly, "The two of you were never happy. The only reason your marriage lasted as long as it did was because of Chase. Once he was at college, Edmond felt there was no reason to prolong the agony and that's why he wanted out."

The color drained from Rosemary's face. Before she could get out a denial, Chase stepped between them. Hope had only to glance at his face to know he had heard everything.

"She's lying," Rosemary accused, point-blank.

"Hope?" Chase asked, impatiently. "What's going on?"

Not about to subject herself to more of Rosemary's insults, or Chase's questions, Hope advised crisply, "Ask your mother."

If Rosemary hadn't been there, Chase would've gone after Hope. As it was, he figured he was better off standing watch over his mother. He knew her penchant for dramatic emotional scenes. Like Hope, he didn't want any there tonight. "Mom?"

"I don't know what she's talking about." Both hands smoothed the ends of her hair; Rosemary stepped back into the elevator.

Chase followed her, prompted by the guilty, distressed look on his mother's face. "What did Hope mean by saying that the only reason you stayed together was because of me?" He kept a hand on the track, preventing the elevator door from closing. He had no intention of descending until they had this settled once and for all.

She looked at him, begging him to be on her side in this latest altercation. "It's true that Edmond and I were fighting a lot before we split up but it was nothing that couldn't have been resolved, given time, and she knows that. If anyone's to blame here, it's Hope." Rosemary continued, a little desperately, "She's the one who pursued Edmond, who convinced him they could have a life together. If she hadn't come along, you and I both know your father and I would have remained married."

Chase studied his mother, aware she was trying a little too hard to get him on her side.

"I've got to go back downstairs and circulate, darling, and so should you."

Before he could stop her, she dashed off and slipped inside the elevator across the hall. The doors shut. The elevator started down.

Chase started after her, feeling frustrated and abandoned. His parents' divorce had never made sense to him, coming out of the blue the way it had. With Hope in the picture, marrying his father so soon afterward, he had never thought to question whose fault it was. He had known it was his father's fault. It had to be.

But now, mulling over Hope's temper-inspired remarks and his mother's shocked, guilty reaction, he had to wonder. Maybe Hope was right. Maybe he had been living with much less than the full story all these years. Maybe it was time he discovered the truth for himself.

HOURS LATER, Chase sat in the store basement, surrounded by Edmond's personal papers and files. He had been right; his father hadn't thrown away anything. It was all right here in front of Chase. There were logs of every business trip his father had taken, notes from clients and colleagues, sales projections, scribbled notes of Edmond's hopes for the future, and notes about a store they'd funded in Oregon in 1963 that had failed. There were calendars, schedules, and expense records.

Chase had to admit that some of the evidence was damning. Prior to the divorce, Edmond had enjoyed a series of lunches for two that were recorded on the credit card he kept for personal use. There was no name on any of the calendars, only the name of the restaurant where he would be lunching.

If it had been a business lunch, Edmond would have recorded it. If it had been an innocent personal lunch with a male acquaintance, Chase felt sure that would have been recorded, too. But it hadn't been.

Chase walked back to the cabinet and pulled out another stack of files from the year Edmond had divorced Rosemary. More bits of paper fell out. Edmond had been a meticulous note keeper, he just hadn't known how to file, and for fear something important would be accidentally thrown away, he hadn't let his secretary touch anything private. Probably everyone had forgotten the notes were here. Even Hope.

Chase stopped when a lavender piece of stationery fell out from between two hotel receipts. The handwriting was bold and perfect. He knew, even before he started reading, to whom it belonged.

Thank you for last weekend. I don't know what I would have done without you. And not just then, but the whole last two months. You are everything to me, and I will never forget you, no matter what happens in the future.

You know you can count on me, too.

Always,
H

Chase stared at the passionately penned words, feeling sick inside.

Hope had said again and again that she hadn't broken up his parents' marriage. Looking at this, it was hard to believe.

Tossing the letter aside, he glanced at the hotel receipts. He frowned, reading the addresses. Cleveland! What the hell had his father been doing in Cleveland? They didn't have any stores there. And what was this? A bill from the Cleveland Clinic, made out in his father's name? Quickly he sorted through the papers. To his frustration, there was nothing else. Then he found a receipt for a two and a half week stay the winter before his parents' divorce. The clinic had charged his father's insurance company twenty-three thousand dollars.

Obviously, Chase thought, his father'd had surgery.

But what kind? And why hadn't he told Chase anything about it? Had either of his parents been honest with him ever?

Chapter Fourteen

"Any word from Chase?" Steve Supack asked Hope late Monday evening.

"No," Hope said. She was worried and very physically exhausted. The store had closed two hours ago, but she had yet to clear her desk enough to even think about going home.

"I thought Chase was going to be here for the sale," Leigh Olney said. She made herself comfortable in the chair opposite Hope's desk.

"I thought so, too," Hope admitted. Especially since Chase knew their All New Barrister's sale could make or break not only the store, but her future as store president as well. But she hadn't seen Chase since last night. She'd left him with his mother. And she hadn't seen him since.

"Anyone ask Rosemary where he is?" Steve asked.

"I don't think she knows, either," Leigh put in. "She asked me if I had seen or heard from him three separate times today."

Steve frowned. "I thought he was more into Barrister's than that, although maybe, considering the way the first day of the sale went, it's good he's not breathing down our necks with the devoted regularity of his mother. Did you see the totals?"

Hope nodded grimly. "Yes. We didn't get anywhere near the figure we were aiming for."

"But it has been the best day we've done so far this year," Leigh pointed out optimistically.

"I don't think that's going to be enough for the Board of Directors," Hope said. Or for Rosemary.

"Well, cheer up," Leigh said. "We've still got three days of the sale left and with the word of mouth of customers who were here today, who knows?"

"She's got a point," Steve said, loosening his tie. "Credit card applications were up forty percent today."

That, Hope hadn't known. It was a fact she could use to her benefit when she faced the Board again. "That is encouraging."

THE GUEST HOUSE lights were on when she pulled in the driveway. If Chase had wanted to see me, he would have been at the store today, she told herself firmly. But the effort to warn herself away from potential hurt failed. She needed to see Chase as much as she wanted to talk to him. There would be no resting until she did.

Not bothering to go to the main house first, Hope walked down to the guest house. Chase opened the door before she even had a chance to knock. In jeans and soft cotton crewneck sweater, he looked as unhappy as she felt. Suddenly, she didn't know where to begin. She only knew she was hurt. He had avoided her so deliberately, not just last night, but today as well. Drawing in a deep breath, she said, "We missed you at the store today."

Shrugging, he sauntered back into his living room, leaving her to shut the door behind her and follow at will. "I had some thinking to do."

Although she had been terribly worried when she had started for the guest house, his dismissing tone and unlaudable attitude sparked the beginnings of her temper. It had been a long two days. "We were counting on you to help out last night," she said. "People know you're in town again and were looking for you. It was awkward, covering for you."

Chase spun toward her, and was surprised at how fragile he looked. Despite his anger, he wanted to reach out to her. And that surprised him, although it shouldn't have. His feelings for her had always been mixed. He'd hated her secrecy, yet yearned to know more. He'd detested her overwhelming need for financial security, yet understood it, given her background. He'd admired her loyalty to his father even while he had jealously wished they had never married, never mind so happily, so the way would have been clear for him.

He had to face it. There had been no other woman who had ever brought him such conflicting emotions, or such deep yearning need, for she made him acutely aware of all that was missing from his life and hers. She made him want to do something about that need. Something that would change them both forever. Something they'd both regret.

Fighting that need, Chase let his surly glance take in the silkiness of her fair skin above the V-neck of her silk blouse and blazer and the trim curves of her hips beneath the slim lines of her skirt. She was one hell of a woman, his Hope. Looking at her, he could understand very well why his father had wanted her. But feeling an urge, no matter how powerful, didn't make it right, he told himself firmly. Slowly he released a long breath and let his glance return to her face. Clearly she still expected an apology. "Sorry," he drawled with a careless shrug meant to infuriate. "It couldn't be helped."

She tried hard to keep the edginess out of her low voice. Something had happened, something bad, for him to be this upset. "What's going on, Chase?"

He case her an ironic look. "Suppose you tell me," he said in a surprisingly silky voice. "You're the expert on lying and hiding and covering up."

At the casually thrown insult, her heart seemed to stop.

"I went through my father's papers last night." The accusing look on Chase's face put her every nerve and her every sense of self-preservation on full alert. He reached into

his shirt pocket and pulled out a piece of lavender stationery. "Recognize this?"

Yes, Hope did. It was the first, and only, letter she had
ever sent to Edmond. It had been written straight from the
heart and meant for Edmond's eyes alone. Realizing Chase
had made her words into something sordid instead of inter-
preting them in the genuinely platonic way they were meant,
she snatched the single piece of lavender stationery from
him. Embarrassed color flooded her cheeks. "This was private."

Chase laughed softly, and then snatched the letter back.
"I'll bet it *was* private." He was damned if he could remember when a woman had ever made him so furious or
light-headed or driven out of control.

He came so close to her she could smell the faint tang of
after-shave mixed with the headier male scent of his skin.
His gaze insolently scanned her face in a way that he knew
annoyed her. After what he had learned about her, she deserved to be looked at in that way. Whether she was willing
to admit it to herself or not, he told himself sternly, she had
sold herself to the highest bidder. "What else did the two of
you have to hide, Hope?" he prodded. His voice was un-
characteristically cool. "Want to tell me?"

She swallowed. He wasn't in the mood to listen to anything she said. Panic edged her voice, even as she sought to
control it. "I can see this isn't the time for us to talk." She
shoved her shaking hands into the pockets of her blazer.
"I'll come back another time."

He moved in front of the door, and found he couldn't be
logical or objective. His look was lazy, predatory and determined. He countered, "Wrong again, Hope. I think it's
the perfect time."

She held her body tense. "You're upset."

"You're damn right about that and with good reason."
He looked deep into Hope's eyes, the more pragmatic side
of him needed and wanted to hear her side of things, even
if he didn't believe her or agree with her. Why had she gone

after a man who was old enough to be her father? Chase had to know if she knew about his father's trip to the Cleveland Clinic. "Did you know about his illness?" he bit out tersely, hoping she didn't.

Hope's eyes widened with shock. "What are you talking about?" she asked cautiously.

Chase's gut told him she knew damn well exactly what he was talking about. "His visit to the Cleveland Clinic," Chase enunciated clearly, with what little patience he had left. "I found the bills, Hope. I know he had some sort of hospital stay, but I don't know for what. You were close to him during that time. Do you know what all that was about?"

A shadow passed over Hope's face, and again Chase had the sharp sensation of being shut out, of being lied to.

"No," she said finally, the lie slicing at her with brutal force.

Chase stared at her in mute frustration. She was hiding something again. Who was she protecting? Edmond? What could be so terrible that they wouldn't want him to know? Had Hope come into Edmond's life at a terribly vulnerable time, when his father wasn't healthy enough to make a sound judgment about his marriage or an extramarital affair? Was that what she didn't want him to know? Or was it something worse?

Again, she moved toward the door, her dignity intact. And again, he moved as if to stop her. "Chase, please, I don't want to talk about this anymore," she whispered. The strain of her long day showed on her face. She held up both hands in silent plea. "It's not going to help anything. You've got to stop asking me for the truth when you know I've already told you all that I can."

Chase knew she was vulnerable now. He was close to tearing down the walls she had built up around her heart, but he felt no satisfaction, only a growing sense of frustration and hurt, at having been shut out by her. "I won't stop, Hope," he whispered, slowly closing the distance between

them. "Just like I won't give you any more time to think up
any more lies. This time—" he touched her shoulders before she could step past him "—you're going to tell me the
truth."

Her heart was a thundering roar in her ears. "I've told
you the truth!"

"You told me you loved him," Chase countered harshly,
keeping his hold firm so she couldn't move away. "You
didn't tell me he was *everything* to you."

"He *was* everything to me, then!" Hope countered hotly.
She splayed both her palms against Chase's chest. "But even
so, I—" Hope stopped and bit her lip, hard. Pushing away
from him, she flushed scarlet and wouldn't meet his eyes.

Chase saw the change in her face. With mounting disappointment he knew, in that instant, she'd stopped being
open and honest with him. And he was determined to get
her back into a truth-telling frame of mind, even if he had
to goad her into it unmercifully. "Dammit, Hope," he bit
out, tossing the note aside, "you told me you didn't break
up my parents'—"

"I didn't!"

"Then what the hell do you call this?" He grabbed the
note and waved it at her furiously. "If it's not interference,
what is?" When she remained stubbornly silent, his fury
mounted. "Are you going to deny the passion you felt for
him, too?"

She clamped her arms, one over the other. "I told you."
She underscored each word with heavy emphasis. "Our relationship wasn't like that."

His face filled with disbelief. Hope's face was only inches
from his own. "Oh, really? And what constitutes passion in
your view, Hope? Does a touch? A kiss?" He pulled her to
him, gave her a long, level look, then watched as she stood
there like an ice goddess. Suddenly, she seemed too good,
too pure, for anything as base as greed. He desperately
wanted answers but he also wanted her—badly. Knowing
how much he wanted her, only added fuel to the flame. He

spected she wanted him, too. And he was determined to
t her in touch with her feelings and his if it was the only
ing he ever managed. "Was it okay to make love with him
s long as you didn't feel anything in return?"

Hope struggled against him. "You have no right—" she
hispered.

But Chase knew, feeling as he did about her, he had every
ght. "What about this?" He slanted his lips over hers. All
e yearning need he had held back was surging to the sur-
ce.

Needing something solid to hang on to, she reached out
o him. She found herself slipping ever deeper into the
byss, being seduced by the promise of a deep, lingering
iss, of the safety and warmth and pleasure of his arms.

"Is this passionate enough for you, Hope?" His mouth
ouched hers, ever so lightly, barely brushing it, and his
reath mingled with hers. "Or this?" he whispered, feeling
er tremble as he parted her lips with his own. She shud-
ered, her legs buckling as her body went fluid against the
ngth of his. He pushed her up against the wall, sliding his
ongue between her lips, drinking deep as his fingers
kimmed along her cheekbones. "Or this?"

Hope moaned. Suddenly it was all too much. Too much
eeling, too much passion, and too much sensation. She
elted against him in total surrender and wreathed her arms
round his neck. That was all the permission, all the en-
ouragement, he needed.

He kissed her as though he meant to go on kissing her
orever. His lips made her feel incredibly alive, wanted and
herished. With a moan of pleasure, she shifted against him
nd surrendered a little more. Then a little more, until they
vere both breathless. Pulses pounding, they broke apart and
tared at each other, stunned and a little in awe.

She knew if he kissed her again, her reason would leave
er and there would be no escape. Need stirred inside her,
ot quite under control. Without a thought to conse-
uences, she wrapped her arms around him.

This was how he had wanted her from the moment he'
been back, Chase thought. He felt weak with pleasure
drugged with desire, and open to anything. And she wa
open to him. Pulling her closer, he trailed his lips over he
jaw to her throat, tasting the softness and flavor of her skin

Hope felt the shudder start deep inside her. It was fol
lowed swiftly by a fire that refused to be quenched. Sun
shine swept into her soul. She felt free and recklessly wild
as she had never been in her youth. "Chase," she whis
pered softly, molding her lips to his. "Oh, Chase."

She felt his fingers tangle in her hair and closed her eyes
giving herself up to the raw jumble of feelings, to the over
powering need to be with him, to be loved. She yearned to
discover the generosity she'd never known and always beer
denied. She felt the desire to give of herself, to give to Chase
as never before.

Chase had never meant to go this far, but now that she
was in his arms, responding, he couldn't seem to stop him
self any more than she could. "I want you," he whispered
the words seeming to burn his throat. "God help me, I wan
you."

"I want you, too." For her, the past no longer mattered
It was finally over and done with. She was ready to move on
with her life.

Chase leaned his forehead against hers and drew a long
breath. In a voice racked with guilt, he closed his eyes and
whispered in a low, tortured voice, "But we can't."

What they couldn't keep doing, Hope thought, was de
nying the powerful wellspring of feelings within them. She
held tight, refusing to let him go, refusing to step back into
the past.

"Chase, my marriage to your father is over."

She knew Chase was leaving again, but it no longer
seemed to matter. If she let this moment go, she would re
gret it forever. Some chances, like the chance to be with
Chase, were meant to be taken.

He wanted to be practical, but the ache inside him was spreading, demanding assuagement, telling him it was now or never and he damn straight wanted it to be now. He inhaled deeply, searched her eyes. "You're sure?" It was important that there be no regrets later. No reprisals. For either of them.

She knew she could offer him the kind of concrete answers he needed about her relationship with Edmond. But she also knew, if she did that, she would be opening up a whole other Pandora's box. "I'm very sure. But we can't think about the past, Chase," she whispered softly, reassuring him with her gaze and the gentle touch of her hands. "We just have to look to the future. It's the only way. Help me move on."

Chase took her hand. She clasped it firmly. And then they were kissing again, moving slowly, inevitably toward his bed in the adjoining room.

His heart pounding, he slowly lowered his mouth to hers once again. He wanted this to be good for her, as much as he wanted it for himself. And yet he knew all too well what was at stake here. If he rushed her, she might never know just how wonderful their love could be. She might never give him a second chance.

She had plenty of time to change her mind as he invited her into his bed, but like a moth drawn to the flame, found herself unable to. And once she'd experienced the first precious feel of his hard body draped against the length of hers, she knew she would never want to change her mind. She combed her fingers through the feathery softness of his hair. As she kissed him, she made a soft unconscious sound and arched closer to him, wanting to feel the muscular planes of his chest against the softness of her breasts. He groaned at the innocent expression of her desire, slid his hands beneath her waist and draped a leg across hers. He drew her even nearer.

The kiss deepened until Hope could no longer tell where her mouth ended and his began. She only knew no matter

what happened in the future, no matter what separate path
they followed, she would always have the memory of thi
night.

Chase had never known he could be so tender, but his lov
for Hope gave him patience and skill. ''You'll have to tell m
what you like,'' he whispered as he slowly unfastened th
buttons on her blouse, undid the front clasp of her bra an
slipped his hand inside.

She gasped as he touched the warm supple curves of he
breasts. ''You like that,'' he whispered softly.

Eyes wide with pleasure and wonder, she nodded. In al
her adult years, she had never imagined lovemaking coul
be like this, so wonderful and filled with rapture.

Slowly Chase's hands slipped lower still, letting her ge
used to the feel of them on her body. With the same pa
tience, they undressed each other and slid beneath th
sheets. Fearing what would happen next, she tensed. An
again he helped her through it. This time, when she over
came her fear, there was only wonder and fulfillment wait
ing for her and for him.

Afterward, he held her tightly, clasped against him. Sh
clung to him tenaciously. A tiny tear slipped down he
cheek. ''If you only knew what you made me feel,'' sh
whispered. As long as she lived she would never forget hi
tenderness.

''Good, I hope,'' he whispered gently.

''Good,'' she affirmed, her voice quavering. ''An
whole.'' I'm a complete woman, at last, she thought. An
if the two of us just stayed together we could have every
thing.

''I'm so glad.'' He held her close.

And she clung to him, wanting never to let go again.

THE NIGHT soothed Chase's soul, but not completely. Wit
the morning, his memories of the past returned. He still fe
very confused and hurt about his father's behavior. H
didn't understand what his father could have been doing i

Cleveland, or why Hope would pretend to know nothing about it when he could tell by the look on her face that she did.

Clearly, Hope thought she was protecting his father; why she felt that still necessary, was less clear. Especially when it hadn't stopped her from making love to him. More determined than ever to find answers, he stuck with his earlier plans to visit the clinic personally. He told Hope nothing about his plans.

Catching the first plane out the following morning, he arrived in Cleveland around noon. Needing answers, he went straight to the chief of staff at the clinic where his father had been treated. "I understand your concern, Dr. Barrister," the accomplished physician said, "but those records are privileged information."

Aware he was operating on far too little sleep and too much coffee, Chase fought to control his exasperation. "My father is dead."

"Even so—"

"I'm his son," Chase continued emotionally, blinking back sudden tears. "If my father was ill, I have a right to know."

Silence fell as the chief of staff studied him. "I'll see what I can do," he said finally.

He returned long minutes later, his expression grim and foreboding. "Don't ever let it be said I gave these to you," he warned. "But if it were my father, I'd want to know, too."

IT WAS A LONG FLIGHT back to Houston. Chase was in shock. He got out the records again. His father had been diagnosed with prostate cancer and had never told him. According to the medical records, he'd had surgery to remove a tumor six months before he married Hope. That surgery had left him irreversibly impotent. Whatever Hope's marriage to his father had been based on, it hadn't been passion. There was no illicit affair. Nor could Edmond have fathered Joey. Yet he had pretended Joey was his son. And so had Hope.

Why? Chase wondered. He felt confused, hurt and filled with a shattering sense of betrayal. Why all the lies? Why hadn't his father trusted him enough to tell him the truth about his illness, if not when he was twenty-one, then later when he was an M.D.? Had his mother known about the battle with cancer and Edmond's resulting impotence?

Worst of all, why hadn't Hope told him last night? She knew how torn up he had been about making love to her. She could have helped him, by telling him the truth about the nature of her relationship with Edmond. She could have spared him all the anguish. But she hadn't. And for that, he wasn't sure he would ever be able to forgive her.

"You KNEW, didn't you?" Chase surmised softly later that same evening as he faced Hope in the guest house. "You knew my father had been sick when you married him."

The breath left her slowly. She had expected to see Chase again, alone. She hadn't expected this. "Yes," she said cautiously, her insides quaking, "I did." How much did Chase know?

"And you also knew he couldn't possibly have fathered your child."

Hope reached out to steady herself, clasping the back of a chair. "Yes," she said softly, looking both terrified and defensive, "I did."

Chase studied her. It was so easy to see why Edmond would have wanted to protect her; in some convoluted way, despite everything, there was a very big part of Chase that still did, too. It wasn't so easy to see how the two of them had ever gotten together in the first place. And Hope, with her closed mouth, wasn't doing a damn thing to help him understand. In fact, she had worked damn hard to keep him in the dark. "The two of you weren't having a torrid affair."

"No," Hope said, in a low voice filled with shame. "We weren't." She had been a fool to think, even for one moment, that Chase could ever understand what she and Edmond had shared. She turned away from him. Although her fingers tensed, her voice was calm. "I told you that from the beginning."

"But you didn't tell me my father was impotent!"

She took an uncertain step toward him, then watched as he moved away. She swallowed hard, trying hard not to let the thick, vibrant silence in the room get to her. "I had promised him I never would."

Chase moved around the guest house restlessly, finally taking a position at the kitchenette counter several feet away from her. He leaned against it, looking anxious and distant. And she knew then that she would either prove her worth to him then, in that minute, in that instant, or lose him forever.

"I don't get it, then." His derisive voice cut like a blade. "If the two of you weren't having an affair, why all the intimate lunches?" he prodded, looking at her in controlled frustration. "Why the clandestine trip to Atlanta? What were you up to?"

He was acting as if she had conned his father, and that knowledge hurt.

"Hope, for pity's sake, let down your guard. Talk to me. Don't you see, I have to know what kind of person you are. I can't go on this way any longer, feeling like I'm operating in the dark about you."

She turned back to him. Their eyes met, hers looking as distant and disillusioned as he felt. Her chin lifted defiantly but her voice carried a thread of hurt. "I thought you already knew what kind of person I was."

He thought about everything she had done, not everything he had thought she was, and forced himself to remain unmoved. He crossed his arms over his chest. "So did I. But I didn't count on everything I found out today, on all the lies." What hurt worse than that, were the evasions she was still enacting. He thought he saw the first hint of tears glimmering in her blue eyes.

She shut her eyes. Her voice trembled as it rose. "Edmond made me promise not to tell."

That much Chase could believe. He'd been a very private, very proud man. But that didn't explain his excluding his son from what must have been the most traumatic time of his life. "Why didn't he want me to know about his illness?"

"He was embarrassed, frightened."

"But *you* knew, from the beginning, what his situation was?" Chase felt a stab of jealousy.

"Not exactly, no."

"Then when?" he demanded roughly.

"I don't know," she responded, her tone defensive. Her pulse jumped, but she stood firm. "It was some time after Atlanta. I had decided to keep my baby and he started talking about marrying me, to give the child a name."

Wanting to rock her out of her implacable calm, Chase demanded tersely, "Why not Joey's father?"

The shades on her feelings went down, shutting him out again. "That wasn't possible," Hope said coolly, her jaw beginning to take on a forbidding, angry tilt.

Chase saw the cold, calculated way she hid from him. That, more than anything she had done, told him she wasn't the one for him. And yet even as he realized that, he wondered if he would ever find the strength to stay away from her. In an effort to clamp his runaway emotions down, he asked, "Was Joey's father married, too?"

She gave him a sharp look that made his heart race. Her brow arched. "I don't have to stay and listen to this."

Turning, he gave her a grim smile and followed her to the door. "No, you can walk away, like you always do. You can hide—"

She whirled to face him, her regal calm vanishing. "My father could have helped you," Chase continued. "He didn't have to marry you. He didn't have to break up his marriage to do it.''

Hope sighed her exasperation, then drew another long, shaky breath. "Initially he didn't intend to," she confided quietly. "In the beginning, we were just friends. He was a father figure, guidance counselor, business mentor and platonic friend all wrapped into one. He found out I was in trouble. He knew marriage to the father was impossible, and he wanted to help me. To that end, he was willing to do everything and anything he could.''

Chase had to admit that sounded like his father. "He could have been your friend without marrying you," he pointed out.

Renewed color flooded into Hope's beautiful face. "Don't you think I know that?" she said softly, begging him to understand. Her voice trembled as it dropped a confiding notch. "But then he fell in love with me." She swallowed hard, sensing how Chase would feel about what she was going to say next. "And as I grew to know him, I began to love him, too, Chase." She turned away from his penetrating gaze, desperate to explain. "Just not the way a woman usually loves a husband. It was kind of a platonic mix." She took a deep breath, that was part sob. "I counted on him. We were partners. And eventually we were tied together through Joey. We were parents to the same child." And that bond had gone very deep, so deep she had been crushed when Edmond had died.

"And he agreed to accept that?" Chase asked incredulously.

The disbelief in his voice cut straight to her heart. "No, not initially," Hope said quietly. She lifted her eyes to his, not caring if he saw the wet sheen in them. "When Edmond married me, he wasn't sure how much time he had left, or even if the treatments were going to work, but he wanted to spend whatever time he did have left happily. That's why he left your mother." Hope paused and ran a shaky hand through her hair. "He also knew we got along.

He wanted to share in the raising of a child again.'' Seeing the skeptical light in Chase's eyes, she finished softly, persuasively, ''We weren't sure it was going to last. We didn't think that far ahead, Chase. We just took it day by day, and it turned into something permanent and enduring.''

Her logic had gotten through to him. Chase was quiet, contemplative. ''Did my mother know about Dad's illness?'' he asked finally, in the same troubled voice with which he had started the conversation.

Hope sighed, wishing there were a less hurtful way to explain it all to Chase. ''Edmond didn't want either of you to know,'' she confided in a thick voice. She met Chase's eyes with as much candor as she could muster. ''I tried to get him to tell you, but he wouldn't.'' She shook her head, remembering. ''He said you had enough on your mind, with just growing up and going to school. He didn't want you worrying about his health, too.'' Hope lifted her shoulders. ''And as it turned out, when the treatments began to work and he went into remission, it wasn't necessary. As for your mother, he didn't want the issue of his illness clouding his divorce. That's why he didn't tell her. And again, I had nothing to say about it. Those were his decisions.'' Just like the decision to keep her baby had been hers, she thought.

Chase was quiet, soaking it all in. Finally he turned to her, his gaze accusing. ''Why didn't you tell me any of this when I first came here?''

''Because I promised your dad,'' Hope said, again.

''Meaning what?'' Chase asked softly, the depth of his anger and resentment even more apparent. ''That your first loyalty was to him, even after we started to become involved? Were you more concerned about promises in the past than the anguish I might be feeling now? Dammit, Hope, you know how I suffered. I fought not to make love to you. How could you have let me suffer like that, Hope? How could you *not* have told me, especially after we made love, when you knew how guilty I felt?'' He'd thought them so close then, so connected. Obviously they were not, not if she'd been able to keep something that crucial and that potentially healing, from him.

Because I'm still protecting Joey, she thought. And because I'm still protecting myself from the pain of your lack of faith in me. Surely if Chase loved her, if he cared about her at all, he'd be able to accept her, without question.

Chase shook his head. "I can't deal with people who are dishonest, Hope. I can't deal with the fact that you didn't trust me enough to level with me, if not in the beginning, at least, when we made love."

Hope stared at him, angry now, too. His thinking the worst of her was all too reminiscent of her past. She had promised herself when she left home under a cloud of disgrace that she would never get involved with anyone who didn't have faith in her, who didn't believe in the goodness inside her. God knew she had never expected it from her parents. They had never given her any reason to think their love for her was unconditional. But she *had* expected it from Chase!

"Do you really think I wanted to hurt you?" she said emotionally. She wanted to tell him everything about Joey's father, but she knew the price of revealing too much. She knew what happened when people who said they loved you turned around and said they didn't believe you. She certainly wasn't going to let Joey be hurt by making his parentage known to anyone but herself. It was enough that she had given herself completely to Chase, made love to him with all her heart and soul, and then been cruelly forsaken.

They faced each other. Chase remained silent, aloof.

But then, she surmised grimly, he didn't have to say anything. Hope saw the guilty verdict on his face. She knew he had tried and convicted her as surely as her parents had. Her heart full of the numbing bitterness that had plagued her for years, she turned and left the guest house without another word. He didn't come after her. She didn't look back.

"YOU LOOK LIKE HELL, darling," Rosemary said the following morning.

Chase felt like hell. He'd just had two sleepless nights and was probably facing another. "May I come in?" he said tersely.

"Of course." Rosemary ushered him into her hotel room. "Would you like me to order you some breakfast? I've already had my coffee but—"

"Got any left?" Locating the carafe, he jiggled it and found it half-full.

"Yes, but there are no cups..." Her voice trailed off. She shuddered in distaste, watching him tear the paper wrapper off a water tumbler and pour coffee into it. "Chase, honestly. I could have called and got you a proper cup and saucer."

"This is fine," he said gruffly, too upset to care about using the proper china for his morning jolt of caffeine.

His mother studied him. "You're still angry with me?"

Chase shrugged, feeling peculiarly close to tears. And he never cried. Never. The one exception being when his father died. "Confused is more like it," he admitted. He needed the kind of heartfelt comfort he wasn't sure she could give. Not knowing where to start, he began by telling his mother about his father's illness. He discovered Hope had been right; Rosemary hadn't known about Edmond's cancer or his surgery.

"I don't understand," she said in anguish when Chase had finished speaking. "Why wouldn't he have told me?"

Maybe, Chase thought sadly, Edmond had known how selfish his wife was and had figured Rosemary was the last person he would want by his side at such a time. Chase took another draught of the hot, strong coffee, letting it beat a scalding path to his stomach. "I don't know, Mom."

"Was I that bad a wife to him? That he felt he couldn't turn to me in what must have been the worst time of his life?"

Chase swallowed hard. He had no answer for that.

"But Hope was there for him," Rosemary ascertained in a shocked whisper.

Chase nodded. "In a way neither of us could be, apparently."

Rosemary buried her face in her hands. "It really was my fault," she murmured.

And in that second, Chase knew what Hope had asserted all along was true. She really hadn't broken up his parents' marriage. Unfortunately she had put her loyalty to Edmond above her loyalty to him and that he couldn't dismiss nearly as easily. If she didn't trust him enough to tell him the truth, what kind of relationship could they ever have?

HOPE WAS HALFWAY DOWN the driveway, toward the morning paper when she saw Russell Morris. He was waiting in a car across the street. "Nice morning, isn't it?" he called. He got out and strolled straight toward her.

Her heart pounding, Hope kept her pace steady. She bent down to pick up the paper. Lately, only Joey had kept her on an even keel. The argument with Chase had left her drained and empty inside. She didn't need a confrontation with Russell on top of that, but it looked as if she was going to get one anyway. When she straightened again, he was right in front of her. "What do you want?" She gave him an ice-cold look.

"Is that any way to greet an old boyfriend?"

Her mouth filled with a coppery taste. Ignoring his provocative remark, she said, "I'm very busy."

"I know," he returned confidently. "I saw the business Barrister's has been doing the past few days."

Hope felt her spine stiffen. "We've had a lot of traffic."

"And a lot of sales."

Not as many as Hope would've liked. "Is there a point to this?" she asked impatiently.

"Why don't you invite me in for breakfast and we'll talk about it?"

"No."

He quirked a brow. "Don't you want your son to se me?"

At the mention of Joey, Hope's knees went weak.

"Now why could that be, I wonder?" Russell continue smoothly. "It wouldn't have anything to do with his no having a father, would it?"

"I don't—"

"Cut the crap, Hope," Russell said roughly. "I know when he was born. I know when we were together and think I might just have a pretty interesting lawsuit to file Custody cases always make such fascinating reading, don they? Especially ones that involve lots of money. Of course if you could see your way clear to give me another loan o another hundred and fifty thou or so then maybe I wouldn' be so determined to see a lawyer. Am I making mysel clear?"

Very, Hope thought, feeling sick.

"Morning!" Chase's cheerful voice sounded in the dis tance. He was wearing swim trunks and a calf-length terr robe; a towel was laced around his neck. He joined them. " thought I heard voices out here."

Hope stood stiffly. Bad enough Chase had discovered al the hurtful specifics surrounding her marriage to his fa ther. She didn't want him drawn into this, too.

The two men greeted one another. "Carmelita needs yo in the kitchen, Hope. Some question about the menu." Chase looked at Russell pointedly. "Sorry you can't com in."

Russell was livid, but controlled himself because o Chase. "Yes, well, I am, too. Hope, I'll be seeing yo around."

"What was that all about?" Chase asked as he fell int step beside her. "What does he want from you?"

Hope was silent.

"Talk to me, dammit. Tell me what's going on." Sh looked unsteady as hell. He waited until they rounded th corner of the house, then stopped beside the nearest tree

She leaned against it weakly, but still said nothing. She just stood there looking as though she wanted to cry.

Chase stared at her in frustration, aware his heart was beating double time. He wanted to take her into his arms and kiss her until she was damn near ready to faint, and until she was ready to confess. But that was no solution.

Hope had to want to let him into her life, all the way. She had to want to open up to him or it wouldn't work. Right now that wasn't the case. He had vague guesses as to what was going on, but nothing concrete. He could help Hope, if she'd let him. But she wouldn't. Hadn't he promised himself he wouldn't get close to people who had no intention of ever opening up to him? Wasn't he through chasing lost causes? And yet here he was again, wanting so much. He was ready to give and yet he was being rejected.

"If you ever change your mind about talking," he said, holding out absolutely no prospect she would, "you know where to find me."

'HOPE, that's the tenth message Russell Morris left for you today," Steve Supack said. "I don't think he's going to give up until he sees you."

I know he isn't, Hope thought, depressed.

"And that's not the worst of it," Leigh Olney said, adding her two cents. "Scuttlebutt is that Rosemary Barrister is trying to get her son and everyone on the Board to vote you out of the presidency. She thinks the sales figures are all the proof she needs."

"They weren't that bad," Steve said in Hope's defense.

Leigh agreed. "I'm happy with them. But you know Cassandra Hayes. She wants profit with a capital *P*, and when she doesn't get it—" Leigh made a slashing motion across her neck.

Hope smiled at her staff's antics. She knew they were trying to be helpful. Unfortunately right now she had the feeling nothing could help. Except maybe Chase.

Why hadn't she confided in him this morning when she'd had the chance? If anyone could scare off Russell Morris, it was Chase. But she had hesitated to tell him the depth of the trouble she was in. Why? It wasn't as if he could think any worse of her. Thanks to Rosemary's half-truths and accusations, he already had a very low opinion of her.

She could set him straight, of course. But he probably wouldn't believe what Russell and his family had done to her, no more than he had believed her when she had told him the truth about his mother. As for Russell, she had no more money and no more jewelry to sell.

"Hey, don't you have to get out of here?" Leigh asked. "Doesn't Joey have a game tonight?"

"Yes. He does. Thanks for reminding me." Jerked back to the pressing demands of the present, Hope forced a wan smile. "I'll see you two in the morning."

Steve saluted. "We'll keep our ears to the ground."

"Are you sure you feel up to playing tonight?" Hope asked Joey when she got home. Clad in his uniform, he was seated on his bed. Mitt on, he was pounding a ball into the center of it with forceful regularity.

"Yeah, why wouldn't I?"

"Well, the Bateman twins, for one thing."

"Oh. Well, they're always going to be around," he offered philosophically, tossing down his glove and adjusting the brim of his hat.

"Yes, but not on your team," Hope pointed out reasonably. "You don't have to go, you know. You could sit the rest of the season out or you could be put on a different team." With a coach who knows how to control his players, Hope added silently.

"Aw, Mom," Joey said, visibly affronted by the suggestion. "Don't coddle me."

Hope hesitated, wanting to do what was best for her son, but uncertain what that was. "Is that what you think I'm doing?"

"Yeah, I do. I don't mean to insult you or anything but, like Chase says, I gotta learn to be tough and stand up for myself."

Hope sighed. Chase, after all, was probably right. "He's talked to you about this?"

"Mmm-hmm. Lots," Joey responded enthusiastically. "When you're not home. He says there are always going to be bullies and that I need to learn to deal with them." Joey shrugged. "As hard as it is, I gotta do it."

Wise advice, Hope thought. If only she could apply it to herself.

"Now can we go?" Joey jumped up, anxious to get a move on. "Hurry and change, Mom. If we don't hustle, we're going to be late."

HOPE CLIMBED UP the bleachers, taking a place near a group of other mothers. As usual, she joined in the small talk, but thinking about the game ahead, her stomach was in a knot of apprehension. On the field, warming up with his team, Joey looked tense, too.

Let him handle it, Chase had said. Asthma or not, you can't fight his battles for the rest of his life. But he's so young, a part of her protested. He's also getting older every day, the more pragmatic part of her answered, and the lessons he learns now will serve him the rest of his life. She sighed. Why was the hardest part of mothering learning to let go?

The game started. Joey's team was first to bat. Because the Batemans were undoubtedly the strongest players on the team, they headed the hitting lineup. The first got a double, the second a triple. Between them, they scored the first two runs of the game. By the time Joey got to bat, the bases were loaded. His team had two outs. It was all up to him. Knowing it, the Batemans were unable to resist. "Hey Barrister," one of them yelled from the bench, "don't blow it for us, okay?"

Listening to the verbal bullying, Hope felt her temper begin to rise.

"Yeah, get us a hit," the other twin yelled. "*If* you can."

Joey turned toward the dugout and dropped his bat. Oblivious to everyone else, he stared at his teammates until they began to squirm and their coach said something in a reprimand to both boys.

Watching how well her son had handled the heckling, Hope felt a swell of pride.

Satisfied, Joey turned back to the pitcher and leveled the bat over his shoulder. The pitch came. Confident, he swung. The bat contacted the ball with a solid smack, and he was off, knocking in another run before the inning ended.

As the teams exchanged places, Hope looked up to see Chase slipping into a seat at the other side of the bleachers. Evidently he'd seen Joey get his hit, for he gave her a thumbs-up sign. She smiled back, then turned away, both glad and disturbed he didn't fight the crowd of parents to take a seat right next to her.

The game resumed. Hope was relieved to see Joey do as well as he had the first inning, but her happiness over that faded when she saw yet another person join the crowd. And this one didn't mind threading his way through the people so he could sit right next to her.

"Hello, Hope," Russell Morris said.

Hope felt her stomach twist miserably. Aware of all the people around her, within earshot, she said as calmly as she could, "Russell."

"That your son playing left field?"

Again, it took all her strength to answer calmly. "Yes."

"Nice looking kid."

A faint pounding began in Hope's temples. "If you'll excuse me, I need a drink." Not waiting for a response from Russell, she climbed down from the bleachers and made her way blindly to the concession stand. She was going to have to take her migraine medicine right now if she wanted to avoid a blinding headache.

By the time she'd ordered a cola, Russell had caught up with her. "You don't look too well," he observed smoothly.

You're making me ill, Hope thought.

"I could help you, you know."

"I don't think so." She moved away from him stiffly. She wished she could just get in her car and leave, but she knew she couldn't, not as long as Joey was still playing his game.

He paused. "Have you given any more thought to what we discussed?"

Out of her peripheral vision, Hope saw Chase standing in the distance, at the edge of the bleachers. Hands thrust into the pockets of his jeans, he was watching her. She knew all she had to do was give him the signal and he would rush in to rescue her, for the moment anyway. But she would also have to tell him everything. He wouldn't keep on operating in the dark. Nor could she blame him.

Hope turned back to Russell. Just knowing Chase was there if she needed him made her feel stronger. "I've already given you all I can," she returned calmly.

Russell shrugged, looking not the least bit dissuaded. "Custody suits are such nasty affairs, don't you think," he pointed out. "Especially when the mother hasn't ever told the father of the child's existence." He waited a moment, for his words to sink in. "Think about it, Hope," he said heavily, "then get back to me. Tomorrow, noon at Maxim's. I'll be waiting."

Hands still in his pockets, he sauntered off.

Hope took her paper cup of cola and headed straight for the ladies rest room. It was deserted. With trembling hands, she pried open the cap on her medicine bottle and downed a tablet. Glancing into the mirror above the sink, she saw her skin was ashen. A fine sheen of perspiration dusted her face. She mopped it dry with a tissue.

I never should have given Russell that first payment, she realized with sickening clarity. I knew better. Blackmailers are never satisfied with just one payment. This would go on and on until she was penniless unless she put a stop to it right now. But how? She had no doubt that Russell was every bit as cold-blooded as he said. He wouldn't hesitate to make their past a current public scandal if she didn't cooperate with him. She couldn't have cared less about herself at this point, but she didn't want Joey hurt.

Her mind awhirl, she walked back out of the rest room. Chase was standing fifteen feet away, a curious, concerned look on his face. She knew he wanted to help, but he wouldn't interfere. It was all up to her now, just like it had all been up to Joey in the first inning.

It was her choice. She had let Chase down once, by withholding the truth from him. She didn't have to do it again. Did she have the courage to tell him everything?

Chapter Fifteen

Rosemary was waiting for Chase when he returned to the guest house after the game. He heard her out impatiently. "Forget it, I'm not voting to have Hope ousted as store president."

Rosemary stared at him incredulously. Impeccably coiffed and attired in an ice-blue Chanel suit, she looked as impeious and controlled as ever. Chase couldn't help comparing her to Hope. He couldn't help wishing that Rosemary had but a fraction of Hope's warmth.

"You saw what she's done," Rosemary continued persuasively. "Sales aren't half what we needed to get the store on a firm footing again." To her, the solution was obvious.

Fortunately for Hope, Chase didn't agree. "They're not as bad as they were, either," he countered reasonably. "I vote we give her another six months, minimum."

His mother's gaze narrowed suspiciously. "What's gotten into you?" When he didn't answer right away, she continued, "Are you involved with her?"

To be involved with her, Chase thought, I'd have to be close to her, and there's no way Hope will ever let that happen. If he'd had any doubts, it had been hammered home to him during the game when he'd seen her sitting with that creep Russell Morris. Judging from the tense, ill look on Hope's face as she'd fled the bleachers, she'd been about to get another migraine. Chase had wanted to grab Russell

Morris by the collar and toss him out of the park, but he'
also known what a hopelessly pointless act of violence tha
would have been. Hope would have just let Russell Morri
get to her again when he wasn't around.

He had to face it. He couldn't help someone who didn'
want to be helped. And Hope had demonstrated more tha
once she wasn't about to confide in him or anyone else. Sh
just wasn't the sort of woman who could open up to a man
really let him into her heart and her life. He wasn't inter
ested in cursory, superficial relationships. He'd had enougl
of those growing up. No, when he became involved with
woman again it was going to be because it was the real thing
Because she loved and trusted him with all her heart an
soul. Because she felt she could tell him anything and coun
on him to understand. And though it hurt him to admit it
Hope couldn't give him that. Wouldn't give him that, h
corrected.

"Chase," Rosemary demanded impatiently, breaking int
his thoughts. "Stop woolgathering and answer me. Are yo
romantically involved with Hope?"

Resignation twisted the corners of his mouth down. H
looked his mother straight in the eye and said calmly, "No
I'm not. Not the way you mean, anyway." He amended si
lently, *I would be if I could.* "I am her friend, however."

His mother uttered a short, repudiating laugh. "You ex
pect me to believe that?"

"I don't care what you believe," Chase said shortly
Then, on impulse, he decided to go for broke and reall
speak his mind. "Frankly, Mother, it's none of your busi
ness."

Rosemary's mouth opened in a round "oh" of surprise
Her porcelain-perfect skin reddened with outrage. "I can se
I'm going to have to talk to you another time, when you'r
in a more reasonable frame of mind." She stormed out.

Hope stood in the shadows, watching Rosemary stalk t
her car. Judging from the wrathful look on his mother'
face, perhaps now wasn't the best time to approach Chase

But then what choice did she have? She knew if she didn't talk to him soon, she would lose her nerve. For Joey's sake, and her own, she couldn't afford to let that happen. She needed him. He was the only person who could help her, the only person she trusted enough to even approach.

He flung open the door on the first knock. "Look, Mom, I told you I wouldn't—Hope." He stopped, chastened. "Sorry," he amended gruffly. "I thought you were someone else."

Hope swallowed and said, "May I come in?"

He gave her a steady look, then as if recalling all that had happened between them, he shrugged indifferently and gestured her in.

Knowing she'd hurt him, she hoped with all her heart it wasn't too late. Lifting her eyes to his, she said in a trembling voice, "I need your help, Chase," and then everything came tumbling out.

He listened to the details of Russell's blackmail and her complicity as if he had known all along. And maybe he had, Hope thought. Or at least suspected.

"What does he have on you?" Chase demanded frankly at last. He was filled with helpless anger. It was so damn senseless, he raged inwardly. All she would have had to do was ask for his help and he would have given it. But she was here now. And he had to concentrate on that.

For Hope, this was the worst. She knew Chase might not believe her about what had happened that fateful night any more than anyone else had. And the thought he might not was devastating to her. Swallowing hard, she said in a trembling voice, "You remember I told you I dated Russell a couple of times?"

Chase nodded, looking every bit as grim and apprehensive as she felt.

Struggling to remain calm, she took a deep, steadying breath and plunged on. "The first date everything was as I expected it to be. We went out for a pizza and saw a late movie. He was a gentleman. But on the second, it was a

completely different story." She shuddered violently at th
memory and rubbed her hands up and down her arms, t
warm herself. "We were supposed to go to dinner." Sh
lowered her eyes briefly, feeling pathetic in her naiveté. T
her relief, Chase remained calm and empathetic. That, i
turn, enabled her to go on, to tell him things she had neve
even told his father.

"Instead Russell took me to a popular bar in Lubbock
He said we were going to wait there and meet up with som
friends of his before dinner. It soon became apparent the
weren't going to show. Meanwhile, he proceeded to get ver
drunk, very fast." She shuddered again, reliving the awfu
tension she'd felt that night. Swallowing hard, she said, "H
ordered drinks for me, tequila sunrises, and when I refuse
to drink anything, or to even take a sip, he drained th
glasses for me and ordered another round." She lifted he
eyes to his. They were dark with the pain she felt.

"I was really scared." She shook her head in abject mis
ery. "I knew I was in trouble and if I'd been smart I woul
have called my parents then and there and asked them t
come and get me. But it was a fifty-mile drive one way, an
I knew they'd be furious, that they wouldn't understand, s
I decided to drive him home, and walk back to my plac
from his house." Her face flamed as she heaved a derisiv
sigh and admitted to him that giant mistake in her judg
ment, one that had been motivated by pride more than any
thing else. "I figured that way no one would ever have t
know what a fool I'd been."

Sensing this was becoming too painful for her, Chas
covered her hands with his own. "Hope, you don't have t
go on if you don't want to," he said. Suddenly it wasn't im
portant to him that he knew every detail, just that she wa
there, just that she was willing to talk, to share.

But Hope shook her head defiantly. "No," she sai
softly, "I want to tell you. I need you to know this." Onl
if he could accept it, accept her, could they be close.

"Everything was okay until we got out of the city, but once we were on the country highway that led back to his parents' ranch, he started—well, he wouldn't leave me alone. He kept pulling at the hem of my dress, touching me." Her face burned at the helplessness she had felt. "I tried to get him to quit but he wouldn't listen and with my hands on the wheel . . . I thought about pulling the car over but I was afraid to do that because we were so far from help. I knew he was stronger than I was and he had this crazy look in his eyes."

Chase tightened his grip on her hands. What she was describing made him livid. Worse, it sounded exactly like something Russell Morris would do. Bullies like him never played fair. "You did the only thing you could," he soothed, wishing he could make Hope feel better, yet fearing in his gut the worst was yet to be told.

"I thought so, too," Hope replied in a voice that was both numb and sad. Tears welled up in her eyes. "But he grabbed me again, harder this time. The next thing I knew, the car left the road and we ended up in a ditch. Luckily, neither of us were hurt, just shaken up a bit. I was scared and furious, but he just thought it was funny. We started to get out of the car, to go for help. We knew we were just a few miles from home by then. And that's when he—he did what he'd been wanting to do all night. He dragged me down into the ditch and—" She choked up, unable to go on.

And Chase found, she didn't have to. The next he could imagine with no trouble at all. A killing rage started in him, lessened only by his need to comfort her.

Running both hands through her hair, she related miserably, "Afterward, I got away and walked the rest of the way home. Once there, I tried to tell my parents what had happened, but they didn't believe me. Russell told everyone that we'd both been drinking that night and that we'd been trying to make love while we drove and that was how the accident had happened. He'd explained the grass stains on my clothing by saying we'd been so drunk that we'd finished it in the ditch." Tears flowed down her face. She couldn't look at him. "I tried to go to the police anyway but they didn't believe me, either. The doctors at the hospital knew I'd been violated but couldn't guarantee that my bruises were from the rape and not the wreck."

The incompetence of the officials was infuriating. "Couldn't they tell you'd been forced?" Chase asked.

She shrugged as if it no longer mattered, and released a bone-weary sigh. "Russell freely admitted to the fact he'd been very rough." She shut her eyes, gritting her teeth against the memory. "He told the police I—" she swallowed hard, looking ill again "—liked it that way."

Oh God, Chase thought. She'd been through so much, without even her parents to stand by her.

Bitterly she continued, "The bartenders at the bar only remembered serving us both drinks and taking away empty glasses. I was so hysterical by the time I got to the emergency room hours later that no one thought to give me a blood test, so we had no proof later that I hadn't been drinking." She shook her head miserably, whispering, "It was such a mess, Chase, and it didn't end with that night, either." Her lower lip trembled. "His insurance company sued me for the loss of his car because I'd been driving. I lost my license. His parents, livid about the whole thing, threw my family off the tenant farm and then spread some money around, insuring that the case would never make it as far as the grand jury for indictment. They told everyone that I was trying to milk their family of money, that Russell was the victim of my drunk, irresponsible actions, not the other way around. And because we'd had those two dates, because I was poor and he was rich, everyone believed him." Her voice broke. "Everyone thought the worst of me, including my parents."

"That's why you got so mad at Mr. Bateman at the baseball game," Chase said slowly, recalling her vehement reaction to a similar injustice.

Looking pale and drawn, she clenched her fists. "Yes. I can't stand it when people use their power and position and wealth to hurt others. It brings it all back."

"I'm sorry, Hope." He put his arms around her, and gently turned her face to him. She saw only understanding in his face for what she'd been through. "And that's why you broke with your family?"

She nodded, admitting, "I couldn't stay."

And, Chase thought sadly, they hadn't wanted her. How had she been through so much, he wondered, and come through with her heart and soul intact?

"I came to Houston and I got a job at Barrister's." She took a deep breath. Now came the really hard part. "It was only later I realized I was pregnant." She teared up again, looking heartrendingly vulnerable. "For Joey's sake, I wish I could say that it hadn't bothered me how he had been conceived, but it did," she said. "I couldn't bear the thought of having Russell Morris's child. I decided to have an abortion. And so I went to Atlanta to have an abortion."

Suddenly it all made sense to Chase. Edmond, in a blue funk himself about his own situation, had reached out to help someone else. And he'd been drawn in by Hope's beauty and warmth and innate capacity for love. "And my father went with you," he said.

Composing herself slightly, Hope nodded. "Yes. Only once I got there I realized I couldn't go through with that, either." She sighed tiredly. "I realized I wanted the child because it was my child." Tears ran down her face and she wiped them away. "And that's when Edmond came up with the idea to marry me. It was only supposed to be for a little while," she confided hoarsely. "He was just going to give the baby a name, but in those first few months we grew to love each other. Not passionately, but deeply." She shrugged, not knowing if he would understand, but wishing desperately that he would. "I know we were years apart in age, but we had so much in common, Chase, our love of the store, of Joey. He was so good to me and I tried to be good to him.''

She didn't have to convince him. Chase knew she had done that and more. She had loved Edmond and he had loved her. "You knew about the consequences of his illness when you married him?" he asked kindly. He only felt a little jealous that Hope had been closer to his father than he had been at that point in his life.

Hope nodded. "Yes, I knew he was incapable of making love with me, but it didn't matter." She gestured helplessly. "I was never a physical person prior to that and the rape left me with an aversion to even the idea of trying to make love." It was an aversion she had kept until Chase held her in his arms. Then, something different, something magical, always seemed to happen. She had felt guilty at first, but now she accepted it. It had nothing to do with Edmond and everything to do with Chase.

"He gave me everything I wanted, all the security, all the love. He was like a parent to me and a best friend and a father confessor. And I loved him with all my heart and soul."

"And you were happy," Chase said softly, suddenly glad his father and Hope had been blessed with each other.

"Yes," Hope affirmed. "We were."

His feelings in turmoil, Chase thought about all she had told him. And the danger still ahead. "Does Russell know about Joey?"

Her face drained of color and she clung to him. "He's just recently figured it out." Tilting her head back, so she could look deep into his eyes, she confessed honestly, "Chase, I'm scared. I've already paid him one hundred thousand dollars. That's why I sold my jewelry. I was trying so hard to get rid of him, to get him out of my life and Joey's once and for all."

Chase had figured as much. Still, it was a relief to hear her say it. She was finally telling him everything; she trusted him, after all. "But he still wants more," Chase ascertained grimly. He was thinking ahead to possible solutions.

Hope nodded. "Yes." Her eyes darkened and her mouth took on a brave, determined line. "I realized tonight I can't pay him again. If I do, it'll never end." She hesitated, looking to him for the answers she didn't have, needing him as ever before. "What am I going to do?"

He held her close, stroking her hair, glad he was able to be there for her. As he contemplated the future, his mood was both troubled and thoughtful. He had to find a way to help her out. He wouldn't rest until he did. "We'll figure something out, Hope," he said, gently reassuring her. "I promise you we will."

RUSSELL WAS WAITING for Hope when she walked into Maxim's. Seeing Chase by her side, his expression soured. His mouth compressed in a furious line, he looked at Hope for explanation.

"I've told Chase everything," Hope said simply.

"And I'm here to tell you to back off, pal," Chase continued. He turned a chair around, slipped into it backward and folded his hands across the top. "The Barrister name wields a lot of influence in this state. Extortion is against the law."

Russell looked at her, pressuring her to back up his claim. "Hope's just been helping out an old friend," he said.

Telling Chase the truth had exorcised a lot of demons within her. Hope knew she didn't have to be afraid anymore, not of the truth and not of Russell. She still didn't want Joey to know, but if it came to that, she knew they would find a way to handle it. She smiled at Russell, her eyes carrying the same dangerous glint as Chase's. "I'm calling in my loans," she informed her nemesis quietly.

Chase fumed like a volcano about to blow as he faced Russell. "We'll give you twenty-four hours to come up with the cash she so kindly 'loaned' you," he said. The smoothness in his voice didn't lessen the threat in his eyes one iota. "Then we go to the police and talk extortion."

"You wouldn't dare," Russell said smugly. The dots
perspiration on his upper lip belied the put-on confidence
his voice.

"Yes," Hope said firmly, saying what she had known sl
should have said from the very first, "I would." For the fir
time in weeks she could face Russell without the fear of
migraine coming on.

They stared at one another. Equals now. No longer th
defenseless poor girl and the overbearing rich stud.

"Be at our attorney's office tomorrow at ten sharp,
Chase said, passing Russell a piece of paper with the nan
and address written on it. "And be ready to sign some p;
pers." He gave him a crocodile grin. "We're going to mak
sure this never happens again."

Russell looked outwardly unimpressed, though a musc
was ticking involuntarily in his jaw. "And if I don't sho
up?" he asked. His low voice was laced with vindictive fur

"Then be ready to face blackmail and extortion charges,
Hope said flatly, refusing to let him intimidate her. "B
cause I *will* go to the police, Russell."

"And this time," Chase finished smugly, "she'll have th
full power of the Barrister name and all our influence be
hind her and she will win."

Chapter Sixteen

"Exhausted?" Chase asked as he drove Hope home shortly before noon the following day.

"Very," Hope said. The session with the lawyers had been grueling but productive. Russell Morris had not only returned the money Hope had given him, but he had agreed never to seek custody of Joey. She had, in turn, promised never to ask Russell Morris for any type of financial support, or to divulge to Joey or anyone else who his real father was.

Finally, after all these weeks, Hope was free of the blackmail, the threats and the memories. She should have felt wonderful. And maybe she would've had she not been so on edge about the relationship between herself and Chase.

She still didn't know where she stood with him. She wasn't sure *he* knew where they stood. She didn't want to believe the passion he felt for her was fleeting, but she also knew he wasn't a man who, apart from his one brief, failed engagement, had ever professed a need to be tied down to any one woman or any one place. She was still very tied to Houston and to Barrister's. She also still had a son to raise. Even if she wanted to follow Chase to the ends of the earth, she couldn't.

"Why don't you go up and lie down?" Chase asked as he let them in the front door. "I'll go in and get Carmelita to make you some tea."

"Thanks. I think I will."

Once upstairs in her bedroom, Hope kicked off her sh[o]
and lay down on the bed. She shut her eyes. As she did [s]
she was confronted with vivid images of Chase and hers[e]
in the guest house, in his bed. Her face burned as she [r]
called how passionate they had been, how uninhibited. S[h]
had never guessed lovemaking could be like that. Never. B[t]
with Chase it was.

Chase walked in, tray in hands. "Tea for m'lady."

Perspiring slightly at the nature of her thoughts, she s[at]
up. He reached behind her to prop up the pillows and not[e]
the moisture on her brow. "Not getting another migrain[e]
are you?"

Hope smiled her relief, glad she was at last able to sa[y]
"No, I think they're all gone."

"Good." He straightened and looked around aw[k]
wardly.

"Chase—" There was so much she wanted to say, but s[he]
didn't know where to begin. Or even if now was the tim[e]
"You don't have to stay with me," she said softly.

Gently he tucked a strand of hair behind her ear. "I kn[ow]
that. I want to." Seeing all the questions in her eyes, [he]
confessed in a low, intimate tone that let her know he real[ly]
did understand her, "I know what it is to handle the ha[rd]
stuff alone, Hope."

Hope took in the firm, very masculine line of his mout[h]
Remembering what it had been like to kiss it, and be kiss[ed]
by that mouth, the warmth of desire flowed through he[r]
Trying to distract herself into paying attention to the co[n]
versation, she asked, "What do you mean?"

He shrugged. If he was entertaining the same type of l[i]
centious thoughts, he didn't show it, Hope thought. H[e]
traced a pattern lightly on the back of her hand. "Growi[ng]
up, it seemed my parents were always fighting and I had n[o]
one to turn to." His hand clasped hers tenderly and his ey[es]
met hers. "I don't want that for you, not anymore," he sai[d]

eminding her of all the storms she had previously had to
veather alone in her life. "I don't want that for me."

Hope looked up at him, her heart in her throat. They
tared at each other. They both longed to make love again.
Only neither was sure what it would mean. Hope wasn't sure
he wanted to risk what had been a very pleasant, very
vonderful, very giving memory.

Reading her fear, he slowly and deliberately stood, picked
p a gift-wrapped box she had failed to notice and brought
forward. "I almost forgot," he said with care, his hazel
yes calm and searching. "Here. This is for you."

Aware of his gaze on her, she opened it with trembling
ingers. Inside was all her jewelry. Each piece conjured up
different memory, of life with his father, of life before
Chase. Overcome with emotion, she didn't know what to
ay.

"I knew you didn't want to part with it, so I bought it
ack for you," he said.

Only he had waited until now to give it to her. Earlier he
adn't trusted her enough. Now that he did, he found he
eally didn't want her to have it, not if it meant she became
is father's wife again. His unwilling stepmother.

"You really do think of everything," Hope observed in a
haking voice.

He studied her reaction, finding her not nearly as happy
s he would have expected her to be weeks ago, when he had
orrowed against the principle on his trust, and arranged to
uy the jewelry. "It upsets you to have it back?"

Hope shook her head slowly. No, it upset her to know he
vas leaving. But knowing how he had hated having bur-
lens put on him—how his father expected him to take over
he store and his mother expected him to be a social butter-
ly—she didn't see how she could put demands on him, too.
Not after all he had already done for her and for Joey.

"It's not the jewelry," she said, finding it hard to speak
around the tightness in her throat. She was so afraid they

were going to lose everything they'd found, and she didn
think she could bear it if they did.

"What then?" Chase prodded patiently.

With effort, she summoned up all her courage and trie
to cope with her feelings. "It's about that night in the gue
house." She didn't want a marriage like she had had b
fore, with him marrying her because he knew she neede
someone and wanted to help out. She wanted him there b
cause he wanted to be there. Because he loved her as a ma
should love a woman.

Chase studied her, looking suddenly as afraid, as wary, a
she felt. "Are you angry with me?" he asked simply. "D
you think I took advantage of you, the situation?"

"No," she said, aghast. She stretched her legs out in fro
of her, smoothing the crocheted white afghan from knee t
waist, as if by making herself more physically comfortabl
it would be easier to admit something that was emotionall
uncomfortable to her. "No, I wanted that to happen." Sh
had for a very long time.

"So did I," Chase said softly, watching as she dipped he
fingers restlessly into the intricate white weave of th
afghan.

It's now or never, Hope told herself firmly. Be brave an
lay it all on the line or die wondering what might have been
She had to find the courage to talk openly and honestly t
him today. Right now, right this minute, while their feel
ings were still fresh. "Where do we go from here?" Sh
lifted her face to his, her eyes telling him she really cared.

He studied her a moment longer, his eyes roving over he
slightly mussed hair and unglossed lips. He flashed her a
crooked grin and said with simple, heartfelt optimism
"How about forward?"

She looked at him, almost afraid to hope she could hav
everything.

"I can't promise you what kind of husband I'll make,"
he continued honestly, clasping both her hands in his and
lifting them to his mouth for tender kisses. "The truth is

n't know." He squeezed her hand and put his mouth to
er palm, planting a warm kiss squarely in the middle. "I
ever felt I was the marrying kind." He grinned again at the
ixture of shock and happiness on her face. "Until now,"
e amended.

Hope went into his arms. "Oh, Chase," she sighed, feel-
g as though all her dreams were finally coming true.

He hugged her back tightly. "Is that a yes or a no?"

Grinning from ear to ear, she hugged him back, just as
onfidently. "What do you think?"

Epilogue

"Joey, have you seen the canteens?" Chase asked, from corner of the garage.

"No. Aren't they with the rest of the camping gear?" fi teen-year-old Joey asked, a perplexed expression on his fac

Hope looked up from the sleeping bags she was shakii out. Beside her, three-year-old Kevin played contented with three Sesame Street figures. He repeatedly droppe Bert, Ernie and Big Bird in an empty cooler, then rescue them all moments later. "I think the canteens are in th supply cabinet next to the freezer."

Chase opened it. "Right again, as usual."

Hope smiled at her husband and oldest son, then co sulted her list of Things To Do. The list was never more im portant than when she was trying to organize their family c four for any group activity. Without a master plan, sh would be lost, she knew, and so would her circle of thre loving "men." She checked off dinnerware and went to th next item. "Are the tents all ready?"

"Yep." Joey answered for Chase. He looked at Hop importantly. "I took care of that myself."

"We're going camping!" Kevin cried excitedly, runnin over to embrace his daddy around the knees. "Yeah, yeah yeah!" he cheered.

Chase picked Kevin up and embraced him in a warm bea hug. "Yes, we are. Think you can handle it, big guy?"

"Yes!" Kevin cried. "But I get to sleep next to Joey!"

Joey moaned in mock aggravation. "Oh, no," he said, etending to be in great pain. He pointed a teasing finger his three-year-old brother. "You snore!"

"I do not," Kevin said indignantly. "You snore, Joey!"

"Do not!" Joey teased, and they were off, laughing and changing loving insults.

Watching them, Hope thought back to the changes the st five years had wrought. She had a solid marriage to a an she loved very much. Joey had a brother twelve years s junior, Chase two sons and a wife to take camping. hase still left for the rain forests, spending several months year total there, but because he only left for two weeks at time Hope didn't mind.

The store had slowly become profitable again, with the anges Hope had implemented becoming chain-wide. And ope was still president. Chase had tried to get Rosemary sell her shares to him, to no avail. However, she was not vocal about the running of it as she had been. And Hope preciated that.

Joey's asthma was better. He still couldn't have a pet, but liked having a younger brother better. Or so he said. rong and fit, he had shed his glasses and was now wear- g contacts and playing on his high-school baseball team. hese days, if anyone teased him, it was usually about the rls who were chasing him.

It would have been better had Chase's mother approved f their marriage, Hope supposed, but she was also realis- c enough to know that Rosemary would always harbor me resentment against her. However, things were better ow than they had been five years ago, when she and Chase ad first married, largely due to the reconciling event of evin's birth. Hope had every reason to expect things would ntinue to improve, very gradually, over time. Currently, osemary was living in Europe but she did visit them in louston from time to time.

"Well," Chase said, looking around at the gear they ha scattered all over the garage. "I guess it's about time we sta loading up the Jeep."

"I'm ready." Hoisting one of the rolled-up tents over h shoulder, Joey stalked to the Suburban parked in the driv way.

Chase handed Kevin to Hope. "You can be in charge our budding frontiersman," he said.

Hope happily accepted her son's thirty-pound weigh balancing him on her hip. For the next few minutes, they were busy loading the car, Hope admittedly doing more su pervising than carrying. Finally Chase shut the rear con partment. Joey held out his hands to Kevin. "Okay, big gu we're going to take a last look around and see if there're an other toys you want to bring."

Chase looked at the crammed rear compartment of th Jeep. "Just so long as it's not too big," he cautioned pra tically.

"Got ya," Joey said, sauntering off, Kevin in his arms.

Feeling incredibly content, Hope watched the boys wal inside then laced her arms around her husband's neck an stood on tiptoe to give him a kiss. "Days like today," sh confided in a tender whisper, her eyes meeting his affec tionately, "I feel like I have everything."

Chase smiled down at her, contentment radiating from him. "I know what you mean," he confessed softly, an dently tightening his grip. "Except one thing."

Hope's brow furrowed and she flushed warmly. Sh couldn't think of a thing. "What?" she prompted cur ously, her pulse beginning to race at the close proximity o her body to his.

"A daughter." He paused, eyes twinkling, his strong bod radiating resolve. "Kevin's three now. Maybe when we ge back, we can get started on that."

Hope grinned in anticipation, easily reading the desire
and love in his eyes. Two qualities that were emanating from
her own. "Now that," she said standing on tiptoe and kissing him soundly once again, "sounds like a very worth-
while project indeed."

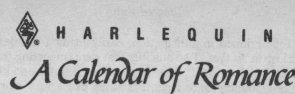

HARLEQUIN

A Calendar of Romance

Be a part of American Romance's year-long celebration of love and the holidays of 1992. Experience all the passion of falling in love during the excitement of each month's holiday. Some of your favorite authors will help you celebrate those special times of the year, like the romance of Valentine's Day, the magic of St. Patrick's Day, the joy of Easter.

Celebrate the romance of Valentine's Day with

#425 VALENTINE HEARTS AND FLOWERS by Muriel Jensen

Read all the books in *A Calendar of Romance*, coming to you one each month, all year, from Harlequin American Romance. COR2

my VALENTINE 1992

Celebrate the most romantic day of the year with
MY VALENTINE 1992—a sexy new collection of four
romantic stories written by our famous Temptation
authors:

> GINA WILKINS
> KRISTINE ROLOFSON
> JOANN ROSS
> VICKI LEWIS THOMPSON

My Valentine 1992—an exquisite escape into a romantic
and sensuous world.

 Harlequin Books

VAL-92-R

Harlequin Intrigue ®

It looks like a charming old building near the Baltimore waterfront, but inside 43 Light Street lurks danger ... and romance.

Labeled a "true master of intrigue" by *Rave Reviews*, bestselling author Rebecca York continues her exciting series with #179 ONLY SKIN DEEP, coming to you next month.

When her sister is found dead, Dr. Kathryn Martin, a 43 Light Street occupant, suddenly finds herself caught up in the glamorous world of a posh Washington, D.C., beauty salon. Not even former love Mac McQuade can believe the schemes Katie uncovers.

Watch for #179 ONLY SKIN DEEP in February, and all the upcoming 43 Light Street titles for top-notch suspense and romance.

LS92

Take 4 bestselling love stories FREE

Plus get a FREE surprise gift!